PERFECT REPSONSES

Margaret K Johnson

Prologue

Corrinne Walker woke up laughing. She'd been having the most ridiculous dream in which God, sporting the traditional white hair and beard, was dressed in a bright yellow felt duck outfit, complete with webbed feet and an orange beak protruding from above his forehead.

How ludicrous! Why on earth would she dream that?

More memories of the dream returned, causing her smile to slip quickly away. Goodness, God had been presiding over a court of law, and despite the ridiculous outfit, he'd been imperious. Terrifying, in fact. What's more, she had been the prisoner in the dock.

Wow, what a very vivid dream. She could still picture every detail of it. The court full of onlookers, the stern-faced, wig-wearing clerk, bellowing, 'The prisoner in the dock will rise.' The way everyone in the courtroom had looked at her; all of them accusing and judgemental. Just thinking about it now made her feel sick to her stomach, which was a pity really, because actually, she felt very well. Better than she had done for a long time.

Still with her eyes closed, Corrinne wriggled up

slightly in bed, reaching for the glass of water she always put on the bedside table before she went to sleep. When she couldn't find it, her hand shifted slightly, searching. Still no glass. Squinting through the half-light, Corrinne realised there was no glass of water there. And not only was there no glass of water, but there was no bedside table either.

Finally she sat up to take a look around. This wasn't even her room. Where the hell was she?

A door opened, and a woman came in; a woman Corrinne seemed to remember was called Nessa. She frowned, pulling the duvet up to her chin, trying to place her. She'd seen her very recently. But where?

'Good morning, Corrinne,' Nessa said, and Corrinne noticed she was carrying a document file. 'I hope you slept well?' She crossed the room to pull the curtains with her free hand, letting the morning light stream in.

Corrinne sat up straighter, regarding the woman with confusion as she remembered where she'd seen her before. In her dream. But how was that possible if she were here now? Was she still asleep? She must be.

Nessa came over to the bed, patting Corrinne's legs sympathetically through the duvet. 'I woke up for a full week thinking it had all been a dream,' she said. 'It's all part of the transition process, dear. The mind takes a while to catch up with the body, I'm afraid. Death's a mighty big adjustment to make.'

Death? Was this woman actually saying she was dead? True, she hadn't felt well lately, but she would know if she'd died, surely? And in any case, far from being the black cotton wool nothingness Corrinne had always imagined death to be, this reality was extremely detailed and technicolour and, well … very much *alive*.

'This isn't really happening,' she said, but Nessa nodded.

'It is, my dear, I assure you.'

'You mean the court trial? And God? All of it? It was all real?'

Another nod. 'Yes. All of it.'

'But God was dressed as a duck,' Corrinne said. 'Why was he dressed as a duck?'

'That must be how you pictured him once. Everyone sees God differently. For me, he looked exactly like my Uncle Norman.'

Corrinne groaned, cursing the Ugly Duckling play she'd been forced to take part in at primary school. Blind terror had prompted her to imagine God as a proactive guardian angel, taking part in the play alongside her to give her confidence. And of course, if he was taking part in the play, then he had to fit in, hence the outfit.

Her thoughts moved on, God's voice booming around her head as she recalled him reading out the charges against her in the court room.

'Corrinne Jemima Walker, you are charged with three counts of failing to live by your strategies for life as detailed in your book, *Staying in Neutral, Responses to Change Your Life*. Witnesses report that when your

3

husband revealed to you that he had met another woman and wished to end his relationship with you, you completely and unequivocally failed to live by the creed that you directed the readers of your book to live by in said book, namely that of remembering that, *"Your thoughts are everything. You can choose to feel good at every single moment. At any time, you have the power to reach for your highest-feeling thought."*

'You made no attempt to reach for your highest-feeling thought when you were presented with your husband's infidelity. You did nothing to view it as a so-called neutral event the way you directed your readers to do. Instead, you vindictively cut the crotches from every pair of your husband's trousers and filled his suit jacket pockets with Valencian paella. Furthermore, you made arrangements for daily deliveries of incontinence pads, enemas and halitosis cures to the flat he was sharing with his new girlfriend. You then proceeded to bed your husband's employer and your subsequent revelations about said seduction on the Internet resulted in the breakdown of this man's marriage, the plummet of the company's shares and your husband's subsequent forced resignation.

'Since these activities were all as far as it is possible to be from your concept of the neutrality of the event, which formed the whole basis of your book, this court deems that during your lifetime you consistently misled and defrauded the public.'

'Oh, but your honour, I mean your Godness, I mean

God –' Corrinne found the courage to interject.

Immediately, a thunderclap echoed around the room. 'Silence!' bellowed God, raising his hand, and Corrinne, who fully expected him to issue a lightning bolt at her at any minute, cowered in the dock, wishing she had died in anything but her favourite nightdress, the one she had washed and worn so many times the fabric was practically transparent.

'It is the verdict of this court that you shall remain in uncertain limbo for a period of thirty days. During that time, an agent shall be sent down to earth to test the theories of your book. I have, myself, selected three individuals from your country of origin. These individuals are Janet Thornton, her daughter Debbie Thornton, and Kate Mitchell, soon to be Kate Bramling, all of Shelthorpe-on-Sea, Norfolk, United Kingdom. I shall be dispatching my agent forthwith to make contact with them. Should all three said individuals be seen to benefit significantly from your theories by the end of the thirty-day period, the charges against you will be dropped, and you will be permitted to pass on from this place. However, should just one of these individuals fail to benefit, you will be confined to Limbo forever to reflect on the error of your ways.'

By this time, God's voice had been ricocheting off the walls of the cavernous courtroom. It had been truly terrifying.

'Did I faint?' she asked Nessa now, unable to remember anything after God's terrible sentence.

'Yes. But don't worry, that's not unusual. I think you caught God in a bad mood. He was particularly almighty last night. I'm not sure he was too happy with his outfit.'

Becoming aware of a slight twinkle in Nessa's eye, Corrinne sunk down in bed, pulling the duvet over her head. 'Nothing about this is funny,' she said from beneath it, her voice muffled by goose down. 'Nothing.'

She felt the pressure of Nessa's hand on her shoulder through the duvet. 'Of course it's not. I'm sorry. But please try not to worry. I'm going to do everything in my power to make certain that the three women God has selected fully engage with the message of your book.'

Corrinne threw the duvet back to stare at her in horror. '*You* are?' she said.

'Oh, of course, you don't know, do you?' Nessa said. 'You'd already passed out when God appointed me. Yes, I'm his selected agent. I shall be leaving to make a start this morning.'

'Why you?' Corrinne couldn't keep the dismay from her voice. She was sure Nessa was a perfectly nice woman, despite her taste in fussy floral fabrics, but it really would have been better to have someone more personable looking to take on her cause with so much riding on it.

She saw Nessa do her best to keep her face neutral – *neutral*, that dratted word! – but nevertheless, Corrinne could detect a flicker of hurt on her face. 'It's my turn; simple as that,' she said, and Corrinne did her best to put her doubts aside, since there didn't seem to be anything she could do about God's selection.

'Who are these three women?' she asked instead. 'And why did God choose them in particular?'

Nessa opened her file. 'They're called Kate, Janet and Debbie. Janet and Debbie are mother and daughter, and all three women know each other. I'm not sure why they've been selected in particular. I imagine God's aware that they're about to be challenged in their lives. Also, one of them, Janet, I believe it is, is currently in a country I happen to be very familiar with.'

Corrinne frowned. 'Wait a minute. They're not even all in the same country? Surely that means it will take longer, if you've got to travel here, there and everywhere?'

Nessa smiled. 'Don't worry,' she said. 'These days I don't need to use public transport to get around. But you're right; it does make the logistics more complicated. Obviously, I can't decide on my best strategies until I've met them all, but my initial plan is to introduce the two-UK based women to your book, and to leave it to do its work on them for a few weeks while I concentrate my efforts on Janet, in Africa.'

'Africa?'

Nessa nodded. 'Yes, The Gambia. Actually, I have to say, I'm most grateful to God for appointing me, because this is going to allow me to tie up some of my own loose ends at the same time.'

Corrinne didn't like the sound of that. 'Hey! You're not going to get distracted, are you?'

Once again, Nessa smiled. Did she ever do anything else? 'No, I promise you, I won't get distracted. All will be well. Now, if you want me to have the best chance of success, then maybe you ought to put me in the picture about the big idea of your book. I'm all packed and ready to head out.'

Corrinne felt exhausted by the prospect of trying to explain the concepts of *Staying in Neutral, Responses to Change Your Life* to Nessa. It was years since she'd even given the book a proper thought beyond lamenting the dwindling amount of royalties it earned her.

She sighed. 'Can I have a cup of tea first please?' she asked, and Nessa smiled.

'Sweetie,' she said kindly, 'of course you can't have a cup of tea. You're dead. The only way you'll be able to drink tea again is if you're selected to be an agent for someone the way I have been. Then you'll get sent down to earth, and you'll be able to do the things a living person can do all over again. God watches you though. One hint of scissors near a pair of trousers and you'd be back up here with your licence eternally revoked.'

'He really didn't like the trouser crotch cutting, did he?' Corrinne said, recalling the thunder in God's face with a shudder.

Nessa gripped her hand, the twinkle in her eyes making Corrinne like her a bit more now. 'No, dear, he did not. But *I* certainly did. Almost snorted with laughter right there in the court room, I can tell you! And that would never have done. But listen, you need to tell me about your book right now, because if I miss my travel slot, there might not be another one for twenty years, and you don't want to be in Limbo for that long, do you?'

'No,' Corrinne agreed miserably.

Nessa sat down on the bed. 'Go ahead then, dear. Explain it all to me. I'm listening.'

So, taking a deep breath, and still unable to believe that she wouldn't wake up at any minute to find out this had all been a horrific dream, Corrinne plunged in.

One

Shelthorpe-on-Sea, Norfolk

They were waiting, all ten of them, each clutching their freshly-baked baguette, the backs of their waistcoats catching the sunshine like oil on water. It seemed strange to see them so well turned out, Davey's shirt tucked in, Kyle's hair tied back. Even Michael McBride had removed his nose stud.

Debbie knew none of them would have done any of it for anyone but Geoff, their favourite bakery tutor at Shelthorpe Further Education College. It was a testament to the man Kate was marrying. *Had* married in fact, because now Debbie could hear the swell of the Wedding March music starting up in the church behind the waiting boys.

'This is it,' she told them. 'Positions, please.'

As the teenagers faced each other in two rows of five to form a wedding arch outside the church, Debbie was grateful for the rehearsals she'd insisted upon. All the jeers of *Miss, how hard can it be?* she'd ignored.

'Right, one two three, lift!' she said, and on her cue, ten hands holding ten baguettes shot into the air like swords to form the arch, just in time for the church doors to open. Debbie scuttled out of the way to allow the photographer to capture Kate's expression of surprised delight, and there she was, her mouth, with its unfamiliar lipstick, dropping open before it planted a smacker of a kiss on her new husband's cheek.

'Did you plan all this?' Debbie heard Kate ask him.

'Might have done,' Geoff replied smugly, and then they were both dipping their heads to make their way beneath the baguettes, the arch wobbling above them as the students finally gave way to their laughter. By the time Kate and Geoff emerged, beaming, the arch had pretty much collapsed, and the photographer had to beg the students to get back into position so he could get his photos.

As baguettes and boys were hastily arranged behind her, Kate caught Debbie's eye and grinned. Debbie smiled back, taking in the picture of her mum's friend, unashamedly dressed in flowing scarlet for her wedding day, the soft fabric lovingly describing her swollen belly. No way on earth was this a typical wedding, and Debbie knew her mum would have loved it. If she weren't off who knew where, gallivanting around the world with her new boyfriend.

'Geoff looks very pleased with himself,' a deep voice said, and Debbie turned to see a tall man dressed in a suit that didn't look quite big enough for him, the sleeves of his jacket ending a few inches short of his wrists.

He saw her looking. 'I don't normally wear suits these days,' he explained. 'Mind you, nor does Uncle Geoff, and he's scrubbed up well.'

The triumphal arch had disintegrated again, and two of the students were having a sword fight with their baguettes, sending flakes of bread everywhere.

'All right, all right,' said Geoff in his booming baking lecturer's voice, 'put your weapons down, lads. And thanks for your help.'

'I didn't know Geoff had a nephew,' Debbie said to the stranger, and he put his hand out for her to shake.

'I moved here from Colchester a few months ago. I'm Paul.'

'Debbie Thornton.'

'Ah, you must be Janet's daughter,' he said, and she looked at him with surprise.

'You know my mum?'

'Yes,' he said, and she noticed suddenly how green his eyes were. 'She leased her shop to the charity I work for.'

The interior design shop that her mother had been going to call Janet's Dreams. The shop she had never actually opened and that was currently a Cat Calls UK charity shop, complete with second-hand mannequins and photos of abandoned cats.

Smokey, 4 year-old tabby. Nervous disposition. Needs a patient owner with no other pets.

Debbie was about to ask Paul what he did for the charity when a woman in a low-cut dress threw herself at him, effectively blocking Debbie out.

'Paul! How great to see you! But whatever are you wearing? Did you get it from the charity shop?'

'Yes, I did, actually,' Debbie heard Paul reply before she moved away to take some photos of the happy couple.

She wasn't sure why the idea of her mum's shop being a charity shop upset her so much. It was stupid really, because it wasn't as if she'd offered Janet support when she'd had her grand plan to open an interior design shop. The whole project had felt too wrapped up with her parents' divorce somehow, even though her mum had used the money she'd inherited from Gran's will to buy the lease. But it had been a rubbish time while the divorce was going through, with Debbie feeling as if both her parents were trying to get her on their side.

It couldn't have come at a worse time for Debbie personally either, with all the stuff she'd been dealing with in her own life at the time. Not that either of her parents knew anything about that, because she had kept it to herself.

But whether Debbie liked it or not, the divorce had gone ahead, the family home was sold and the money was divided up. Two months later, Janet had decided to go on some sort of glorified gap year with Scott, her new man, and her dad had bought a new flat in

Norwich. Suddenly, there was nothing to remind Debbie of her past at all.

'Hey!' Debbie looked round to see Kate, her arms spread. 'Give me a hug.'

Debbie smiled, moving willingly into Kate's arms. She might disapprove of some of the decisions her mum had made lately, but she had to admit that Janet had some excellent friends; especially Kate. With Kate, what you saw was what you got. Debbie liked that, and it was one of the reasons she'd felt okay about becoming Kate and Geoff's lodger when Janet had set off abroad with Scott. Although she wasn't sure how much longer this arrangement was going to work out for, with the baby on the way.

'Congratulations,' Debbie said as she was squashed against Kate's baby bump.

Kate grinned at her. 'Mad, isn't it? I'm actually married. Again. Honestly never thought I'd do that.'

They both turned to look at Geoff, their arms linked. His hands were on his hips as he exchanged some banter with his baguette-wielding bakery students, a pose designed to emphasize his belly.

'Hey, I wonder who'll give birth first, eh?' Kate giggled. 'Me or him?' And Debbie laughed, as she knew she was supposed to do.

At the reception, Debbie was seated at one end of the top table with her mum's friend Estelle and her partner Mark. Another of their friends, Reenie, was nearby, with her husband Ted, but Debbie didn't know either of them very well. She liked Estelle though, even though she found her a bit intimidating at times.

'So,' said Estelle now. 'Are you going to be able to stand continuing to live with the lovebirds now they're married, do you think?'

Debbie waited for one of Geoff's booming laughs to die down before she replied. 'No,' she said without hesitation, thinking of night after night of trying to tune out the sounds of Geoff and Kate's unrestrained love-making.

At first, when Kate had become pregnant, there had been a bit of a respite, since all she'd wanted to do when she got back from work was sleep. But that phase seemed to be well and truly over now, and besides, *everything* about Geoff was whole-hearted and unrestrained. It was one of the things that made him so endearing, but it didn't make for a peaceful home life.

'It was only ever supposed to be temporary anyway; just while I found somewhere of my own. Geoff and Kate won't want me around when the baby comes.'

'What about the flat above your mum's shop?' Estelle suggested. 'Surely Cat Calls UK isn't using that? Maybe you could come to some arrangement with them.'

Automatically, Debbie's eyes sought out the man in the ill-fitting suit. Paul. He was seated at a neighbouring table, suit jacket off now, deep in conversation with the man to his left, his hands moving expressively as he talked. 'Yes,' said Debbie, 'maybe that's worth a try. Thanks, Estelle.'

Estelle smiled and was about to say something else when Kate called over, holding up her iPad. 'Debbie! It's your mum, on Skype!'

Reluctantly, Debbie went over, getting there just in time to hear her mother say, 'Congratulations, Kate! I so wish I could be there with you!'

'Thanks,' said Kate, sounding emotional. 'I wish you could be too.'

Staying to one side, Debbie heard her mum ask, 'Are you having a good day?'

Kate grinned. 'The best day in the history of days since records began,' she said, and Janet laughed.

'Ah, I'm so pleased. And you look amazing. I love the red.'

Kate laughed. 'Well, I'm a fallen woman, aren't I? Might as well be upfront about it. And it looks as if you've worn the white for me.'

'Er, yes … ' said Janet, and Debbie, who'd heard that evasive tone of voice before, moved a little closer so she could see her mother on screen.

'Well, actually, Kate, the thing is … '

Suddenly another face appeared next to Janet's, forcing her to move sideways. Scott, his face freshly shaven for once, but coated in a sheen of African heat. And something else. Excitement.

'We decided to steal some of your thunder and get hitched ourselves!' he announced, and Debbie's heart gave a lurch. No! Mum and Scott? It was impossible.

'Scott!' Janet was saying. 'We aren't trying to steal anybody's thunder. Honestly, Kate, it's not like that. You inspired us, that's all. We're not trying to eclipse you and Geoff, we just – '

Geoff had joined Kate, his hairy cheek pressed close to hers. 'Janet!' he boomed. 'Good to see you, girl! And what's all this about eclipses?'

'Janet and Scott are getting married too,' Kate told him.

'Blimey O'Reilly!' Geoff said. 'When?'

'They're waiting for us right now, actually, mate,' answered Scott. 'In fact, we'd better go, Janet.'

'Not just yet, Scott, I haven't spoken to Debbie. Is she there, Kate?'

Kate looked round at Debbie, and Debbie knew she was completely aware of her feelings. Why wouldn't she be? The two of them had discussed Scott often enough, neither of them thinking he was good enough for Janet, and both hoping that somewhere on their round-the-world-trip, Janet would come to realise it. And now she was marrying him.

'Yes,' Kate said, 'she's here.' And she held the iPad out to Debbie with a sympathetic smile.

Debbie took it with reluctance, forcing a smile onto her face. 'Hi, Mum.'

Janet looked back at her with a slightly fearful expression. It seemed to have become her mother's default expression where Debbie was concerned, and it exasperated and saddened Debbie in equal measures.

'Hi, sweetheart. Are you having a fun day?'

Like she was twelve. Ten.

'Yes, thank you.'

Janet paused, obviously waiting for Debbie to say more, so she added, 'It was a lovely ceremony.'

Janet smiled. 'Good. Kate and Geoff deserve the best. And listen, sweetheart, I'm sorry if this – I mean me and Scott getting married – has come as a bit of a shock to you. I had no idea he had this in mind when we came out here; none at all! But when he told me about all the arrangements he'd made, oh, Debbie! It was just so romantic! He really bowled me over. I'm just so sorry you can't be here. Kate, Estelle and Reenie too. That would make it perfect.'

The smile on Debbie's face was beginning to hurt. She badly needed to go. Now. 'Look, Mum, it's fine, okay? It's your life.'

'All right, love. Have a nice time. Oh, and we're going to be travelling around the country for a few weeks, so don't worry if you don't hear from me. I don't think there's going to be much of a mobile signal.'

Scott came on screen, interrupting before Debbie could make any reply. 'Janet?' he said. 'We really need to go now, love. It's almost time for the ceremony.'

'Bye, Mum,' Debbie said, keen to avoid saying anything to Scott. 'Good luck.' And, handing the iPad back to Kate, she moved quickly away.

'Everything all right?' Estelle asked as Debbie

passed her on her way outside.

'Sure,' Debbie said with a fake smile. 'Just going to get some air.'

She walked out of the hotel, and across the road to the seafront where a breeze had blown up and the waves were breaking against the pier. Here there was air in abundance, but as Debbie hugged her arms around herself, she realised it wasn't air she needed at all, but forgetfulness. Not to have to think about her mother gazing into creepy Scott's eyes and saying 'I do.' Christ, the ink was barely dry on her divorce certificate from Dad.

Debbie took her phone from her bag and switched it on, waiting impatiently for it to come to life. After a minute, a message come through. Exactly the message she'd been hoping for.

Meet me? I need you! Adam X

Where? She typed, not giving herself time to think about it.

The answer came almost straight away. *Beach hut. Thirty minutes.*

OK. X she replied, then she headed back across the road to get her jacket and to say her goodbyes, every one of her recent resolutions about ending it and never seeing him out of work again trashed as surely as the baguettes which had been used in the post wedding-arch sword fight.

Two

The Gambia

It had seemed a good idea to Janet to phone Kate so she could be part of the wedding, even though she couldn't physically be there. But all she'd managed to do was make herself long to be a proper part of it all. To be there to give them both Kate and Geoff a huge hug and to throw confetti. *And* to conspire with Estelle and Reenie to present Kate with some sort of exotic lingerie. Nothing they'd imagine her actually wearing of course, with her pregnancy bump, but something that would give her and Geoff a good giggle.

One thing was for sure, when she'd come up with the plan to Skype Kate at her wedding, she certainly hadn't expected to be wearing a wedding dress herself when she did it. Getting married again – at any time of her life – hadn't featured anywhere on her agenda. And just now, telling Kate about it, Janet had almost felt as if she were speaking about some other woman, not herself. The whole thing seemed utterly unreal. *Had* Kate thought she was trying to eclipse her own big day? She hoped not.

Oh, who was she kidding? Why should the happiest day of Kate's life be spoiled by anything Janet did? Geoff and Kate were made for each other, and Kate's face had been glowing with happiness. Unlike Debbie's.

Debbie. Janet sighed, suspecting that the news of her imminent marriage to Scott had just pushed her prickly daughter even further away than ever.

'Oh, Scott,' she said now, looking at him. 'The look on Debbie's face. Did you see? She was so upset we were getting married out here, away from her.'

'She'll be all right,' he said. 'We'll make it up to her when we get back.' And he shrugged.

Janet's hands were in his as he waited to pull her to her feet, but she froze, suddenly unwilling to move. That shrug; it had said so much. Scott might ostensibly be reassuring her that everything was going to be all right, but unless she was imagining things, his shrug had clearly said *I don't give a shit.*

'Janet?' Scott's hands were pulling impatiently now. 'They're ready to make a start. We mustn't make them wait for us.'

She stared at him as if she'd never really seen him before. And perhaps she hadn't. 'You don't care, do you?' she said slowly, as the truth really began to sink in. 'You don't care about Debbie and what she thinks about us.'

Scott's face wore exactly the same stiff smile it had worn when they had been trekking on the mountain paths in New Zealand, while he waited for her to catch up with him. Most of the time he'd been slightly ahead, but every now and then he paused to wait for her. Then, almost as soon as she'd puffed up to him, he said, 'All right?', gave her arm a squeeze, and set off before she had the chance to get her breath back, or spend any time admiring the view.

'Well, Debbie hasn't made much of an effort with me, has she?' he said now, and Janet realised it was the exact same matter-of-fact tone he'd used back home when she expressed regrets about leaving her business plans to go travelling.

'The shop will still be waiting for you when you get home, Janet,' he'd said. 'You can rent it out for a while. Charities are always looking for vacant high street shops. We're not properly out of the recession yet. It's hardly the best time to start up an interior design business anyway, is it?'

And Janet had allowed herself to believe it, and to be whisked away around the world.

Not that she regretted it really; these past few months had been amazing. Mostly. And when Scott had proposed out of the blue, revealing all the secret intricate plans he'd made for the ceremony and honeymoon in The Gambia, it had seemed like a glorious continuation of the adventure. Janet had found herself saying 'yes', her heart swelling at the pleasure on Scott's face.

'Janet?' he said again now, and she noticed that the flower in his button hole was drooping in the heat.

Had it, in fact, been a bit presumptuous of him to arrange all this without consulting her properly first? Leaving no space for her to say, 'It's a lovely idea, but maybe in a few years' time when we know each other better?' Or, 'Let's wait until we get home so our friends and family can be with us.' Or even, 'No.'

Suddenly, Janet felt sick. 'Scott,' she started, and he swallowed, his dark eyes searching her face.

'You're not going to go through with it, are you?' he said. 'You aren't going to marry me.'

'No,' she whispered. 'I'm so sorry. I can't.'

Lips twisting with displeasure, Scott dropped her hands and ripped the flower from his button hole, tossing it to the ground.

'Well, fuck you, Janet,' he said viciously. 'Fuck you!' And he turned and walked away.

Janet was horrified. Where had that vicious stranger come from? 'It's too soon, that's all,' she called after him. 'Scott! Come back, please! Let's talk about this.'

Without a backward glance, Scott strode through the garden and into the hotel. With his fists clenched at his sides, he looked frightening, reminding her of Ray, her ex-husband, when she'd told him she wanted a divorce. Suddenly, Janet was afraid of what Scott might do. After all, Ray had gone berserk, ransacking the house and chucking pot plants out of the windows. How did she know Scott wouldn't do something similar?

'Scott!' she called, and as she ran after him, the flower began to slip from her hair, so she tore it out. When the wedding official stopped her, she was clutching it in her hand, her knuckles white.

'Madam, I'm so sorry, but is the wedding cancel?'

Intent on preventing Scott from doing any harm to her belongings, Janet was reluctant to stop. Until now, he'd always seemed quite a mild, easy-going man; quite good company most of the time, if a bit over-controlling. But she hadn't imagined the hatred in his eyes just now, she knew she hadn't.

'Yes,' she told the official. 'The wedding is cancel. I mean, cancelled.' And she started to hurry past him as he tried to offer her sympathy, explaining that no refund would be available.

'That's okay,' she said quickly. 'That's okay.' Janet tried to jog, but her dress was tight around her thighs, and all she could manage was a queer sort of shuffle, her lower legs coming slightly out at the sides. She was fully aware she looked ridiculous, but she didn't care. She just had to see Scott. Explain to him. Find out what he was doing. And it hit her then, how little she did actually know him if she didn't know whether or not he was up in the room right now shredding her passport or chucking her clothes out of the window.

But by the time Janet reached the hotel lobby, Scott was already getting out of the lift with his luggage, his face still like thunder. 'Scott!' she called, but he just pushed past her as if she wasn't there.

'Wait, please!' she called after him, but he continued on without a backward glance, and by the time she'd managed to hobble to the entrance again, he was climbing into a taxi. 'Scott!' But the taxi door slammed, and a second later, it was on its way, leaving her staring after it.

Now what? Now the hell what?

Trying to stem a gathering tide of panic, Janet went back into the hotel lobby. Avoiding the openly curious gaze of the receptionist, she asked for her key and tore upstairs the minute she got it. The room door was slightly open. Hurrying inside, Janet went straight to the wardrobe to check that her bag was where she had left it, hanging from a coat hanger inside her walking jacket. It was. And her purse, phone and passport were inside it.

Thank goodness.

But what now? They'd planned to stay in The Gambia for a fortnight, travelling around. Janet sank onto the bed, her hands covering her face. Think. She had to think. Her flights; maybe she could change them? Return home early. But then what? The house was gone. The shop was rented out to the cat charity. Debbie was bunking down at Kate and Geoff's. Estelle? Could she stay with Estelle and Mark? No, that would never work. Love her friend as she did, Estelle and Mark needed their privacy.

Just to talk to Estelle right now would be bliss though, and Janet reached immediately for her phone. Then she remembered the wedding. No, she couldn't ring Estelle now, present her with all this drama. Her friend didn't drink a lot, but when she did, she really did, and Janet had the feeling that Kate's wedding would prove to be one of those occasions.

Tomorrow. She would phone Estelle tomorrow. She would just have to manage by herself until then.

But suddenly, sitting with her head in her hands on the king-sized bed, Janet thought of a possible solution all by herself. The flat, above the shop. They'd kindly let her store her mother's belongings in a room they weren't using, so surely they wouldn't mind her living there? They were a charity after all. They wouldn't look after stray cats and leave humans out on the street. Of course not.

First thing tomorrow morning, she would phone Estelle and ask her to go round to the charity shop to sort it out for her. Everybody listened to Estelle. It would be all right.

Relief at having some sort of plan made Janet sit up to take a deep breath, leaning back on her hands. As they encountered the expensive cotton sheets, Janet sighed, smoothing down the fabric. How was it possible for so much to have changed, so quickly?

Scott might be the kind of man who got impatient on mountain paths, but he was a good lover. Or at least, he was compared to her ex-husband, who had never managed to satisfy her properly. Thinking about it, the sex was probably one of the main reasons she'd said yes to this world trip in the first place. The reason she'd put her business dreams on hold, and even entertained the idea of getting married so quickly after her divorce.

Janet sighed. Yes, she would certainly miss making love. And the intimate companionship that came with it. Waking up with Scott's arms still around her. The late night chats and giggles. All the things she'd hoped to find when she'd decided to sign up to the online dating agency. Marriage might have been lonely, but so had divorce, especially with all her friends in fulfilled, loving relationships. Now she was going to be alone all over again.

What if she had been meant to marry Scott? What if this was her last big chance for happiness, and she'd just turned it down? What if she had, in fact, just made the biggest mistake of her life? After all, he was right about Debbie; she hadn't been friendly to him on the few occasions they'd met. In the circumstances, Janet could hardly blame Scott for not feeling affectionate towards her daughter when she'd always behaved like a sulky, surly teenager when he was around.

Oh, God, she had to find Scott; try to talk to him. Persuade him to give her a bit of time. It wasn't too late. It couldn't be.

Decision made, Janet hurried to the door, intending to go straight out, but caught sight of herself in the mirror on the way. Hell, she couldn't go searching for

Scott dressed like that. Even though her wedding dress wasn't the long, formal type, it was still white with a beaded bustier bodice. Hardly suitable for chasing around town looking for Scott. Quickly slipping on a soft, floral-print dress instead, Janet shoved her feet into a pair of travel-stained espadrilles and headed for the door, leaving the wedding dress on the bed.

Where to look though? He'd been in a taxi. Which meant he could be anywhere by now. The airport even. But Scott loved her, didn't he? Okay, he was hurt, but after he'd got over that initial disappointment, surely he would have a change of heart? This was the man who'd haggled over the price of a wooden carving in the market the previous day for a full half hour, after all. He wasn't a man to give up easily when he wanted something.

The market! Perhaps he'd gone to the market. Yes, he'd said he wanted to return there before they left the country. She'd look there first.

Like the previous day, the market was a bewildering mass of sights and smells and kerfuffle. Yesterday it had been rich and exciting; a colourful, crazy, incredible feast to the senses, with the pungent smell of cooking food, animal dung and sweat. Steaming pans of stew and rice she and Scott were invited to try. A stall of stunningly bright fabrics Janet had wanted to completely buy up and ship home. The clamour of life and people and easy smiles – a communal bath of humanity to soak yourself in.

Now, today, everything had changed. The market was no different, but Janet was, and, trying to make progress through the crowd while simultaneously looking around for Scott, she constantly stumbled and knocked into people. A woman walked past holding four chickens by the feet, heads down, like a noisy bunch of macabre roses. The mix of smells made it difficult to breathe, and the cacophony of voices made her already throbbing head throb still more.

Distorted sounds came at her in waves, and Janet wanted to put her hands up to her ears to block them out. Scott wasn't here. Why would he be here? She'd been stupid to think he might be. He wouldn't do a spot of souvenir shopping right after he'd been jilted. He would just leave.

'Lady? You all right? Here, sit. Sit.'

Somebody's hands were on her shoulders, steering her, pushing her down onto a rickety chair. When Janet opened her eyes, she caught a glimpse of a woman's round, kindly face. Then suddenly a wave of blackness washed over her, and she had to put her head down between her knees to avoid passing out.

'You be okay,' the unknown woman assured her. 'Just take a minute. It is the heat. No good for you toubobs.'

The blackness was passing now. Janet even managed to smile a little at the use of the Gambian word for tourists. She'd heard it over and over again since she and Scott had arrived in the country. Toubob. Toubob. Scott had laughingly explained to her the word's origin; the word came from the Gambian habit of begging for 'two bob', or 'two shillings'.

Scott … Anxiously, Janet began to get to her feet.

'Wait a little, lady,' her saviour advised. 'No need to hurry. You're on Gambian time now. Here, drink.'

'Thank you.' Janet took the cup the woman offered her, recognising the bitter-sweet tang of the local drink called attire. 'Thank you for helping me,' she said again. 'I'm sorry to be so much trouble. I don't know what came over me. I felt faint suddenly.'

The woman smiled. She was broad-beamed, and about thirty years old, Janet thought, dressed in a floor-length traditional African grandmuba in red fabric printed with bright yellow flowers. It was beautiful material, and, looking beyond her, Janet saw with surprise she was at the fabric stall that had so impressed her the previous day.

'I see you, lady,' the woman said, instantly claiming Janet's attention back from the brightly-coloured cottons. 'You lost. Looking around, not finding what you want to see. You panic.'

Lost. Yes, that's what she was. A forty-four-year-old woman, alone in Africa, without even a home to go back to. Lost for sure.

'Hey, lady, you don't cry at my stall please,' the woman said. 'People don't buy here if they see a crying lady.'

Janet hadn't realised she was crying. She hastily wiped her eyes with the backs of her hands and stood up. 'Oh, I'm so sorry,' she said, but the woman only laughed and pushed her back down again.

'I make a joke with you, lady,' she said. 'Stay. You stay with Fanna for now. That's me. Fanna. What is your name?'

'Janet.'

'Janet. That is nice. A nice name. And what you want to find in this market, Janet?'

Janet looked down into her cup of attire. 'My … my … friend,' she said. 'I was looking for my friend.'

'Well,' said Fanna. 'Your friend want to be found, he look for you. For now, you stay here. Okay?'

Janet smiled wanly. 'Okay.'

Sipping her drink, Janet watched Fanna at work, selling her fabrics, and gradually relaxed into her bones again. Yesterday, gazing in rapture at the stall, Janet had stroked the lengths of cloth and wanted to buy a piece of everything to take home with her. 'Aren't they gorgeous, Scott?' she'd said, but Scott had just given her arm a little squeeze, glancing over at the stall with scant attention.

'You'd hardly be able to wear any of them in Shelthorpe-on-Sea, would you?' he'd said, kissing her on the top of her head. 'You'd stick out like a sore thumb. Come on, I want to look at that carving stall over there.'

And reluctantly, Janet had abandoned the fabric stall

to trail after him, where he'd proceeded to haggle ruthlessly to get the price of the carving he wanted to a rock bottom price.

'This one would be good for you,' Fanna told her now, holding up a bolt of fabric. 'Stand, Janet, let me see.'

Obediently, Janet stood for Fanna to drape the fabric against her. It was a deep jade green colour with a print of white flowers and butterflies. Over-the-top. Completely unsuitable for Shelthorpe-on-Sea, as Scott had said.

'Yes, that very good for you.'

'I'll take it,' Janet said, and paid the first price Fanna mentioned without even thinking about haggling.

After the fabric had been folded up for her, Fanna regarded her. 'You look better now.'

'Yes,' agreed Janet. 'I feel a lot better now. Thank you for being so nice to me. I really appreciate it.'

Fanna smiled her broad smile. 'It's nice to be nice,' she said. 'You come to visit me again. And I hope you find your friend, if this is what you wish to do.'

'Thank you,' Janet said, and as she moved away, smiling and waving, she wondered if that was, actually, what she did want.

Three

Shelthorpe-on Sea, Norfolk

At their wedding reception, Kate and Geoff were dancing together.

'Did you see Debbie's face when Janet said she was going to marry Scott?' Kate said. 'The poor girl looked gutted.'

'She'll be all right,' Geoff said, and she smiled at him, reaching up to stroke his newly-trimmed beard. How lucky she was to have someone who totally got her. A man she could share her passion and the depths of her soul with, who was also her best friend, her old mucker, her drinking mate.

'I love you, Mr Bramling,' she said, kissing the tip of his nose.

'Love you too, Mrs Bramling,' he said, cinching her in even closer for a passionate kiss.

'Watch it, you'll squash Bradley,' she joked, using their nickname for the baby growing in her belly, and

Geoff laughed, snuffling her ear with his mouth in a way that sent so many shivers down Kate's legs, it was difficult not to squeal out loud.

'Bradley best get used to being squashed,' he whispered. 'I've booked the bridal suite at the Country House Hotel for us tonight.'

Kate pulled back from her husband, gobsmacked. 'But we said we wouldn't have a honeymoon; not until after we'd got the house sorted.'

'It's only one night, Katie,' Geoff soothed her. 'If you want to know, I got a bargain deal because of a last minute cancellation. But I'm going to make it the best night of your life.'

Every night with you is the best night of my life, she wanted to say, but she had a feeling it would sound too cheesy even for her wedding day, so she gave him a fierce kiss instead.

After they'd pulled apart, Kate suddenly noticed a woman standing at the edge of the dancefloor watching them. 'Who's that woman?' she asked Geoff.

'What woman?'

'Over there, next to your Cousin Toby. Wide lady with a pink fascinator and matching lipstick.'

Geoff took a look. 'No idea. Spotted her earlier on. Thought she must be someone you'd invited.'

Kate frowned. 'No; never seen her before in my life. Oh look, she's holding a present up. Perhaps she wants to give it to us.'

'Well, that's very nice of her, but she can bloomin'

well wait. Nobody's interrupting my first dance with my new bride, present or no present.'

'Ah!' said Kate, snuggling close again.

By the time Kate remembered the woman a little later on, she was nowhere to be seen. There was only a beautifully gift-wrapped package with Kate's name on it, lying on a table next to her wedding bouquet.

As Kate began to open the package, her mind was only half on the task, because Geoff was acting the fool, taking his best man Tom in a clinch and attempting to waltz around the dancefloor with him.

Laughing at Tom's attempts to wriggle free, Kate pulled the final piece of wrapping paper from the present. It was a book. *Staying in Neutral - Responses to Change Your Life.*

What the heck? Why on earth would anyone give her a self-help book for a wedding present? Kate turned the book over to glance at the earnestly-smiling portrait of its author, Corrinne Walker. How strange. She was about to wade into the blurb to see if it offered any further insight, when Geoff called her over. Putting the book down on the table along with the discarded wrapping paper, she went to see what he wanted.

And a little later, when an over-zealous waiter scooped both book and wrapping paper into a black plastic sack along with the party-popper detritus, Kate didn't notice. She was hell bent on sucking every last bit of pleasure out of this, her big day to end all big days. Besides, she was desperate for the loo.

When Kate came out of the toilet cubicle, she found her friend Estelle touching up her make-up, her back glamorously bare in her chic linen dress.

'Hi, sweetie,' Estelle said, turning as soon as she saw Kate in the mirror. 'Are you having the wedding of your dreams?'

'I certainly am.'

'Good. It's just a shame Janet can't be here too.'

'She's only gone and got herself hitched to Scott,' Kate told her friend. 'She skyped me just now.'

Estelle shook her head. 'Silly girl. Still, I'm not surprised, are you? I thought she might. If she'd been here, the three of us would probably have been able to make her see sense, but out there with all those sandy beaches fringed with palm trees ...'

Kate nodded. 'Yeah.'

Estelle squeezed her arm. 'Janet will be all right. She's pretty strong, you know. I don't think we need to worry about her.'

'Yeah, you're right,' Kate sighed. 'Hey, you'll never guess; Geoff's booked the Country House Hotel for us tonight!'

'How fabulous,' said Estelle. 'You'll love it.'

Kate pulled a face. 'Might have guessed you'd have already stayed there.'

Estelle squeezed her shoulder. 'I've never stayed in the bridal suite though, which I assume is what Geoff's booked?'

Kate grinned. 'Yeah.'

Estelle smiled back. 'Well, have an amazing time, all right? You deserve it, the two of you.'

'Thanks.'

Leaving the ladies, the two women embraced. 'I suppose Geoff and I better circulate,' Kate said. 'See you later.'

'Yes, and do me a favour, will you? When you throw that wedding bouquet of yours into the crowd, don't aim for me. Adore Mark as I do, I'm not ready to get married yet.'

Kate laughed. 'Got you.'

Estelle moved away, and Kate stood, still smiling, looking around for Geoff and putting a hand up to her back, which was starting to ache. Since this was nothing compared to the relentless sickness she'd experienced for the first four months of her pregnancy, Kate didn't mind. She could put up with a twinge in her back, which was just as well, because the scans showed that Bradley was already breaking records on the size front. And *that* was hardly surprising, when you looked at her and Geoff. They were hardly petite, either of them. Although in Geoff's case, that probably had quite a lot to do with bread, cakes and beer.

Beer. What she wouldn't give right now for a perfectly poured pint. But she had given up drink as soon as she'd learned she was pregnant.

'Bradley,' she said, with one hand on her bump, 'you'd better be worth all this sacrifice, d'you hear?'

With Geoff nowhere in view, Kate began to tour the room by herself, thinking how difficult it had been to give up her pints of bitter. She'd done it right away, cold turkey, but it had only been the onset of morning sickness that had chased away the cravings.

It was tricky really, with her and Geoff starting out as drinking buddies the way they had. Kate knew he felt a bit guilty about drinking in front of her now. No doubt that was where he was at the moment; enjoying a crafty pint with Tom. It didn't seem to matter how often she told Geoff she didn't mind about giving up the drink – that it seemed like a miracle to her that she was with him and pregnant when not so long ago she'd been alone, feeling as if she had nothing to live for – he still felt bad about it. But what did a few missed beers matter when she was so thrilled to be expecting their baby?

Still, she could certainly murder a pint right now.

Suddenly, Kate spotted Tom at the bar. Geoff wasn't with him, but she went over anyway. If anyone knew where Geoff was, it would be Tom. When she got there, Tom was in the act of raising a fresh pint to his lips, and when he saw her he put the glass down and swooped in for a kiss, leaving the tantalising taste of Broadland Best on her lips.

'Hey, gorgeous! How's it feel to be married to old Geoff?' he asked.

'Lonely, at the moment,' Kate confessed. 'D'you know where he's got off to?'

'Not a clue,' Tom said. 'Thought he was with you. Want me to help you look?'

'Nah,' Kate said. 'It's all right. You enjoy your beer.'

'Cheers!' Tom said, raising his glass to her, and Kate moved on, smiling ruefully.

It was several minutes later before Kate finally tracked Geoff down. He was out on the hotel balcony, sitting looking out to sea.

'Geoff?' He didn't look round when she called to him from the doorway, so she went right out and closed the door behind her, shutting out the wedding noise. The sun was starting to go down in a fiery show that put him in silhouette, making it impossible to see his expression. But something about his stillness and the way he hadn't turned round made Kate feel suddenly frightened. What was he doing out here, all alone? Geoff wasn't the run-away-from-the-party-to-be-alone type.

'Hi, you,' she said, moving to squat awkwardly down in front of him, holding his arms as she looked up into his face. From this angle, his features were lit by the glow of the sinking sun, but the light didn't quite hide their tiredness. Or something that looked scarily like despair.

'What's wrong?' she asked, really frightened now. 'Not regretting marrying me already, are you?'

He drew in a breath and let it out again slowly. Then, finally, he turned to her, reaching out to stroke her hair. 'Get real, Katie,' he said slowly. 'You're the love of my life. Why would I ever regret marrying you?'

Relief brought tears to her eyes, and she shook her head. 'I don't know. Just trying to work out why you're sitting out here on your own looking like an old git who's lost his bowling balls,' she said, and although her tone was flippant, she could still sense some big emotion in him, and the fear wouldn't quite leave her.

He looked away again, out to the west, where the sun was slowly disappearing. Kate sensed he wasn't so much looking at the spectacle as avoiding looking at her. 'It's so good, Katie,' he said, and now there was no mistaking the emotion in his voice. 'It's so fucking good. You, the baby; it's all more than I thought I'd ever have in my life. Overwhelms me sometimes, it does. Yes, that's what this is. You overwhelming me.'

She still had hold of his arms, and now she gave them a little shake. 'And is that a good thing?' she asked. 'Me, overwhelming you?'

'What do you think?' He was still talking to the disappearing sun, making her want to give him a harder shake; for him to start rabbiting on about having a second crazy stab at beating the world record for the biggest ever trifle with his students at college or some other rot like that. Anything but this scary philosophical stuff.

'I don't know, Geoff,' she said, 'that's why I'm on my frigging knees with Bradley's weight threatening to topple me over, asking you.'

He turned then, blinking, seeming to see how she was positioned for the first time.

'What are you doing down there?' he asked. 'You'll ruin your dress. Let alone squash Bradley's bits.'

Kate closed her eyes gratefully. He was back from whatever bleak, alien place he'd gone to, and as he helped her to her feet, relief made her lips wobble.

'Ah, Katie,' he said softly, noticing and kissing her mouth. 'My Katie. My wife.'

She sniffed, wiping away a tear. 'I might not have agreed to marry you if I'd known it was going to turn you to mush. Now, are you coming inside to have another dance or not?'

'I'll come in, but not for a dance. Got a bit energetic while you were titivating in the ladies, I think. Pulled something in my back.'

'Was that why you were out here?' she asked. 'Because you pulled a muscle?'

'Yeah, but it's nothing much. Just wanted to rest it so it didn't get in the way of the rest of the evening's entertainment, if you know what I mean.'

He gave her a wink, and she smiled, reassured. 'It better not do,' she quipped.

But in the end, it wasn't either of their bad backs that got in the way when they got to their honeymoon suite. It was the drink. Or at least, Kate assumed it was the amount of drink he'd consumed that made Geoff fall asleep open-mouthed in his boxers on top of the king-sized bed while she was in the bathroom.

Whatever, he was out for the count, and Kate pulled a cover over him, snuggling up and trying not to mind too much. It was difficult to get to sleep though, and she wished she'd brought something to read with her. Anything would do, some mindless paperback that would bore her eyes into closing. Only it had never occurred to her that a paperback, boring or otherwise, would be something she'd have need of on her wedding night.

Lying awake in the darkness, listening to Geoff snoring loudly beside her, Kate suddenly remembered the book the strange woman had left for her. What had it been called? Neutral something. What had happened to it? Put with all the other presents probably. Not here, anyway, where she could do with it, that was for sure.

Four

Extract from Staying in Neutral, Responses to Change Your Life by Corrinne Walker.

You're late for work because someone has thrown themselves onto the railway line. You feel sympathetic, glad it wasn't you up there, finding the courage to leap.

But then it happens again, the next day. And the next. They're like lemmings up there, with their shitty lives, waiting to jump. And always in the rush hour. Never at 10 a.m., or 11 a.m., when it's just the tourists en route for the London Dungeon, or their free trip up the Cheese Grater to see the view of the Tower of London like a model far below them.

No, they've got to make the most possible impact with their final gesture, and they couldn't care less about your blood pressure, sat there helpless on that train, somewhere between Colchester and bloody Kelvedon.

They couldn't give a monkey's that you could lose your job because you're consistently late. That you'll no longer be able to afford the au pair, and you'll have to bake cakes and do voluntary work and pretend to the world you're happy being an earth-mother-stay-at-home-mum. And all while your husband's at large in the world with his immaculate suit and Creed aftershave, and never so much as a whiff of baby sick or mustard-bum poo.

He'll return home after a day of exciting deals and flirtatious banter, expecting a tasty, well-presented meal and willing sex, and it will be as much as you can do to growl something primeval at him before you head for the bath tub in a vain attempt to scrub away your frustration and resentment. You're so suffused with them both, the bath water fairly fizzes, and much of the steam on the expensive floor to ceiling mirror has come out of your own ears.

And all because of a string of suicides by some selfish, down-on-their-luck losers. The injustice of it all makes you want to scream. Either that, or grab your coat, put it on over your bath-wet body and clomp down to that sodding railway bridge yourself.

Sisters, stop.

We've all been there, with that spiral of self-destructiveness. We've all blamed others for our misfortunes, and slumped with despair and self-pity. But unless you want to be a martini-quaffing martyr or a hatred-haggled harridan, flailing at the injustice of the world and watching your former friends cross the road to avoid you and your negativity, you need to take action. You need to do something about your reactions to the bad, the irritating, the stressful and the downright disappointing happenings of life. To understand that, if you're alive, shit happens.

Because this is life we're living, not some happy-ever-after movie. Your car will break down on your way to the airport for your dream holiday. You'll be the only one at your Weight Watchers group to put on weight. Your boyfriend will always be busy when you call him. You'll get gout. You'll be first in the queue for the Liberty's sale and a security alert will force you to vacate the area.

Shit. Happens.

Let me tell you, the day I realised that – truly embraced the fact and decided I would no longer let it affect me – was the day I really started living.

When shit happens, we have two choices. We can let shit have power over us and our emotions and responses. But who wants shit to have power over them? Not me. Alternatively, we can keep hold of our power and choose our own reactions. Because all those shitty things that happen to us are events, just as all the good things that happen to us are events.

You find your daughter's lost hamster alive and well under the fridge. That's an event. You give an amazing presentation and win your company a lucrative contract. An event. You get the flu and miss a music concert you bought the tickets for a year ago. An event. Your mother dies. An event.

Yes, I know what you're saying. That missing a pop concert and your mother dying are hardly in the same league. Well, I guess that depends to some extent on the quality of your relationship with your mother.

Only kidding! Of course one outweighs the other. But they are both still events, and I put it to you that we can – and should – choose how we wish to react to events.

Events – and this is very important – are *neutral things*. Like a closet full of beige clothes. The trouble is, many of us have such chaotic closets – colours all jumbled up, red next to lime green, summer dresses next to winter coats, jeans we'll never fit into again next to shorts that make us look like geriatric ramblers. And when shit comes calling, we reach into the mess of a closet to snatch up something red or purple or angry orange, and we wrap it closely around us until it feels like a part of our skin. When actually, what we need to do is to stand back, and give ourselves a little space. Keep hold of our dignity and our emotional control. Recognise that shit for what it is. A stinky, unwanted interruption in our lives.

Five

The Gambia

After she left the market, Janet wandered down to the beach. The sun was starting to go down, and the sky was tinged with glowing pink. It was beautiful. Peaceful.

Janet loved walking by the sea. At home, a walk by the tide's edge often helped when she felt churned up about something. She'd practically worn the beach out during her divorce. And, through it all, her friends had been there at her side, strong and straight-talking. Estelle and Kate might be ten years younger than her, but the age gap had never made any difference. Neither had it mattered that Reenie was older. All of them had been such a support. Especially Estelle.

Sod it. Waiting until tomorrow to speak to Estelle might be the sensible thing, but Janet didn't feel sensible. Two minutes speaking to her friend would calm her down, whether Estelle were off her face or not. She would call her now.

But, to Janet's disappointment, the call went straight through to voice mail. She left a message, doing her best not to sound too desperate. 'Hi, Estelle, it's Janet. Hope you and Mark are having a good time at the wedding. Look, something's happened. Something big. I'll ring you again tomorrow to tell you about it. Okay, 'bye for now. Make sure you give them both a good send off. Hope your hangover doesn't hurt too much in the morning!'

Putting her phone away again, Janet sighed. Then she walked some more, imagining that Estelle were here with her, saying, *Come on now, Janet. Shoulders back. Take a big breath. It will all be okay. You can do this!*

Janet took the deep breath the imagined Estelle had advised her to take, feeling slightly better. Somehow, just thinking about those hard times and all the support her friends had given her had helped.

She would come through this. She could do it. Scott had made a booking in a fancy restaurant for them this evening. Why not go there to eat anyway and sod the expense? If Scott did end up having a change of heart, he'd come there looking for her. And if he didn't … Well, if he didn't, she'd decide what she was going to do next in the morning.

'Hey, lady,' said a male voice. 'Hello, how are you?'

He was tall and good-looking, in his early twenties

she guessed, dressed in western clothes – jeans and a T-shirt with a picture of a motorbike on the front. He saw her looking. 'You like it? That's a Harley Davidson. One day I will own a Harley Davidson. For now, I only have the name. Davidson, this is me.'

'Davidson?' she said, because it seemed so unlikely. 'That's your name?'

He flashed a huge smile at her, clearly delighted she'd spoken instead of telling him to get lost, and suddenly Janet remembered the advice about dealing with bumsters she and Scott had been given by the hotel when they'd arrived. To be polite but firm, and to just walk on. So far, Janet hadn't needed to take this advice, because she'd been with Scott. Now, remembering it, she began to walk back up the beach.

'Yes, Davidson is my name now,' he said, tagging right along beside her. 'David for short. But when I was born, my name was Massaneh.'

'Massaneh is a nice name,' she said, keeping to the 'be polite' part of the hotel's advice.

'I can be Massaneh for you,' he came right back. 'If you prefer it. Or David. Or Davidson. Where are you from?'

'England,' she said, offering the information reluctantly.

'England, that is nice. I know another lady from England. Very nice lady. Binta, she is called here. I don't know her name in England. What is *your* name?'

Goodness, this being polite but firm was difficult.

Would it be rude not to tell him? Surely it couldn't do any harm? 'Janet,' she said. 'My name is Janet.'

'Jan-net.' He repeated her name slowly, relishing both syllables with reverent care, and it sounded so ridiculous, having her humble name rolled out in that way, that she burst out laughing.

'Why you laugh?' he asked, smiling at her. 'Are you laughing at me, pretty Jan-net?' His eyes were all the time seeking to make a connection with hers, his hand hovering, as if he'd like to stroke her arm.

'No,' she said, suddenly feeling exhausted. 'I'm not laughing at you. 'It's just been a crazy day, that's all. I'm probably a bit ... '

Hysterical; that was what she was, very likely. This whole damn day had been surreal, and it seemed to be continuing that way.

Davidson was looking at her expectantly, waiting for her to finish her sentence. 'How it been crazy for you today, Janet?' he asked. 'Tell David. It will help to talk.'

It was tempting to spew it all out, the way she'd wanted to do with Estelle. But she couldn't.

She sighed, summoning some strength from somewhere. 'Look, I have to go now, okay? But it was very nice to meet you, David. Goodbye.' And she began to walk quickly away.

He caught up with her in two easy lopes. 'Where you go? A restaurant, to eat? I take you there, make sure you're safe. There are lots of men here who want to speak to a pretty lady like you.'

Once again, Janet wanted to laugh. Clearly, it didn't occur to David to put himself into this category.

'No thank you,' she said. 'I'll be fine. Goodbye, David.'

But when she walked on, he followed her and she turned to face him. 'Goodbye, David,' she said again, making her tone as firm as she possibly could. 'I'd like to walk on my own. Thank you.'

Finally, he seemed to accept it. 'Okay, Jan-net.' He smiled. 'You have a good evening. Enjoy this beautiful country of mine.'

'I will,' she said, and as she went on her way, confident he wouldn't continue to follow her this time, she thought regretfully of all the places she and Scott were to have visited while they were in The Gambia and sighed. If only he hadn't got it into his head to marry her. He'd ruined everything.

Half an hour later, Janet was sitting at the table Scott had booked for them.

'You are ready to order now, madam?' The waiter was back. She'd fobbed him off once already, but now it was twenty past eight. Crazy day or not, she was hungry, and Scott clearly wasn't going to come. It had been daft to even think he would. After all, if he wanted to find her, he could just go to the hotel. Or phone her, come to that.

Janet forced herself to smile. 'Yes, thank you,' she

said. 'I'll have the shrimps fried in garlic, please. And a glass of white wine. Your house wine is fine. Thank you.'

The waiter bowed respectfully and took her menu from her. Janet's table was outside, on the terrace. Presumably Scott had requested it, but it was cooler now, and Janet was glad she had her piece of material from the market. It made quite an effective wrap.

Arranging the fabric more comfortably around her shoulders, Janet smiled to herself, remembering her encounter with Fanna. The woman had been so caring, even if it had resulted in a sale for her. Did she feel passionate about the fabrics she sold? Janet hoped so.

Once, Janet had possessed a huge collection of fabrics; all waiting for her to do something with them. Her husband had moaned about them continually, but Janet had put up with his complaints, refusing to get rid of them. Where were they now? She sighed, thinking bleakly of all her possessions in storage. It was symptomatic of how chaotic her life had been in recent months that she had no idea where the bag of precious fabrics was.

And yet, in the depths of all that chaos, she had seriously contemplated getting married again. Sitting alone at her table, Janet shook her head at herself. What had she being thinking of? She must have been living in some sort of a bubble since Scott's proposal. Or maybe even longer than that. Maybe since she had first met him.

Well, if she had been living in a bubble, then it had most definitely burst with his casual reaction to Debbie's disappointment and his vicious response to Janet's change of heart. It was as if he'd turned into someone else. Either that, or he'd revealed the true person he was.

Perhaps it was just as well she hadn't been able to find him while she'd been full of panicky remorse about her decision. Yes, definitely.

There was a vase of large-petalled flowers in the centre of the table. Janet reached out to touch the petals, uncertain whether the flowers were real or artificial. They were real, and silken to the touch. Wondering what the flowers were, Janet looked round at the other tables to see if they had the same flowers. As she did so, she realised that the balcony was full of couples – every single table was occupied by a man and a woman gazing into each other's eyes.

If she had never skyped Kate at her wedding, then she would never have seen the expression on Debbie's face. If she had never seen the expression on Debbie's face, then she would have married Scott. And if she had married Scott, then they would have been a couple like all the other couples here, gazing at each other and holding hands across the table. No doubt she would be feeling exhilarated; fresh from the glow of love-making, finding every little thing Scott said fascinating, with the veil over her eyes intact.

A voice interrupted her thoughts. 'Hello, again, Jan-net.'

It was David, from the beach. Davidson. Mass something. Massaneh?

'David,' she said, somehow not feeling surprised to see him. Not surprised, but not pleased either. 'What are you doing here?'

He shrugged expressive shoulders. 'This is a restaurant. People come here to eat. No different for me, pretty Jan-net.' And he proceeded to settle himself down at the empty table for two right next to her.

Janet shook her head, smiling. He was cheeky, she'd give him that.

'You are laughing at me again?' he asked, and his smile was so appealing, she did just that.

'Yes, David, I am.'

He laughed, the sound deep and attractive. 'Well, that's okay. I don't mind. But, Janet, we are friends. It is so silly we do not sit together. Shall I move to your table?' And in a flash, he was in the seat opposite hers.

'David,' she said, and he lifted innocent eyebrows.

'What?' he said, spreading his hands. 'You like for me to move back again?'

'Yes,' she said firmly, 'I think that's best.'

'Okay,' he said. 'Anything you say. I want only that you are happy.'

'Good.'

David returned to his own table, but when he continued to stare at her with that smile on his face, she sighed.

'Please don't stare at me like that,' she said reprovingly. 'I want to be able to relax and enjoy my meal.'

'So sorry, Jan-net,' he said. 'It is hard for a man not to stare when a lady as pretty as you. But tell me, where is this meal, you talk about? I see no meal. I think the waiter he has put it in the wrong place? Maybe under the table instead of on top of the table?' And he made a big show of looking under the table.

Janet supressed a smile with difficulty, reminding herself yet again of the hotel's advice. Firm but polite and keep on walking. Well, short of leaving before she'd eaten, the keeping on walking option was going to be difficult. And she had to admit, she liked him, despite everything. He was amusing, even if he did have some ulterior motive for talking to her. Which, clearly he must have, since she had to be almost twice his age.

Come to think of it, when she'd taken a look around the other tables, there had seemed to be a large disparity between the ages of most of the couples. Janet looked quickly around the terrace again to check. Goodness, yes; there was definitely a disparity. Sex tourism was rife in The Gambia, she was aware of that, but this was blatant.

'Listen, David, just so we understand each other,' she said, in her best pretend-you're-Estelle voice, 'I'm not going to pay for your meal. Or … for anything else.' Janet made herself look straight at him so that he would believe her, and willed her cheeks not to go red.

But of course they did. They really shouldn't do; not after completing the course about confidence and sensuality on which she'd met her best friends. But hey ho, sensually confident or not, she was still herself; a woman who blushed easily. All the courses and workshops in the world weren't about to change that.

'Jan-net, I am shocked that you think this of me,' David said. 'Shocked.' And he did, indeed, look shocked. For the first time since she'd met him, his face was serious, and she wondered if she'd misjudged him. 'This was not in my head for a minute. I have my own money. I can pay for me myself.'

She nodded. 'Then, good. That's good.'

The waiter appeared with her glass of wine and took David's order. After he'd left, she and David sat at their neighbouring tables, self-consciously not speaking. After a while, Janet couldn't help herself from glancing discreetly over at David and found him looking down at his phone. Not that she was really convinced he was interested in it. In fact, he looked a bit miserable. Lonely, even.

She sighed, twisting her napkin in her fingers. Oh, hell. Would there really be any harm in talking to him? If he accepted what she'd said about her not paying for anything?

'Are you from Banjul, David?' she asked, and instantly he put his phone away, his face breaking into a smile.

'No, Jan-net, I am not from here. I came to Banjul three years ago, when I finished school. My family is Upriver. You been Upriver yet, Jan-net?'

She shook her head regretfully, thinking again of all the trips she and Scott had planned to do. 'No. We were going to go next week, to do some exploring.'

David frowned. 'Who is this we you speak of? You have a friend here?'

She looked into her glass of wine, wishing she'd been more careful about what she'd said. 'No, not anymore.' She sighed. 'To be honest, we argued.'

'Oh, Jan-net,' he said with a shake of his head. 'This is not good.'

She sighed again. 'I know.' She forced herself to smile. 'But that's life, isn't it? These things happen. We wanted different things.'

David nodded. 'You married, Jan-net?' he asked.

She looked up at him, surprised by the question. 'Not anymore, no. I'm divorced. That was why I fell out with my ... friend. He wanted to get married, but I didn't. I ... changed my mind.'

Why on earth was she telling him all this? Why hadn't she got more control of her words? A quick glance down at her wine glass showed that it was almost empty. Perhaps that was why. Or perhaps she was just bloody well lonely and alone.

'Maybe he is not the right man for you, Jan-net?' David suggested, and she shrugged.

'Maybe.'

There was a brief pause while they both contemplated this. Then David asked, 'You want to be married again, Jan-net? If it is the right man?'

She shook her head. 'No. I don't know. Maybe, one day.'

'Me, I would like to marry one day. But not like my grandfather. He has four wives. I do not wish to have four wives.'

'Four?' Janet repeated, astonished.

He nodded. 'Yes. In Gambia, a man can have up to five wives. My father, he has only one, but my grandfather,' and he paused to shake his head, 'I think he will find another new wife one day. He never thinks about the children, and how they will eat, my grandfather.'

Janet was intrigued. 'And do you think about those things then?'

'Of course. This is my country, but one day I will leave here. My family is very poor. Everyone here in The Gambia is poor. The tourists, if they stay in one place, they do not see so much. Life here is very hard, and this is not what I want for me. So yes, Jan-net, when I can, I will leave and make a good life; send money back to my family. I hope that it will be soon. You remember the English lady I tell you about? Binta? She paid for my education.'

'She did?'

'Mm hmm. When I first met her, she worked for a charity. I see her a lot of times when she came to my village. One day, when I was nine years old, I ran after her truck to throw a note into it.'

Janet was captivated, imagining the scene. 'What did the note say?'

David's laugh sounded slightly embarrassed. 'It say, I am Massaneh. Please help me go to school. And, you know what, Jan-net? She did. Binta, she pay for everything for me. For six years.'

Janet felt tears in her eyes. 'That's amazing,' she said, feeling humbled.

'But Jan-net, I do not want to make you cry!' he said, and next moment he was back in the seat opposite hers clutching her hand across the table.

Carefully, Janet removed her hand and rummaged in her bag for a tissue. 'You didn't. I mean, it's just so moving. And I cry very easily. But tell me, do you still see this Binta?'

David shook his head and looked genuinely sad. 'No, I have not seen Binta for many years now. I think she stopped coming to Gambia, but I do not know why this is.'

Once again, Janet felt moved. Clearly David had been very fond of his sponsor, and the whole story made her feel quite inadequate. Apart from the odd donation into a charity box and a phone-in fundraiser, she'd never done anything much to help those less fortunate than herself. Apart from rent out her shop to a cat charity, she supposed.

'Yes,' David continued. 'Without Binta, I would

never have received an education. My family is too poor to pay for books and clothes and exams. This is why I want to do lots of things with my life, you see, for Binta. So she not waste her money.'

Janet smiled at him. 'That's such a great goal to have, David,' she said. 'Really great. And I'm sure you will.'

The waiter brought Janet's food to the table. And when, soon afterwards, David's meal arrived, it seemed churlish to ask him to return to his own table. Besides, his story about throwing the note into the charity worker's truck had changed things.

'Tell me about your life in England, Jan-net,' David asked, and so she did.

She talked about her daughter and the seaside town she lived in. About her shop, and her future plans for it. Somehow, she even found herself telling him about her fabric stash and how she'd always loved sewing. He was easy to talk to. Interested.

'I like you, Jan-net,' he said when at last there was a pause in the conversation. 'I like you a lot. You are a very interesting lady.'

Janet shook her head, blushing slightly. 'Oh, I don't really think so. No, I'm not really very interesting. I've had an interesting few months, it's true. Well, an interesting year, I suppose, but really … '

'You are interesting,' he insisted, interrupting her. 'This afternoon, as soon as I see you at Fanna's stall, I know that I will like you.'

Janet frowned, suddenly feeling cautious all over again. 'You saw me at Fanna's stall?'

He nodded. 'Yes, I see you there. And at other places in the market before that. I see you searching, and I think to myself, that lady, she is looking for a man.'

Still frowning, Janet had a sudden mental view of what she must have looked like as she searched wildly around the market. 'Yes, well, I told you. I was looking for my boyfriend.' She broke off, looking at him. 'Wait a minute, if you saw me in the market, then … '

But she had guessed the answer to her question before she'd even asked it. They hadn't met by chance on the beach at all. It had all been premeditated. David had followed her there.

Janet sighed, glancing down at her half-empty plate as she analysed her feelings. Did it matter? Yes, since she felt flat and let down, then apparently it did.

Not appearing to realise that anything had changed, David reached for her hand across the table again. 'It is so funny, Jan-net, you know? I see you do a lot a lot of searching, all over town, and all the time, there is a man for you right here.'

Oh, well. It had been good to talk to someone who seemed to be genuinely interested in everything she had to say. For twenty minutes, she'd even been able to forget about the current disaster of her life. 'Oh, David,' she said sadly, 'now you've gone and spoiled it all.'

His face fell. 'How is this? You don't like me?'

'No, it's not that. I'm just not looking for anybody in my life. I already told you that. And even if I were looking for someone – which I'm not, then you're so young; far too young for me. My daughter's older than you are.'

He smiled, making a dismissive flapping gesture with his hand. 'Age means nothing unless you say it means something. I like older women, Jan-net. And you are not so old anyway, I think.'

'I'm forty-four. How old is your mother?'

He shrugged. 'This is not important. My mother is my mother, and you are you.'

Janet tried to pull her hand away, but he wouldn't let her. Stupid to feel offended. He was poor, that was all. This was what David did to earn a living; tried to seduce female tourists. Perhaps it was best that his Binta had lost contact with him. Janet couldn't help thinking she'd be disappointed.

'Let go of my hand, please,' she said, trying to pull it away, but he still he wouldn't release her.

'You and me, we have good times together, Jan-net,' he said, staring into her eyes, and she thought she could detect a slightly desperate note to his voice now. 'Come on, you know this is what you want too.'

'No,' she said firmly, shaking her head. She tugged at her hand again, finally managing to get it free. 'I don't want that. Not in the way you mean. And now, I'm going back to my hotel. Alone. Goodbye, David.'

'But, you haven't finished your food.'

'I'm not hungry any longer,' she said, standing up.

He stood up too. 'You are angry with me. Please don't be angry with me, Jan-net.'

She sighed again. 'I'm not angry with you, David; not really. I want to go back to my hotel, that's all. It's been a long day.'

The waiter came over. 'Everything is okay, madam?'

She gave him a tight-lipped smile. 'Yes, thank you, everything's fine. I just have to leave now. Here, this is for the bill.' And she put some notes down on the table and began to walk away.

'Jan-net!' David called after her, but she kept on walking, hoping against hope he wouldn't follow her.

To her surprise, he didn't. But she hadn't been on the street for more than two minutes before someone else did.

'Hello, pretty lady, where are you from? You have a nice holiday? You want to have a drink with me?'

This time, Janet walked quickly on without speaking or making eye contact. She'd learned her lesson.

'Hey, lady, you no speak to me? Why you in such a hurry? I only want to talk to you!'

He kept on and on at her, not giving up, so she walked faster and faster until she was almost running, panic beginning to spiral in her chest. But no matter how fast she ran, she couldn't seem lose him.

Speaking to David in the restaurant had been fun,

but she'd ended up feeling foolish and used. And now, out in the dark street, it was all too much. 'Oh, leave me alone,' she said. 'Please, leave me alone. I just want to get back to my hotel.'

'What's the matter, lady? Are you a racist?' The man's tone had developed a nasty edge, and his accusation stunned Janet into looking at him.

'No, I am not a racist. Not at all. Look, it's been a bloody awful day, and I just want to get back to my hotel, that's all.' There was a catch in her voice, and suddenly it was a job to keep the tears at bay.

Then suddenly someone else spoke up. A woman. 'You heard the lady, Petey. Run along.'

Janet looked around to see where the voice had come from and saw a short, dumpy European woman wearing a traditional African outfit.

'I not do anything. I only speak to the lady.'

'I know, Petey, but the lady doesn't want to speak to you right now. Try again tomorrow, okay? Maybe she'll feel different after a good night's sleep.'

The man laughed. 'Okay, I go now. Thank you for the tip.'

'You're welcome, Petey. Suto Yediya.'

Janet was breathless from her panicked hurrying. 'Why did you say that?' she asked, looking at her saviour. 'About me feeling different tomorrow?'

The woman shrugged. 'It got him to go away, didn't it? Besides, it might be true.'

Janet shook her head. 'No way. I was really

frightened by him. He seemed quite aggressive.' Finally she remembered her manners. 'But thank you anyway, for stepping in. I appreciate it.'

The woman smiled. 'That's no problem. I know Petey; he's all talk. Anyway, where's your husband? Why isn't he here to chaperone you?'

They were outside her hotel now, standing beneath a rustling pair of palm trees. Just four short hours ago, Scott had got into a taxi here, bound for who knew where.

'I saw you this morning, in your wedding outfit,' the woman was continuing. 'You looked gorgeous, I must say.'

'Oh,' said Janet.

'Oh? He didn't ditch you, did he? Surely not!'

The woman may have saved her from the persistent Petey – and Janet was extremely grateful for that, she really was – but somehow she was still pretty annoying. Janet really didn't want to have to offer explanations right now.

'No,' she said. 'We decided not to proceed, that's all.' Somehow she managed to summon up a smile from somewhere. 'Now, if you don't mind, thank you so much for stepping in back there, but it's been a long day, and I just want to go to bed. Good night.'

'Goodnight, dear. I hope you sleep well.'

Janet began to turn away. 'Thank you.'

'But before you go,' the woman detained her, 'I want you to remember something.'

'What's that?' It was an effort now to be polite, the compulsion to get to her room was so strong.

'Just something I've been reading up on lately; something I find really helpful. The idea that everything that happens in our lives – every event, whether it seems good or bad – is neutral. It's completely up to us to choose how we react to it.'

What? Janet's brain reeled as it tried to deal with this statement. It was so utterly ridiculous in the face of everything she'd been through that day that she turned round to face the woman, shaking her head as she did so.

'Look, I'm sure you mean well, and I don't mean to offend you, but I've got to say that that is the biggest load of *tosh* I've ever heard in my life! I've broken up with my fiancé, been left all alone in a strange country, and been propositioned for sex by two men both younger than my daughter. I'd hardly call any of those events neutral.'

The woman didn't appear to be in the least put out by Janet's anger. 'I don't suppose you would, dear. And believe me, it took me a long time to take the whole neutral concept on board. When I did, I have to say, it transformed my life. Completely. But we haven't been introduced; how remiss of me. I'm Nessa. Nessa O'Brien.' And she stuck her hand out for Janet to shake.

Reluctantly, Janet did so.

'Aren't you going to tell me your name?' Nessa

asked, and Janet sighed, her annoyance dissolving. Being annoyed just took more energy than she possessed right now.

'Janet,' she said. 'My name's Janet Thornton. And now I am going to bed. Good night.' And she turned her back and walked away.

Six

Shelthorpe-on-Sea, Norfolk

Debbie's route to work from Kate and Geoff's house took her past her mum's shop, which was now the Cat Calls UK charity shop. If she had time, she usually paused to look at the window display. Today it was, in her view, as uninspiring as ever. Did the man from the wedding – Paul – know how rubbish the window display was? Though possibly it might not even be his responsibility. Maybe he drove rescue cats about in vans or something. His suit hadn't exactly shouted management after all, and that cleavage woman had asked him if he'd bought it in the shop.

Returning her attention to the window, Debbie saw that the focus of this week's display seemed to be books and bric-a-brac. It looked a lot like the jumble sales her gran had favoured. Debbie had often gone along to them with her, and she smiled now, remembering how good her gran had been at elbowing people out of her way on her quest to add to her collection of gravy boats and ornaments.

As a child, Debbie had loved to gaze at these treasures in her gran's china cabinet. The china donkey with his cruet saddle bags. A shepherdess in a crinoline dress. What had her mum done with those things? Though actually, now she came to think of it, that donkey cruet next to the large mixing bowl in the window looked similar to her gran's. The pepper and salt had hung from the straw saddle bags exactly like that. Debbie shielded her eyes from the sun's glare with her hand to take a closer look. Surely Janet hadn't just dumped Gran's treasures here, in the charity shop, before she went away? Maybe she had, and they'd taken all this time to surface.

Frowning, Debbie quickly scanned the display for more evidence of her mother's uncaring treachery and gasped. The purple glass vase! That had been her absolute favourite of her gran's treasures. It had a rainbow lustre to it when the light caught it right. If it was Gran's, it would have a tiny chip on the rim where Debbie had knocked it over one time. Water had spilled all over Gran's best tablecloth, and the whole freshly-laid table had had to be cleared.

Was that a chip on the rim? It might be, she couldn't be sure from this distance.

She checked her watch. Almost five to nine. There was no time to do anything about it now, and in any case, the shop wasn't open yet. She'd have to come back during her lunch break. Whether the vase turned out to be her gran's or not, it would be a memory. It was almost a year since she had died, but Debbie still missed her every day. She'd always felt at ease with her; not ever-so-slightly irritated and on edge the way she was with her mother.

It began to rain, a sudden deluge drawn from the sea, instantly soaking through her clothes, and Debbie hurried along the street, trying not to think about Janet and Scott on their honeymoon in the African sunshine, or about how everything had completely changed in the past year. Gran dying, her parents' marriage breaking up, the family home sold. And now her mum with a new husband.

Reaching the further education college where she worked, Debbie ran towards the administration block through the pouring rain, arriving soaking-wet and breathless and in time to see Adam, the Deputy Principal she worked for, leaving for a meeting. Automatically, her heart skipped a beat. The last time she'd seen him had been in a borrowed beach hut with the sound of the breaking waves in her ears as they'd made love.

'God, you're beautiful,' he'd said, ripping off her expensive wedding outfit and tossing it into a sandy corner of the hut alongside a child's bucket and spade.

Now, he was speaking to the Principal – or rather, she was speaking to him, and he was nodding seriously as he listened, apparently intent on what she was saying. But just for a moment, his deep brown eyes connected with Debbie's, and she thought of the way he'd gazed into her eyes on Saturday evening as he moved inside her, her body instinctively responding to the memory.

'Good morning, Debbie,' said the Principal. 'Goodness, you need a towel-down, don't you?'

'Yes, I think I do,' answered Debbie, still looking in Adam's direction, but the Principal was on the move now, drawing him along with her.

'Now, Adam,' she was saying, 'about that inspection report. I don't know that it's a good idea to share every last detail with parents. If they're really interested, they can go to the Ofsted site.' And she turned away, her hair-sprayed hair not moving a millimetre as she whisked Adam along the corridor towards the meeting.

Debbie waited for just a moment, hoping he would look back, but when he didn't, she took off her sodden suit jacket and headed to the ladies to dry her hair under the hand dryer. At least there had been that one, possessive glance. Sometimes, even though they worked so closely, there wasn't even that.

She and Adam had been having an affair for almost six months now, and it was both the best and the worst thing to have ever happened to her. The best because, when they were together, she felt as if she owned the world, and experienced more pleasure than she'd ever thought possible. The worst, because Adam was married, and it was so difficult to find places they could meet. She could hardly take him back to Kate's house, since Kate and Geoff obviously knew him. And his wife. She'd known he was married right from the start of course, but, until recently, had kidded herself she could deal with it.

In this year of changes, why was it that the one thing she most needed to change in her life remained stubbornly, resolutely the same? Would she and Adam ever be able to be public about their relationship? Sometimes, despite what he said, she wondered.

Seven

The Gambia

Considering everything that had happened the previous day, Janet slept well and woke with new clarity.

Sod it, she wasn't going to run back to England straight away with her tail between her legs. Why should she? After all, it had been her idea to come to The Gambia in the first place. The tiny country hadn't originally been on their schedule, but somehow, when she'd seen it on the map, she'd felt compelled to visit. Scott had agreed, and now here they were. Or rather, here she was. And she was damn well going to make the most of it, while her money lasted anyway. Starting with going on the trip to Kachikally Sacred Crocodile Pool she and Scott had booked onto for this morning.

But first, breakfast.

As soon as Janet went into the dining room, she saw Nessa. Of course. Silly to hope she could have a peaceful breakfast and wake up slowly.

'Yoo hoo!' Nessa called over straight away.

'Morning, Janet.'

Reluctantly, Janet went over to her table. Nessa was wearing another outlandishly patterned African outfit this morning, complete with a scarf around her hair. If it weren't for the extreme pallor of her skin, she would have looked very authentic.

Janet forced a smile. 'Morning.'

Instantly, Nessa burst out laughing and had to hold a hand up to her mouth to prevent herself from spraying grapefruit everywhere. 'Sorry,' she said. 'It's so obvious what you're thinking.' She put an irritated voice on. 'Oh no, not that crazy woman; not first thing in the morning, with all her talk about neutral events and all that other shit.'

Janet laughed. She couldn't help herself. Somehow, it was just so funny to hear the word shit coming from Nessa's mouth. 'Sorry,' she said. 'My friends are always telling me I'm transparent.'

Nessa hooted with laughter. 'Well, they're certainly right about that, dear. It must've got you in real trouble at school.'

Janet's lip twisted some more. 'Frequently.'

Nessa laughed again. 'Well, listen, you can't offend me. I'm not offendable. I've got a hide like a rhinoceros. By the way, did you get to see any wildlife before your man took off?'

Janet shook her head. 'No, not in Africa. We just got here from India.' With her amusement over, Janet looked longingly over at the breakfast buffet. She so wanted to sit quietly and eat.

'You want a table by the window, madam?' asked the waiter, indicating a table set for two. Instantly, Janet imagined herself there with Scott, giggling over some private joke and sharing intimate glances.

'Why don't you join me?' Nessa invited, and Janet sighed.

'All right,' she said, then remembered to add, 'thank you. I'll just go and help myself to some food.'

When she returned with cereal and fruit, Nessa smiled at her, popping a last piece of grapefruit into her mouth.

'There are lots of beautiful birds here,' she continued as if Janet hadn't been away. 'Animals too. None of your plains animals, elephants, giraffe or lions, but plenty of monkeys, hippos and crocodiles.'

Janet bit into a juicy piece of pineapple. 'You sound very familiar with the country.'

Nessa nodded. 'I started up a charity here a while ago supplying bicycles to girls in the isolated villages Upriver, so they could get to school. I was here two or three times a year with my work, so I got to see plenty of birds and wildlife while I was distributing the bikes and helping those girls learn to ride them.' She looked at Janet and began to laugh. 'You've got your jaw dropping open again, Janet,' she said. 'I bet you can't imagine me on a bike, can you?'

'Well –' started Janet, embarrassed, but Nessa flapped a dismissive hand.

'That's okay,' she said. 'I told you; I'm not easily offended. And I have packed on the timber a bit since my bike-riding days.'

'It's a surprise, that's all,' said Janet. 'I mean, the bikes and everything.' She thought about her conversation with David the previous evening and wondered how he had got to school. She was going to mention her meeting with him, but Nessa was speaking again.

'Upriver girls often don't get to go to school unless they've got a bike. It can be a three hour walk there and back, and their families can't spare them for that long. The girls do all the chores. A simple thing like a bike can transform a girl's life.'

Janet put her empty fruit plate aside and began to eat her cereal, thinking of the hundreds and hundreds of times she had driven her daughter to school over the years. Debbie had always been so slow to get ready in the morning, it had been easiest just to jump into the car. That way Janet could be sure her daughter arrived on time, even though none of the schools she'd attended had ever been more than half a mile away. To think of having to travel for three hours to get to school, and another three to get home again … You'd have to really want an education to do that. Clearly Nessa had made a real difference to people's lives with her work.

She looked at her companion with new respect. 'Don't you work for the charity any longer then?' she asked.

Something changed in Nessa's face. Janet thought she looked suddenly sad, although almost immediately she was smiling again.

'Not any longer, no. I had to stop because … well, for health reasons. But it's great to be back for a visit. Really great. I'm so looking forward to catching up with family.'

Once again, Janet was surprised. 'You have relatives here?'

Nessa's smile turned into a grin. 'Oh, yes, lots of them. Hundreds. All adopted, of course; we aren't related by blood. But adoptive relatives are the best kind in my view, because we've chosen each other.'

Janet immediately thought about Estelle, Reenie and Kate; her wonderful friends. In a way, they were like adoptive relatives. She loved all of them dearly, and couldn't imagine them not being in her life. 'That's nice,' she said.

They ate in companionable silence for a while, and then Janet asked, 'Is the charity still continuing with its work? Now that you aren't working for them?'

Nessa smiled. 'A different charity set itself up to do similar work. Although I did hear they had a staffing problem at the moment. Their main worker, Sarah Ann, had to go back to the States suddenly because her son got arrested on a drugs charge.'

'Oh, dear,' said Janet. 'How awful.'

Debbie had never got herself mixed up in a drugs

charge. To Janet's knowledge, she'd never even tried drugs. Not, she supposed, that she would know about it if she had. But Debbie was a good person, she was pretty sure of that. And self-sufficient. Independent. Maybe a bit too independent at times. Janet couldn't remember the last time she'd asked her for advice.

Not that she wanted Debbie caught up on a drugs charge, obviously. But it would be good, every now and then, to feel needed. Debbie so rarely told her anything about her life. Yesterday, when she'd shown her obvious feelings on that Skype call, had been a real rarity.

Janet sighed. What she wouldn't give for a better relationship with her daughter. To be able to really communicate with her. To ask, *what do you want from life? Do you want to get married? Have children? Are you happy typing letters and arranging meetings at that college? Do you love me? Do you even like me? Will you ever forgive me for divorcing your father?*

Oh, well.

'You're thinking about your stuff, aren't you?' observed Nessa, and Janet suddenly felt irritated by the woman all over again.

'I wonder if Sarah Ann was able to view her son's arrest as a neutral event?' she asked, and Nessa burst out laughing.

'I don't imagine so!' she said. 'But maybe she'd be a convert if she read the book.'

Janet stared at her. 'Your neutral event theory's in a

book?'

'Why, yes, dear, didn't I say? It's a book called *Staying in Neutral - Responses to Change Your Life.* By Corrinne Walker. She's dead now, poor woman, but I heard her speak once. She was very inspiring.'

Staying in Neutral! What a title.

'But was her life testing?' Janet wondered out loud. 'This Corrinne? I mean, it's one thing to have theories, and to write about things being neutral. Saying all that about us being able to choose how to react to things. But it's quite another actually doing it, isn't it?'

Nessa laughed, spreading butter on her toast. 'Of course,' she agreed. 'From what I learned, her life certainly gave her plenty of opportunities to test her theories. And in case you're wondering about me, about whether I've been tested in life, then I can tell you I have.'

'Have you?' Janet asked reluctantly, sensing that some sort of confession was imminent.

'Yes,' Nessa nodded. 'My husband was crushed to death twenty years ago. He was a farmer, and his tractor rolled over on him.'

How utterly awful. 'I'm so sorry.'

Nessa shrugged. 'Silly sod,' she said. 'It was entirely his own fault. The tractor was stuck on a slope, and when he got out to check the wheel, over it went. This was way before I discovered Corrinne's book, actually. I burned in the hell fires of grief for a long time before that.'

Janet had gone right off her breakfast. 'I'm so sorry,' she said again, unable to think of anything else to say.

'Don't be.' Nessa wiped her mouth on her napkin and looked at her watch. 'I tell you what, I'll lend you the book. I'm sure you'll find it very interesting. But right now I have to get going. I'm out for the day today, and I've got a few things to sort out before it's time to set off. Have a fantastic day, won't you? See you later, if you're still here.'

'Yes,' said Janet, feeling as if her mind were fizzing. 'See you later.'

Eight

Shelthorpe-on-Sea

In the Staffroom, Kate was catching up on paperwork. There was a lot to tie up before she went on maternity leave, but her heart wasn't in it. She never enjoyed paperwork, but today she was finding it even more difficult to concentrate than ever. It was all such an anti-climax after the build-up to the wedding.

'Are you and Geoff all right, Kate?' Tom asked, stopping at her desk on his way out to a class. 'Tell me to mind my own business, but Geoff looks like a kicked dog, and you've been snapping everyone's head off all day. I'm thinking that all's not well in the Bramling household.'

'Mind your own business,' Kate retorted automatically, then sighed, knowing he only meant well. 'We've got a few issues, if you want to know. But nothing we can't sort out.'

'Good,' Tom said. 'We can't have the college's

most loved-up couple having difficulties. Else what hope is there for the rest of us?' He lifted a hand in a farewell salute. 'See you later.'

'Yeah, see you.'

Left on her own, Kate threw her pen down and gazed miserably out of the window, all pretence of getting on with paperwork abandoned.

She hadn't intended to argue with Geoff on Sunday. But then she'd fully expected to wake up next to him at the Country House Hotel, have a giggle about the way he'd fallen asleep with his wedding clothes on, and help him to take them off. She'd expected to experience some passion between the expensive sheets – in short, to consummate their marriage.

But when she woke up, Geoff was already up and showered and expressing a noisy need for breakfast. Afterwards, she thought as she got dressed, lethargically pulling on clothes she hadn't expected to wear until much later. We'll make love after breakfast. I'll haul him back up here after he's had his full English and ravish him.

Only Geoff didn't have a full English breakfast. He just toyed with a croissant or two, drank a cup of weak tea, then expressed a desire for a coastal stroll to include a visit to the lifeboat station at the end of the pier.

'Since when have you been so interested in lifeboats?' Kate retorted.

'Part of our heritage round here, Katie, they are. Did

you know Henry Blog saved eight hundred and seventy-three lives during his time on the Cromer lifeboat? Now, that's a worthwhile way to spend your life, if I ever heard of one.'

'You do know we have to be out of our room by twelve o'clock?' Kate told him at the lifeboat station.

'Do we?' he said vaguely, leaning over the railing inside the boatshed to get a better look at the lifeboat. 'Well, we'll saunter back after this and pack up, shall we? It's a lovely day. Maybe we could stop off at Felbrigg Hall to take a look at the walled garden?'

'Since when have you been interested in flippin' lifeboats and walled gardens, Geoff Bramling?' she stormed, drawing gazes of other people inside the boatshed.

Geoff smiled at them in a 'don't mind her' sort of a way that made Kate madder than ever. 'Just trying to explore the culture while we're in the area,' he said.

'What about exploring your new wife's body while we're in the area of the honeymoon suite?' she came straight back at him.

'Katie,' he said under his breath, flushing bright red and walking away, leaving her to do a walk of shame past their audience on her own.

Bloody hell. How was this even possible? Her and Geoff, like this. They'd never really argued, not even before they'd got together as a couple. They were soulmates – everyone said so. So why did it feel as if she'd suddenly discovered a side of Geoff she'd never been aware of before?

She found him downstairs in the gift shop, his head bent as he examined something. Should she go in and sneak her hand into his? No, she'd be better off waiting outside, taking some deep, calming breaths of sea air. Then, when he came out, she could apologise and everything would be all right again. It was probably only the pregnancy stirring things up again. People had fallen over themselves to tell her about back ache, morning sickness, and the wonders of ginger tea, but they hadn't said anything about pregnancy being like a truth drug; that she would feel even more compelled than usual to express whatever was on her mind.

When Geoff finally emerged from the RNLI shop, he was holding a giant seal soft toy. 'Thought Bradley might like this,' he said sheepishly.

'That thing's going to be bigger than Bradley for a good three years, you great lummox,' she teased, giving him an affectionate push. 'Probably scare the poor kid to death.' Then she took his arm and squeezed it to show she was joking, and they walked back up the pier by the side of the theatre, a pair of young sea gulls wheeling over their heads in search of discarded chips.

'Sorry,' they both said, turning to each other at the same time, and then they smiled, and Geoff kissed her on the end of the nose. Without discussing it, they sat close together on a seat backing on to a view of the rolling ocean.

'I was a right bitch back there,' Kate said with a

sigh, watching the larger sea gull wobble in the air, testing its wings.

'You were disappointed in me, that's all,' said Geoff, squeezing her hand.

He looked such an idiot with his free arm around the giant seal toy, but he was her idiot, and she was absolutely, madly, crazily in love with him.

'I was a bit, I suppose,' she admitted.

Geoff sighed. 'Sorry,' he said, then sat looking out towards the shore, his face half-turned away from her.

'Well?' she said, doing her very best to stifle her impatience. 'Aren't you going to tell me why you chose a French continental breakfast over ravishing me in my new, specially-bought maternity lingerie?'

The seagull flew off with a loud squawk, and Geoff watched it go. Kate felt him shrug. 'I don't know,' he said. 'Maybe I'm self-conscious about Bradley. Best thing that's ever happened to me, he is. Apart from you of course. Don't want to do anything that might hurt him.'

What? Was he serious?

'Geoff,' she said, 'we've been going at it hammer and tongs ever since I managed to get my head out of the toilet with the morning sickness.'

He avoided her gaze, stroking some imaginary sea spray off the giant seal's face. 'Well, maybe we shouldn't have been,' he said.

'But at the hospital they said –' she started, but he got up with the seal toy under his arm.

'I know that, but I can't help how I feel, can I? Just got a huge sense of responsibility about it all of a sudden.'

'Well,' she said, pushing herself up from the seat. 'Since the only thing that's changed is us getting married, maybe we shouldn't have got married.'

He turned to her then, his face stricken. 'You don't mean that, do you, Katie?'

She sighed, feeling sudden tears in her throat. 'Of course I don't, you idiot. I want my red-hot lover back, that's all. Bradley won't mind; I know he won't.'

But Geoff didn't answer her, and they left the pier in silence, returning to the hotel to collect their things, and the closest Kate got to red-hot anything all day was the red hot poker flowers in the walled garden at Felbrigg Hall.

Things were still cool between them now. And Geoff kept disappearing too, holing up in the bathroom, or going out into the back yard, or out for a walk. As if he were avoiding her. Kate had no idea what she was supposed to have done, if anything, or any idea how to get her friend and lover back again. She just hoped things improved after Bradley was born.

Nine

Shelthorpe-on-Sea

'Could you change this report, please, Debbie? I think it would look better if the text had a ragged right edge instead of being justified. It looks a bit dry the way it is.'

The report was dry; she'd almost fallen asleep at her computer typing it up.

It never failed to amaze Debbie how different Work Adam and Non-Work Adam were. Although if he were to read his report on the eco-management of student science laboratories out loud to her in his deep, honeyed voice, she'd probably go weak at the knees. Even if she didn't understand a word of it.

'Debbie?'

She blinked and smiled at him. It was just the two of them in the office – Rosemary, the Principal's PA, was in a meeting. 'Sorry,' she said. 'I keep getting flashbacks of the other night, down at the beach hut.'

Adam put the report down on her desk and moved away. 'Remember the rules,' he told her.

She sighed. 'Sorry. It's difficult sometimes.'

'I know, but it's the only way. Three copies please.'

Debbie looked at him blankly.

'Of the report. I need three copies by Thursday.'

He was at his office door. It was one o'clock, and she knew he had a lunchtime conference call followed by an afternoon out at a neighbouring college. She wouldn't see him again until tomorrow morning. They hadn't arranged when they would be meeting up next, and suddenly she very much needed to know. Sod the rules. The rules sucked.

'When will you be able to get away?' she asked, but just at that moment, the door opened and Rosemary appeared, her meeting over.

Adam smiled at Rosemary before turning back to answer Debbie. 'I shouldn't think I'll be leaving the Hurst until six at the earliest, so I'll see you both tomorrow. Now, I'd better get to that conference call. Howard's never late.'

Rosemary laughed. 'Now, isn't that the truth. You can set your watch by Howard.'

Adam smiled his agreement, then went into his office and shut the door. Sometimes, being her boss's secret other woman was bloody torture. 'Are you all right, Debbie?' Rosemary asked. 'You look a bit peaky.'

Debbie took her bag from her desk drawer. 'I'm fine

thanks. Hungry, that's all,' she said. 'See you later.'

'Don't forget we need to work on that stationery order this afternoon.'

Debbie gave Rosemary a stiff smile. 'No,' she said. 'I hadn't forgotten.' It was the highlight of her flipping week.

Making her way past a noisy group of students gathered outside the college building, Debbie wondered, as she so often had before, how it had come to this. Typing dull reports and making stationery orders.

She'd only meant to work at the college for a short while as a temp, while she considered her options. But now, because of Adam, her options were limited. She was addicted to the man, and at least while she was working here, she got to see him. Got to be indispensable to him, as she efficiently organised his work. To smell his aftershave as he stood close to explain what he wanted her to do.

But boy, did it come at a price. Working with him and having to keep their relationship secret was playing havoc with her health. It took half a stick of concealer a week to cover up the dark circles beneath her eyes.

Sighing, Debbie did her best to push away her miserable thoughts and walked along the High Street towards the charity shop, eating her sandwich as she went. As with many small towns, charity shops were beginning to take over. The community had resisted plans for a superstore for a long time, fearing the death of the small independent shops the tourists liked so well in the summer, but the supermarket giant had finally managed to get its plans through the previous year, and now this was the result.

Debbie, along with most of the town's young residents, had been all for the superstore. It was so much easier to go there to get everything you needed instead of having to go into several different shops and stand in lots of queues to get served. It was progress.

But still, it was sad to see all the empty shops with their To Let signs. Though plenty of people welcomed the wealth of charity shops. Including Debbie herself at that moment. If it weren't for her habit of browsing in windows for bargains on her way to work, her gran's vase might have been lost to her forever. She just hoped it was still there now.

Speeding up, Debbie slung her empty sandwich wrapper into the nearest bin and jay-walked between the cars to cross the road, arriving outside the shop slightly out of breath to scan the window anxiously for the vase. Yes! It was still there. Oh, but a woman was walking over it to it now. Shit! She was picking it up. What if she decided to buy it? She couldn't. Not Gran's vase.

But the woman had replaced the vase, and now she was putting a book down on the table next to it. Perhaps she worked in the shop? Or maybe not. She looked like a tourist with her shorts and sunhat.

Debbie left the window and went to the shop door.

But she had to wait to get inside because the woman was coming out now, filling the entrance with her bright colours and considerable bulk. When Debbie stood back to let her get past, she was rewarded by a huge smile.

'Thank you so much, dear. You have a wonderful day, won't you?'

'Er, thanks,' Debbie replied vaguely, feeling discom-forted by the piercing way the woman's eyes were connecting with hers. They were a very bright blue, and piercing. So much so, it felt to Debbie as if her soul was being examined.

'Do we know each other?' Debbie asked, starting to feel embarrassed.

'I was just asking myself the same question,' the woman said with a chuckle. 'But no, I don't think so. And yet somehow it feels as if we ought to have met before. Perhaps we'll meet again in the future, hmm? Anyway, I've got to go now. People to see, lives to save and all that. Bye!'

And off she went, her floral, shorts-encased bum waddling as she walked. Debbie stood and stared. What a very unusual woman. *Lives to save?* What on earth was that about?

Consigning the woman to a 'bit mad but harmless' category in her mind, Debbie went inside the shop, soon forgetting all about her.

Going straight over to the table, she picked up the purple vase, examining it carefully to see if it had the tell-tale chip on its rim. It didn't. Not Gran's vase then. Feeling bereft, Debbie put the vase back on the table, realising how much she had wanted it to be a connection with the past. Should she buy it anyway? To remind her? Undecided, she picked it up again.

'Lovely colour that, isn't it, love?' said the sales assistant from behind the counter. 'I shouldn't think it will hang around in the shop for long. It's the kind of thing people snap up to sell on eBay, that is.'

That decided her. It may not be her gran's vase, but it had probably belonged to someone else's gran, and it deserved better than someone making a quick buck from it on the Internet.

'I'll take it,' she said, but before she could go and pay, the title of the book the strange woman had put down on the table caught her eye.

Staying in Neutral - Responses to Change Your Life. Whatever was that about? Maybe she'd get that too. Yes, why not?

Taking the vase and the book over to the till, Debbie suddenly imagined herself sitting on her bed reading the book back at Kate's house, with Kate and Geoff arguing in the room next door. They'd seemed annoyed with each other since the wedding for some reason, which surprised her, since they were usually so lovey-dovey. But she could hardly ask Kate if everything was all right. They got along really well, but Kate was really her mum's friend. Suddenly she remembered Estelle's suggestion at the wedding about her moving into the upstairs room in the shop. Why not ask now, since she was here?

'I was wondering,' she said, putting the vase and the book down on the counter, 'is the room above the shop still free? My mother owns this building, you see; she's leased it to the charity. Only she's away at the moment, and I'm looking for a flat. Quite urgently, actually.'

The sales assistant stopped in the act of wrapping up the vase. 'Oh, it's your mum's shop, is it? I don't know, I'm afraid. I'd have to ask Paul. He generally comes in about this time on a Monday with a poster of the latest cats available for rehoming.' She broke off as the door opened, a smile lighting up her face. 'Why, here he is; the very man himself. Paul, this young lady was just enquiring about the room upstairs. She's looking for somewhere to rent.'

Debbie turned to look too, and saw the man from the wedding. Geoff's nephew.

'Hello again,' he said, recognising her.

'Hi.'

He was wearing jeans and a T-shirt today instead of the ill-fitting wedding suit. She'd forgotten how tall he was, and yet somehow so youthful looking. It was perfectly possible to imagine him smiling that lopsided smile as a little boy; using it to get more sweets, or an hour longer to watch his favourite TV programme.

'Is it free?' she asked. 'The room?'

'Well, it depends what you mean by free. No-one's using it, but there's quite a lot of stuff in there. Why don't I take you up to have a look?'

'Thanks.' She began to follow him towards the back of the shop, forgetting all about her purchases at the counter until the sales assistant called after her.

'D'you want to pay for these things when you come down again?'

She glanced back. So did Paul. The book was face up, and she saw him notice the title. 'No,' she said, reaching for her purse and feeling embarrassed. 'I'll pay now.' She glanced in Paul's direction. 'If that's okay?'

'Of course.'

Was that an ordinary smile, or was he amused by her buying a self-help book? And why did she even care?

'Oh, while I think of it, here's the latest cats for rehoming to go in the window, Sheila,' he said after the assistant had given Debbie her change.

'Thanks, Paul. I'll put it up straight away.'

'Thanks.' He turned to smile at Debbie. 'Right, then. Shall we go up?'

Debbie followed him out through the door marked Staff Only at the back of the shop, past the bags of donations waiting to be sorted, and then on up a narrow staircase with a threadbare carpet.

'The room's got a nice bay window,' he told her as they went up. 'No sea view though, I'm afraid.' And he turned to smile that lopsided smile towards her. 'But there is a good view of the bakers.'

'The view doesn't matter.' Too late, Debbie realised she'd spoken in a clipped, rather unfriendly way and frowned at herself. What was the matter with her? He was doing her a favour, and she needed this place. So why did she feel so defensive?

'Were there a lot of cats for rehoming?' she asked to make up for her unfriendliness.

'There are always a lot,' he said, glancing at her. 'You're nothing like your mother, are you?'

'What d'you mean?' she asked, immediately realising that she had pretty much snapped at him again.

'Well, you're tall for a start, and your eyes are brown, not blue like hers.'

He was probably only making conversation. She seriously needed to get a grip and to stop imagining he had some kind of an agenda. Why should he have an agenda? He hadn't even known she was going to be here.

'Anyway,' he said, before she could think of a reply, 'here's the room.' He led the way into what must be a large room, since it took up almost half the space of the shop below. But Debbie soon saw he hadn't been exaggerating about the amount of stuff. There were so many boxes and bulging black sacks, the room seemed a great deal smaller than it actually was.

'I did tell you there was a lot,' he said, watching her reaction.

'Would you be able to get rid of it?' she asked,

attempting to see beyond the junk to imagine where she would place a double bed.

'I expect so, if your mum said it was okay.' He saw her face. 'Oh,' he said, 'didn't I say? This all belongs to Janet. She asked if she could store it here while she was away. I said it would be okay, since we didn't need the space.'

Debbie couldn't believe it. 'This all belongs to Mum?' she asked, looking around at all the bags and boxes. 'I thought she'd put everything in storage.'

Paul nodded. 'Actually, I think some of it might be your gran's. Things your mum hadn't found the time to finish sorting through before she left on her travels.'

'These are Gran's?' Debbie placed a reverent hand on top of one of the bags, aware that she must sound like a parrot, repeating everything he said, but unable to help herself.

'I think so. That's what Janet told me, anyway. I suppose you could ring her to see what she wants you to do with it all?'

'She's on her honeymoon. But I suppose I could move it all to one end of the room for now. I only need to get a bed in here, and a few other bits and pieces.'

'Right,' he said doubtfully. 'I didn't realise Janet had got married.'

'Yes.' Debbie turned away, not wanting to talk about it. Her hand was still resting on one of the bags of her gran's belongings. How wonderful it would be to be able to immerse herself in it all for the afternoon. To

96

make some excuse not to go back to work and the grinding boredom of the stationery order.

'Well,' Paul was saying, 'I'll show you the bathroom and the kitchen, such as they are. The place hasn't been refurbished for a good while. You'd have to share the kitchen with the volunteers of course, but obviously they won't be around in the evenings or on Sundays.'

Ten minutes later, Debbie left the shop feeling very pleased with herself. The rent she and Paul had agreed was very reasonable, and not only that, she could move in as soon as she liked. All she needed to do was break the news to Kate and Geoff and sort out a bed.

She found the opportunity to speak to Kate that evening, when they were cooking dinner together. Geoff had a late class, and hadn't returned yet, so it was just the two of them.

Debbie was chopping onions, Kate was peeling potatoes, and the radio was on in the background, playing some eighties tune Debbie didn't know the title of. Every now and then, when she remembered the lyrics, Kate burst into song. She seemed a bit more relaxed than of late, and Debbie knew she would miss this. But she also knew that time spent alone with Adam would more than compensate for its loss.

'Kate,' she said, deciding it was time to broach the subject, 'I hope you don't think I'm ungrateful, but I've been given the chance of a flat of my own, and so – '

'You're going to pack up your stuff and get away from me and Geoff as fast as your little legs will carry you. Don't blame you.'

'It's not that, I just –'

Kate sighed, turning from her potato scraping to look at her. 'Listen, love, it's fine. I completely understand. I'm only sorry things have been so rubbish around here since the wedding, with me and Geoff sniping at each other the whole time. It's probably best we have some time alone to sort things out anyway. As long as it's what you really want, and we're not forcing you out.'

For all Kate's brave words, Debbie could sense her sadness, and felt awful. 'Well, I'm twenty-four, aren't I? It's time I had my own place. And it's not far away. I'm going to be renting the room above Mum's shop. The charity said I could use it.'

Kate gave her a quick hug. 'Well, that's perfect then, isn't it? But let's make sure we meet up regularly. I'll miss our chats in the kitchen.'

'Me too,' said Debbie, and meant it. 'Maybe we could have lunch together at work sometimes?'

Kate nodded. 'Great plan. Just as long as it's sandwiches. I don't fancy having wine accidentally poured on me by my students in that training restaurant.'

Debbie smiled. 'Okay. Sandwiches it is.'

Ten

The Gambia

It seemed strange to be getting on a coach with a lot of tourists as if she were on a day trip to York or off to sample cream teas in Devon, when she was actually in Africa.

She and Scott hadn't done any of these kinds of excursions while they'd been travelling – he'd insisted they hire guides and taxis and do everything independently. And yet, two days ago, Janet had booked the tickets for this trip of Kachikally without even consulting him about it first. She'd seen the details and badly wanted to go, and so she had booked them on it.

Now, boarding the bus without him, Janet remembered how taken aback he'd been when he found out. 'What on earth made you book us on a bus trip, Janet?' he asked. 'You know how I hate travelling in a pack.'

How parental he'd sounded. How bossy. Well, he wasn't here to have to suffer it now, was he? She was here alone. And, having managed to get here without encountering Petey, David or any other bumsters, she was feeling both relieved and quite proud of herself for not deciding to just hole up in her hotel room all day.

Where was Scott now? Back in England? Over the border in Senegal? Janet was surprised to discover, as she walked down the centre of the bus to find a free seat, that she didn't much care. Yesterday, desperately searching the market for him, she'd cared a lot. But this morning … well, she didn't. Simple as that.

Simple? Nothing about her situation was simple. She had no idea how her feelings for Scott could have changed so much, so quickly. But they had. In twenty-four hours she had switched from almost marrying him to feeling relieved she would never again have to hear the sound of him clipping his fingernails in the bathroom. Or inhale the hot-grease smell of the fried eggs he liked to eat every morning for breakfast. Oh, there had been that initial feeling of panic that had propelled her to the market, but that had well and truly passed now.

'Janet!' a woman hailed her from near the back of the bus. 'You didn't say you were coming on this trip.'

Nessa? Surely not. But it was, and she was patting the empty seat next to her, a look of delight and welcome on her face. Hell.

'Neither did you,' Janet pointed out, taking the

proffered seat.

Nessa smiled. She'd put some lipstick on, the same red as her grandmuba dress. Somehow, it made her face look even paler than ever. 'I always come to Kachikally when I'm in The Gambia. The crocs there are so sweet, as you'll soon see for yourself. They seem almost like pets to me.'

'I'm not sure I've ever heard a crocodile described as sweet before,' said Janet. 'Or as a pet.'

'Ha!' Nessa laughed. 'You wait until you see them. They're irresistible. Especially when they're covered in all that scummy green weed. It makes them look as if they're decked with watercress.'

The bus doors closed, and the driver started the engine.

'I thought Kachikally was supposed to be a pilgrimage site?' Janet said.

'Yes, it is,' agreed Nessa. 'But that doesn't mean the crocodiles can't be sweet, does it?'

'I suppose not.' Janet smiled, imagining herself back at home, telling her friends about all of this. How they would laugh. Especially, Reenie. Actually, she'd probably get on very well with Nessa. In fact, knowing Reenie, she'd probably lend Nessa some of her belly dancing kit and soon get her shimmying in the function room of the local pub.

'What's funny?' asked Nessa when Janet smiled. 'Share the joke!'

But Janet shook her head. 'I was just thinking about

some dear friends,' she said, and promptly stopped laughing because suddenly she missed them all so badly.

She was still missing them when the bus arrived at Kachikally Sacred Crocodile Pool, even though Nessa had done her best to distract her with information about the place the whole way. Janet was already familiar with much of it from reading her guidebook, but hadn't bothered to say so. In an odd sort of a way, it had been quite pleasant to have Nessa's voice wash over her as the bus bumped along.

'There's a story that Kachikally, the fertility goddess, took the form of a woman and pretended that her daughter was drowning in the pool,' Nessa had said. 'The Bojang family, who lived nearby, did everything they could to help out, and Kachikally rewarded them by entrusting the pool to their care, asking them to populate it with wildlife. This they did, releasing a pair of crocodiles into the pool a few weeks later. Those crocodiles are the ancestors of the crocodiles who still live there today.'

Later, after they'd arrived and Janet was standing in front of the pool, she remembered the story and asked Nessa, 'Was there ever a drowning child? Was it true?' As she gazed out at the green water, her imagination supplied young legs desperately kicking about, and she shivered, hugging her arms around herself. She could almost hear a woman's voice, screaming, over and over again. *My daughter! My daughter! Someone save my daughter!*

'Nobody knows,' Nessa said. 'Gambian people are very superstitious, but I imagine they were even more so five hundred years ago, when this story dates from. Perhaps they made their own interpretation of something that happened; something they didn't properly understand.'

Janet's interest was piqued. She thought there had been something vulnerable in Nessa's voice as she'd spoken. Surely she couldn't have lost a child as well as a husband? No; nobody had that much bad luck. Or at least, nobody had that much bad luck in their lives and managed to stay as relentlessly cheerful as Nessa.

'I have that book in my bag for you, by the way,' Nessa told her now. 'Corrinne's book. *Staying in Neutral.*'

'Oh,' said Janet. 'Thank you.' The moment – whatever it had been – had passed. Nessa's face and voice were back to normal, and Janet returned her gaze to the pool. Were those crocodiles moving about where the thick, scummy, green weed was at its thickest? Yes, she thought they were. Yuck. How much more frightening they were, moving, than the statue-still specimens on dry land about ten metres away. Those just didn't look real, even though she knew they were.

'Excuse me, Janet,' Nessa said. 'I must go and say hello to a very dear old friend of mine.' And she walked away, waving at someone as she went.

Looking curiously to see who the friend was, Janet saw a tall Gambian woman with her arms spread wide, clearly overjoyed to see Nessa. Lucky, lucky Nessa, to have a friend to embrace her. And once again, Janet thought about her own friends at home, and wondered if deciding to stay here had been the right thing to do. Perhaps she ought to pack up and go home after all?

Suddenly, there was a loud shriek of laughter from over by the crocodiles, and Janet saw a crowd of tourists posing around the animals, all cheesy grins and hands on the crocodiles' knobbly backs. What did it feel like to touch a crocodile's skin? She wanted to know, but not quite enough to go over to join the noisy group. And anyway, was it really right? How many hands did the crocodiles get on their backs during the space of day? A hundred? Two hundred? Did it bother them? And was it really safe? After all, the crocodiles had to move sometime. They'd emerged from the water to make their way to their current positions at some point. Nobody had placed them there.

Having seen footage in wildlife programmes of crocodiles spinning in the water to tear their prey apart, it was easy for Janet to imagine the still-as-a-statue animal suddenly snapping open its jaws to take hold of a tourist and drag him into the water.

Suddenly, a flash of blue crossed her field of vision, pulling her from her maudlin thoughts. It was a bird – a kingfisher perhaps? – skimming across the green water before disappearing again. How lovely.

A man in a checked shirt had his binoculars out, avidly watching it. Janet gasped. Surely it was Scott? He had a backpack just like that. And the same shirt.

Bloody hell. What should she do? Go over? Or pretend she hadn't seen him? No, she couldn't be so childish. Besides, she was genuinely sorry about the way they'd parted.

But as she was about to go over, the woman standing next to Scott slipped an arm around his waist, halting Janet in her tracks. For goodness sake! He certainly hadn't wasted any time, had he? Knowing she really ought to walk away, go and hide in the museum or something, Janet couldn't stop herself from going over.

'Scott!' she shouted, furious now.

The man didn't turn, so she called his name again. This time, both of them turned – Scott and the woman – and immediately Janet realised that the man wasn't Scott at all. In fact, from the front, he looked nothing like him.

'Oh,' she said, totally embarrassed. 'I'm so sorry. I thought you were someone else. Er, wasn't that a beautiful bird just then? A kingfisher, was it? I'd have loved to have got a photo of it, but it was too quick for me …' Gabbling, Janet pulled her phone from her pocket. Too quickly. In a flash, it had slipped from her fingers to soar through the air, plopping into the murky water.

All three of them stood and stared at the ripples. 'Oh

dear,' said the woman. 'I don't fancy your chances of getting that back.'

'No,' said the man. 'I'm afraid it's crocodile food.'

'Even if I were able to get it back, it would probably be ruined.' Janet groaned, now feeling both foolish *and* dismayed. 'What a clumsy idiot.'

They all stood staring at the water for a few seconds longer, and then the couple muttered something sympathetic and wandered off, no doubt thinking she was mad.

Which she was.

Now she would have to try to buy another phone. *And* she'd lost all her photos and contact numbers. What a mess. What a stupid flipping mess.

'Janet!' Nessa was calling over to her. 'Come and meet my friend.'

Janet sighed, looking over to see Nessa beckoning to her. It wasn't a subtle sort of beckoning – Nessa's hand was fairly swiping through the air in its insistence. But then how else would Nessa beckon? The woman clearly didn't have a subtle bone in her body.

'Janet, I'd like you to meet my friend Ida. Ida, this is Janet from England.'

'Pleased to meet you.' Janet held out her hand politely.

But the Gambian woman wasn't so formal, taking Janet's hand in both of hers, her smile dazzling and full of what seemed to be genuine pleasure. 'I am so very pleased to meet a friend of my lovely Nessa,' she said.

'You know, I begin to think that I shall never see her again, it has been so long, and I tell you, I could not bear the thought of this.'

'Well, I –' began Janet uncertainly, but Ida swept on. 'But come, you must have a blessing. The waters of Kachikally will give you what you most desire in return for this favour.' And, as she spoke, she began to pull Janet towards a kind of concrete cubicle a few metres away.

Janet glanced uncertainly back over her shoulder, but found Nessa grinning broadly at her, and nodding her encouragement. 'Go on,' she said. 'You'll be fine. More than fine.'

There was a concrete step on the ground inside the cubicle. Ida gestured for Janet to stand on it. 'Aren't the blessings at Kachikally for women who can't have children?' Janet queried as she climbed up obediently. 'That's what it said in my guide book.'

Ida had her back turned, filling a cup from a large bowl of water. 'Kachikally blessings are for whatever you desire the most, Janet,' she said, turning with a huge smile. 'We do get the poor ladies who are not able to have children, yes. Often times we get those ladies. But businessmen come too. And boxers who want to win their fight. Kachikally, she listen to everybody who wants something badly. Now, close your eyes please, Janet. Close your eyes and listen to your heart. She will tell you what it is you most desire, if you do not already know this.'

Janet closed her eyes and tried to concentrate on anything other than feeling foolish. She could hear the chatter of the crowd around her. Somebody laughing. The endlessly beautiful birdsong.

What was it she wanted more than anything else?

Home. Estelle, Kate and Reenie. Debbie.

Was that all?

No. She wanted to love someone. Someone who would love her back – just as she was – without trying to change her. Someone who thought – whatever she did – that she was perfect. Unconditional acceptance; that was what she wanted. Perhaps she ought to get a dog.

'Oh!' Janet's eyes flew open as the water from Ida's cup made sudden contact with her skin. She'd known it was coming, but that hadn't stopped it being a complete shock to the system. Ida's own eyes were closed. She was muttering something; Janet couldn't quite make out what.

She closed her eyes again. Another cup of water splashed over her. This time, although she swayed a little, Janet managed not to cry out. Then Ida spoke. 'There,' she said. 'Now you will have your heart's desire, Janet. It is done.'

Opening her eyes, Janet realised everyone nearby was gawping at her as if she were one of the crocodiles, and she was grateful to leave the cubicle when Ida gestured for her to do so.

Nessa came forward to meet her. Which was just as

well, because Janet stumbled a little, and Nessa had to catch hold of her arm.

'Are you all right?'

'Yes,' Janet said. 'It's probably only the heat.' Out of nowhere, a memory flew into her head. Of being in the shop in Shelthorpe-on-Sea. Her shop, before it had become her shop. When she'd worked there as a humble sales assistant for the bitch boss from hell, Carole de Ville.

Janet had been stock-taking when John George, one of their suppliers, had arrived with a delivery. Suddenly, there was a loud buzzing sound from beneath the counter. Her Mule Rutter vibrator – a cheeky gift her friends had brought in for her – had begun to buzz. How she and John had laughed about it together. There had been a definite spark between them, Janet remembered.

But then Janet had ended up buying Carole de Ville out, and John's ex-wife had begged him to give their relationship another try. So that had been that.

And soon afterwards, Janet had met Scott.

Janet shook her head. How very strange, to be standing here in Africa, surrounded by crocodiles, her hair soaked flat to her head by the blessing water, and to be thinking about John George and Mule Rutters.

Eleven

Shelthorpe-on-Sea

'This is a first for me,' said Adam, rolling off Debbie and slumping back against the pillows.

'What? Making love at my place?' Debbie said, smiling and reaching out to stroke his chest, her body still glowing from their love-making.

'No,' he said, looking around at the cluttered room. 'Making love in a junk yard, surrounded by black sacks. Are you going to take all this to the tip?'

Debbie's hand dropped. She thought he'd known these were her gran's things. And how much she'd loved her gran.

'That might be where some of it will end up, but I've got to look through it all and to talk to Mum before I chuck anything out.'

Adam's gaze was ranging restlessly around the room. She knew it was only a matter of time before he swung his long legs out of bed and began to get dressed. Which would be big a waste – not only of this valuable chance to be together, but of the money she'd spent on the very best bedding for their love nest.

'I've always hated the smell of charity shops,' he said now, wrinkling his nose. 'I'm sure it's coming up through the floor boards.'

'Don't think about it,' she said, diving beneath the covers, intent on delaying his departure.

Some time passed.

'God,' he said afterwards, 'you're so good at that. How did you get so good at that?' He was slumped back against the goose down pillows, eyes closed, his restlessness temporarily cured.

Aware that it was a rhetorical question, Debbie didn't think she needed to tell him about the little book she'd poured over recently, when she wasn't reading *Staying in Neutral.*

Written by Jade Gate, the sex therapist who'd run the workshops her mum, Estelle, Kate and their friend Reenie had attended, the book was called *One Hundred and One Ways to Drive Your Man Wild in Bed*, and clearly its tips and tricks were pure gold, if Adam's response was anything to go by.

'You inspire me,' she said against his bare chest, loving the resultant rumble of laughter that lifted her head slightly.

'You can say that again. That was certainly an inspired performance. I'll think about it every time I see you eating your lunchtime banana.'

She propped herself up on one elbow to look at him. 'I didn't think you really noticed me that way when we're at work.'

'Well, I can hardly shove my hand up your skirt with Rosemary or the Principal there, can I?' he said, sitting up.

'No, but ...' she began, but broke off when he began to get out of bed. 'You don't have to go yet, do you?'

He pulled an apologetic face. 'I really should, sorry. I promised Liam I'd take him out on his bike this afternoon. Besides, Caro thinks I've gone to B & Q for a bag of cement. I'll have to drop in to get some on my way home. I'm redoing one of the garden steps.'

He saw her expression. 'What? You knew I wouldn't be able to stay long today.'

If only the sex weren't so good. If only he didn't have eyes she could drown in. A voice that made her insides melt.

'Sure,' she said, with an attempt at a smile. 'It's fine.'

Adam picked up his jacket. 'Listen, Caro's taking the kids to visit her mother soon. We can spend the whole weekend together if you like. Maybe go away somewhere?'

Joy rose within her at the thought. A whole weekend. 'That would be wonderful.' They'd never had a weekend away together before.

Adam smiled at her cheekily. 'I'll get my PA to do some research,' he said. But then he spoiled the moment by lifting his jacket to his nose to sniff it, screwing up his face. 'I reek of mothballs,' he complained.

He was gone, to take his son out on his bike. Then home to a meal with his wife no doubt, some chat about their day. Stacking the dishwasher together. Flicking through the TV channels after Liam was in bed.

It shouldn't hurt so much; after all, she'd known what she was getting into. Except that she hadn't. She'd thought it would just be sex for her too, but it wasn't. Far from it.

Would he even think about her again today? Surely he would. Her body ached after all the things they'd done together. It had to be the same for him.

Debbie sighed, crossing listlessly to the window. So, what now? Go to sleep, as her body was telling her to? No, it was far too early. Get dressed and go for a walk? Somewhere near the park? No, that way madness lay. And Adam would be furious if he saw her sneaking around when he was with his son.

She sighed, moving away from the window. A cup of tea then, and then maybe make a start at sorting through Gran's stuff. Because Adam was right. She couldn't live in this mess.

Sometime later, Debbie had two piles of things – Keep and Ask Mum. Looking at the Ask Mum pile, she sighed. Phoning Janet was the last thing on earth she wanted to do, but, if she wanted to get anywhere with all this stuff, she was going to have to. Might as well get it over with now.

But when she tried to ring Janet's number, the call went straight through to voicemail, and she remembered Janet saying she might be out of phone range for a few weeks. So she left a message asking her mother to call her back, trying not to imagine Janet being too busy to answer the phone because she and Scott were dipping into their own copy of *One Hundred and One Ways to Drive Your Man Wild in Bed*.

Ending the call, Debbie put her phone down on the little table she'd managed to squeeze beneath the window. *Staying in Neutral* was on there too. So far, she'd only flicked through it. Picking it up now, she opened it at random and began to read.

Twelve

Extract from Staying in Neutral, Responses to Change Your Life by Corrinne Walker.

I say it again. Every event is neutral.

But I can feel you resisting it, like a fish on a line, jerking your little tail about as you wing through the air, desperate to get off that hook and back into the familiar water.

Stop resisting.

You won't die, if you allow yourself to be brought into that boat. You won't even find the death of all that is you. Instead, you will find incredible peace and enormous power. You will be in the driving seat of your emotions and your actions.

Your thoughts are everything. You can choose to feel good at every single moment. Yes, honestly. At any time, you have the power to reach for your highest-feeling thought. You just need to make the decision to do it.

I'm fortunate enough to have a wonderful aunt – my Aunt Muriel. Muriel is an architect, and for most of her life, she's been a woman in a man's world. She's never married, and she has thrown everything into her work. But no matter how busy she was, my Aunt Muriel always had time for me, her niece. She listened to my troubles, whether they were about my friend having a better doll collection than I did, or some boy I adored who didn't like me back. Aunt Muriel cared about my hopes and my dreams – more so, in fact, than my mother, who was more of a *pull your socks up, it'll soon be water under the bridge, don't make a spectacle of yourself* type of a woman.

Happily, as I write this, my Aunt Muriel is alive and well and still designing beautiful buildings. But I'm sure you can imagine, that if I were to get a phone call one day, telling me she had died, I would be deeply upset. However, if I told you that Muriel had died, you would not be upset. Oh, you might well feel sorry for me, because I'm sure you're a decent person. But I doubt if you'd feel compelled to dress in black or to attend Muriel's funeral. Why should you? You never met Muriel.

Muriel's death is a neutral event. It changes only because of our perception and the values we apply to it.

What? I hear you scream at me. What about the horrors of this world? How can something like a terrorist attack ever be viewed as anything but pure evil? How can the events of 9/11 be neutral?

Well, just for a moment, think of those terrorists, holding

meeting after meeting to plan the attacks. Of the huge amount of thought and attention to detail that went into the project. Now, don't get me wrong, I'm not condoning their choices for one millisecond. But I want you to imagine how much belief in the justice of their actions went into their plans. How much conviction they had that were right, and the rest of the world was wrong. How they must have celebrated when they saw those towers fall. They had set out to achieve the destruction of the Towers and the annihilation of thousands of Americans, and they succeeded beyond their wildest dreams.

With two such opposing views of one event, the only conclusion to draw is that the event itself – no matter how much it might pain us to accept the fact – is neutral. Whether we decide it was a supremely evil event or a cause for celebration, depends entirely on our values and our beliefs.

Every single thought you have can be changed.

Thirteen

Shelthorpe-on-Sea

Debbie threw *Staying in Neutral* across the room in disgust. What a complete load of rubbish. How could all events be neutral? The Twin Towers, for goodness sake!

And there was no way her lopsided relationship with Adam was neutral either. All the times he'd left earlier than she'd expected him to, or not turned up at all. How could it be neutral to feel as if your heart was breaking? Sometimes she could barely look at her phone in the minutes leading up to their meetings in case he cancelled. Corrinne Walker mustn't have had to deal with anything worse than a broken fingernail or a traffic hold up her entire life, if she really believed the rot she wrote.

Debbie flopped back on her bed and stared at the patchy paint on the ceiling. A group of people walked past in the street below, laughing together, and pain twisted in her innards like a snake. Was she the only person on the entire planet on her own? It felt like it. She was twenty-four years old, and what had she achieved in her life so far? A big fat nothing. No proper home, no proper relationship, not even a job she enjoyed. And no idea of what else she could aim towards either.

Oh, she had to get out of here. Go for a walk or something. The sea; she'd go for a brisk walk by the sea. And maybe if the lights were on in Estelle's apartment, she'd pop in there for a cup of tea. Find some company. Get away from all these boxes and black sacks. And from her thoughts; those most of all.

Quickly getting dressed, Debbie grabbed her jacket and was soon running down the stairs. Neutral event. If she did get to see Estelle, she'd tell her all about Corrinne Walker and her stupid book. Estelle would slate it, she was sure.

But when she unlocked the door to let herself out, Debbie's way was blocked by more boxes and black sacks. Somebody had ignored the sign on the door that clearly stated that donations shouldn't be left outside the shop when it was closed. Again. What were people like? Before long, she would be drowning in black sacks – both inside and outside the flat.

Pushing a surprisingly heavy bag out of the way with her foot, Debbie turned to lock the door behind her, then stopped to listen. What was that? It had sounded like a cat. No, a kitten. Yes, there it was again.

Definitely a kitten. Or several kittens, by the sound of it.

Looking around on the ground, Debbie soon found the source of the plaintive cries – they were coming from a sealed cardboard box which was next to another over-stuffed bin bag. Squatting, Debbie saw that a few air holes had been punched into the box. A tiny foot – with an even tinier claw – was scratching at one of the holes in a desperate escape bid.

How could people be so cruel? The shop was closed, and it would be dark soon. If she hadn't decided to come out, the poor things might have been there all night, and foxes came into town from the nearby common and woods after dark. The kittens might all have been killed.

'Don't worry, kitties,' she told them. 'I'll get some help.'

At the sound of her voice the kittens all came to the end nearest to her and the box immediately began to lurch. If she'd thought they were loud before, now the sound of their cries was almost deafening. Oh my gosh. What should she do?

Suddenly she remembered Paul and quickly reached for her phone, relieved she'd kept his mobile number after she'd sorted out her tenancy for the flat. Please, God, let him be around.

Fortunately, he was. And, even better, he was willing to drive over straight away to help after she'd explained the situation to him.

'Oh and, Debbie,' he said, just before he ended the call, 'please don't open the box. I don't want to be scraping squashed kittens off the High Street.'

'Of course I won't open it!' she retorted. But Paul had already gone.

When he arrived ten minutes later, Debbie couldn't believe it had only been ten minutes since she'd spoken to him. The kittens had begun to scrabble away inside the box, determined to break free, and, terrified they might escape in the street, Debbie had unlocked the door and manoeuvred the box inside. As she did so, a tiny paw broke right through one of the air holes and was quickly followed by a butting head.

'No! Oh, no. No, no, no!' She slammed the door shut, then looked frantically around for something to cover the box with. An old blanket; anything.

There weren't any old blankets, so she grabbed a coat instead. But when she hurried back over to the box with it, she was just in time to see a ginger kitten skittering across the floor to disappear behind the shop counter.

When Paul knocked on the door, Debbie was trying to decide whether the coat would be enough to keep the remaining kittens in the box while she went to track the escapee down.

As it was, she had to leave the box to let Paul in, so when she turned back again after a hurried, 'Watch out, one of them has escaped,' it was to see more kittens emerging.

'I thought you weren't going to open the box?' Paul said, scooping up stray kittens by the handful.

'I didn't. They did it by themselves. And watch where you're putting your feet. One of them's around somewhere, but I don't know exactly where.'

'How do you know it's a he?' Paul asked, head bent, scanning the floor for the kitten.

'I just do. It was him who started the break out. He's a very determined ball of fluff.'

'He might just be hungry. These guys are barely old enough to have left their mother. Oh, look, there he is, inside that boot. The brown one with the red laces.'

Debbie looked, her face breaking out into a huge smile. 'Oh, my goodness, is that cute or what?'

'Can you get him? My hands are a bit full at the moment.'

Debbie went over to the kitten, wishing there was time to capture his unbearable cuteness with her phone camera. But before she could even think about reaching for it, he made a sudden lunge upwards from the boot, attaching himself to her denim-clad legs, his claws like needles in her skin.

'Ow!' she squealed, trying to detach his claws without hurting him.

'What a little brute,' said Paul. And he placed his share of the kittens into a box of scarves that was next to the counter and came to help.

'Thanks,' said Debbie, rubbing her leg when the

final claw came out of her jeans. 'That's a good name for him. Brutus.'

Paul smiled, stroking the kitten, which began to purr against his throat, paddling him with now harmless paws.

'Here,' he said, carefully removing the kitten and holding it out to her. 'Look after him while I bring some cat baskets in, will you? I don't think that lot will get out of the scarves for a little while.'

Warily, Debbie put her hand against the kitten to support him, feeling his vibrating softness as he began to purr. Wow. How pathetic to have got to the age of twenty-four without having held a kitten. Her dad had never wanted pets, and Debbie had always told herself she was quite phobic of cats, shrinking away from her school friends' moggies. But had that just been a defence mechanism? A way of helping herself not to care about their petless home?

'Somebody looks very comfortable,' Paul said, returning with a cat basket in each hand and smiling at Brutus nestled into her chin. 'Perhaps you should keep him.'

Debbie immediately removed the kitten from her neck and held him out to Paul. 'I don't think so,' she said. 'My life's complicated enough as it is.'

Dark eyebrows lifted. 'Is it?'

Debbie flushed, asking, 'What will happen to them?' to fill the waiting silence.

Paul got on with the job of transferring the mewling

mass of kittens from the scarf box to the cat baskets. 'Oh, these guys will be snapped up as soon as I put their pictures on the website,' he said. 'Kittens always are. Even sharp-clawed, leaping ninjas like Brutus. It's the older ones that break your heart; the ones whose owners have died when their cat is starting to need some extra TLC themselves. If those students at that college of yours ever want to get involved in a fund-raising project, you'll find Cat Calls UK very receptive. Who knows? You might even change your mind about keeping Brutus.'

She shook her head. 'I don't think so.'

Paul fastened the last cat basket. 'Oh, well, come and visit the rescue centre if you're ever passing. We're up near the common on Thorney Road; you can't miss it. Thanks for your call. Enjoy the rest of your evening.'

'Thanks.'

As Paul manoeuvred the cat baskets out of the door, Debbie was sure it was little Brutus's face at the front, pressed against the mesh of the carrier, his plaintive cry louder than all the rest.

'Bye,' she said. 'Thank you for coming.' And she double-locked the door, abandoning all thoughts of a walk and deciding on an early night instead. Suddenly, she was exhausted.

Fourteen

The Gambia

'Open your legs, please.'

'*What?*' Janet looked at the tall Gambian man with alarm.

Nessa laughed. 'They're going to carry us through the water to the ferry, Janet. It can't dock any closer. Do as he asks. You'll be fine.' And, as Janet watched, another young Gambian whisked Nessa – and her considerable bulk – up onto his back.

'Open your legs, please,' the man instructed Janet again.

'Er, okay,' she said, and spread her legs with trepidation, squealing as she too was hoisted upwards.

'All right?' Nessa called over as the man carrying her started to splash through the water.

'Yes, I'm okay,' Janet replied, and, much to her surprise, she was. 'But what about my suitcase?'

'Someone else will bring it,' Nessa told her. 'Don't

worry.'

They'd been waiting for the ferry for almost three hours, having arrived in good time to catch the nine o'clock sailing. Now it was eleven thirty, but nobody seemed concerned.

In England there would have been complaints and talk of compensation, but here everyone had just settled down to wait – with their goats, their goods and their babies on their backs – a mass of patient, chattering life and colour.

'Janet,' Nessa had told her with a smile as they waited in the queue, 'I do believe that GMT is sinking into your bones.'

'Greenwich Mean Time?' frowned Janet, confused.

'Gambian Maybe Time. No hurry; it happens when it happens.'

'Perhaps,' said Janet. Certainly, waking up that morning, she'd experienced no sense of panic or urgency to exchange her plane tickets and to fly home early. After all, why should she? There was nothing to hurry home for, and The Gambia was here, waiting to be explored. The only obstacle was her limited funds, but Nessa had offered her a solution to that.

'I'm going Upriver for a week, to visit my families,' she'd told Janet. 'Why don't you come with me? It won't cost you much, and that way you'll get to experience the true Gambia. My friends will be thrilled to have you. They love meeting new people.'

And so, here she was, being carried onto a ferry, any

reservations about spending so much time with Nessa put aside as she said a firm 'yes' to life and experiences. Jade would be proud of her. Her friends would be proud of her. And Debbie … Well, Debbie would probably think she was crazy.

On board the ferry, Janet found herself seated between Nessa and a Gambian woman with a young baby. The boat was packed, and there was a strong smell of goat and body odour. The noise level was high.

'If I'd known we were going to have to wait so long for the ferry to arrive, I could have tried to replace my phone,' Janet said, raising her voice in order to be heard over all the chatter.

Nessa shrugged. 'There's no signal Upriver anyway. The world will manage without you for a week.'

Yes, no doubt it would. After all, everyone thought she was on her honeymoon anyway.

The baby next to her began to suckle on his mother's breast, his huge, serious eyes turned in Janet's direction. She smiled a big, exaggerated smile at him. 'Hello!' she cooed, but the baby's expression didn't change, and it was almost as if he were sizing her up, deciding who was right about her rash decision to accompany Nessa – Janet or Debbie.

Janet looked away, her gaze sweeping over the other occupants of the boat. It was like a patchwork quilt of colour. Cerise. Vermillion. Turquoise. A woman with a flower in her hair. Another with a yellow scarf. A glint of a gold tooth when someone laughed. An awning flapping. A couple kissing.

'Oh, it's so good, so very good to be back. You can't imagine,' Nessa said, her sigh one of deep contentment.

How relaxed she looked; as if she belonged here. Not all hyped up and buzzing like Janet, looking around her with bird-pecking glances all the time, an outsider looking in.

'What brought you to The Gambia in the first place?'

Nessa had her eyes closed. She didn't open them again as she answered Janet's question. 'My parents. They were both in the medical profession, and they used to volunteer here in their holidays before it became the fashionable thing to do. They brought me along with them, and I loved it.' She smiled. 'They were people before their time, my parents.'

'It sounds like it,' Janet said, trying and failing to imagine her gas fitter father and housewife mother doing any such thing. 'Are they still alive?'

'No, they both died a long time ago.'

'I'm sorry.'

Nessa opened her eyes to look directly at Janet. 'Death comes to us all,' she said. 'That's why we must always do our best to make the most of life while we have it.'

The atmosphere had changed suddenly, and Janet frowned. Then Nessa smiled again. 'Later on, I started the Bike2School Project and came back here. I was a keen cyclist in my youth, you see. Always entering competitions. Even winning some of them. Then, when I was older, I wrote a book about keeping fit through cycling.'

Nessa had written a book about keeping fit through cycling? Had entered cycling competitions?

Nessa laughed. 'Sounds unlikely, doesn't it? My trouble is, I didn't take my own advice. I should have practised what I preached, but I didn't. Instead, I piled on the pounds until I could hardly get on a bike any longer. Luckily for me, it's not difficult to prove that cycling's good for your health and for losing weight, otherwise, well, I might have been in big trouble later on.'

Janet frowned, feeling as if she'd missed a thread of the conversation somehow, but was distracted from asking more when the boat suddenly began to rock alarmingly. More people were climbing on board. Was that safe? Surely the boat was already full? Nessa's thigh was jammed against Janet's on one side, and that of the nursing mother on the other. When the baby hiccupped and dislodged itself from the mother's nipple, there was a strong, sickly smell of milk.

Janet put a hand to her face. 'Surely they can't fit anyone else on?'

'These are the men,' Nessa explained. 'They stand around the outside of the boat. Ideas about health and safety are a bit different here.'

Sure enough, there was soon a line of men – visible only from mid leg to waist – lined up around the boat, and, looking over, Janet's gaze connected with someone's crotch. She looked quickly away again.

Nessa laughed, a big belly laugh that, since they were jammed so closely together, vibrated its way right down Janet's leg. 'Don't worry,' she said. 'He can't see you looking!'

Finally, finally, the ferry set off. With the men's crotches lined up to the side, the baby still staring at her, and the broad back of a woman with two goats in front of her, Janet felt extremely hemmed in. It was difficult to know where to look, so she closed her eyes for a moment, belatedly remembering that she could be prone to nausea on the water unless she concentrated on looking where she was going.

'How long does the boat take?' she asked Nessa, carefully drawing in some deep breaths.

'About fifty minutes. Then about two hours by Land Rover. There aren't any proper roads, so be prepared to get bashed about. I'm always grateful for my extra padding when I travel in The Gambia.'

She could hang on for fifty minutes, couldn't she?

Maybe.

She managed fifteen. Then, with shaking hands and her clothes drenched with sweat, Janet turned to Nessa with a hand pressed over her mouth to ask, 'Have you got a bag or something? I feel really sick.'

Nessa had been napping. Now her eyes sprang open.

'No,' she said, 'I haven't, sorry. You'll have to push through to the side.'

Pushing through to the side didn't look possible in the press of people. But Janet knew she was going to have to do it somehow if she didn't want to throw up over everybody.

'Excuse me,' she said to the mother next to her, her hand still over her mouth. After one look at her the woman swiftly moved her legs, pulling her baby quickly out of range. Disturbed by the sudden movement, he began to protest loudly, the sound of his cries crashing around Janet's head as she pushed past.

Please let me make it, she thought. Please.

Somehow she got to the side. But then there were all those men's legs and crotches to contend with.

'Please,' she said weakly, almost weeping with gratitude when someone shouted something, and somebody else pulled at a trouser leg. And finally, there was enough space to push her head through.

Just in time.

'Are you all right, Janet?' Nessa called, but Janet couldn't answer. She was too busy chucking up her entire breakfast, and, it seemed, everything she'd eaten the previous evening and possibly the previous morning too.

Finally, it was over, and the desire to slip over the side to become food for any passing crocodiles had begun to pass. Making her way apologetically back to her seat, Janet tried not to think about the upcoming drive along bumpy tracks. Surely she would be all right now? Oh, she hoped so.

Back next to Nessa on her unyielding wooden seat, Janet smoothed her hair back from her sweaty face. Nessa reached out to push back a strand she'd missed. 'Poor, Janet,' she said.

'I didn't even think about being sick when I agreed to come,' Janet said. 'It's not exactly the high seas, is it?'

'No, it's not. But you know, my friend was sick in paddleboat once when we were kids.'

Janet smiled weakly. 'Really?'

'Yes. Her brother made it go round and round on purpose. I loved it – I was always a fairground ride sort of a girl – but Jeannie couldn't take it. Of course, her brother never let her forget about it. I bet he still trots out that story at dinner parties.'

Janet's smile grew a little stronger.

'That's better,' Nessa said approvingly. 'And listen, everything will be all right for you. I just know it. You made the right choice, and now your new future is beginning to unfurl. Trust it to do so in the way the universe intends.'

Nessa seemed to have a disconcerting habit of switching the tone of a conversation from light to more serious. It made Janet a bit nervous. 'You don't happen to know somebody called Jade Gate, do you?' she asked wryly. 'Only that's exactly the kind of thing she would have said to me.'

'No,' said Nessa, 'I haven't had the pleasure of meeting Jade. What a lovely name she has. Who is she?'

Janet smiled, remembering Estelle once telling her that the name Jade Gate was actually the ancient Chinese name for a woman's most private anatomy. How they'd giggled together as they speculated about what Jade's name might really be. The memory brought with it another sudden, sharp pang of homesickness, and she looked away, avoiding Nessa's gaze.

'Oh, just a teacher I knew once,' she said, wondering suddenly what on earth she was doing here, heading who knew where with a virtual stranger.

If she'd changed her plane ticket, she could be with her friends right now, being congratulated on making a lucky escape from Scott. She might have been sharing amusing details about his habit of pulling his underpants up as far as they would go when he got dressed. Or the way he finished off the process by giving the elastic a ping before he pulled on his socks. And they would have spluttered with laughter, holding their stomachs like giggling girls.

But she hadn't changed her plane ticket.

Another memory of Jade popped into her mind – standing in front of the class in one of her black lace dresses, her arms spread, all evangelistic and charged with passion. 'You have to truly want to give and truly want to take to be your most passionate selves. Find the courage to let go. Take that step into the dark!'

And Janet knew without a doubt that Jade would approve of Janet going on this trip into the unknown. Anyway, she was here now, so she might as well make the best of it.

Hours later, bumping along in the Land Rover, Nessa finally turned to her to say, 'We're almost at the village.'

Janet was mightily relieved to hear it, although she had no idea how Nessa could be so sure, because, squinting out of the passenger door window, all she could see through the red dust the vehicle was throwing up, was some sort of tall crop.

'That's maize,' Nessa told her. 'It forms the main part of the diet of the people here.'

After a while, the maize gave way to rough picket fencing. White chickens scattered as the Land Rover advanced. Then suddenly, there was a shout, and a gang of children appeared from nowhere. Shouting something to Nessa, they began to run alongside the vehicle. Nessa's face was suddenly split in two by a huge smile, and she was waving, waving.

'Please stop,' she told the driver. 'We can walk the rest of the way. I want to see my babies. Oh my goodness, I can't believe how much they've grown!'

The Land Rover came to a halt, and as soon as Nessa had eased her bulk out, she was swamped by children, all of them calling to her and wanting to hold her hand.

'Thomas!' Nessa crooned, stroking an older boy's hair. 'Lily.' Cupping a girl's cheek. 'Oh, you wonderful, wonderful children! Take me to your mamma.'

Feeling forgotten, Janet wasn't sure whether to stay in the Land Rover or to get out and follow behind. In the end, the thought of arriving in the village before Nessa persuaded her, so she climbed out onto the red dirt track.

Ahead, Nessa was barely visible she was surrounded by so many children. Since none of them had been unable to get exclusive custody of her hand, they were each clutching at one of her fingers, making the bottoms of her arms look like bouquets of children. Very lively bouquets, since the children were skipping and dancing, each one of them calling out something to their beloved Nessa.

One older girl of about ten or eleven, who hadn't managed to get hold of even a finger, ran back to take Janet's hand instead, smiling up at her. And as Janet took the dusty hand in her own, she experienced a glow of happiness.

'What's your name?' Janet asked her.

'I am Fatu.'

Up ahead, Nessa looked back to check up on Janet. 'That's my friend Janet,' she called. 'You take good care of her, Fatu. She's a very special lady.'

'Oh, no, I'm just …' Janet began to say, but Nessa

and her gaggle of excited fans were bouncing ahead again, paying no more attention to her.

Fatu was still smiling up at her. 'You are special because you bring our Binta back to us. It has been so long since we have seen her. We begin to think she is never coming back. And now she is here. Binta is here!' And she began to dance, right there along the road, still holding Janet's hand.

Dazzled by the sunshine of Fatu's joyful smile, Janet laughed, a part of her brain snagging on the name she had used for Nessa. Binta. And now she realised that this was what the children had been chanting as they ran alongside the Land Rover. Binta! Binta! It was a name Janet had heard before, very recently. From David.

'Why do they call you that?' she asked Nessa as soon as she was close enough. 'Why don't they call you Nessa?'

'Binta is my Gambian name,' Nessa smiled. 'And I can't tell you how good it is to hear it again. Nobody's used it for years. They'll probably come up with a Gambian name for you too, if you stay around long enough.'

'You don't know a man called David, do you?' Janet asked, fearing the answer, but any answer Nessa might have given was cut off by a woman running towards them from the village, sending children flying in her enthusiasm to take Nessa into her embrace.

'Binta! You have come back to us!'

'Sukai!' cried Nessa.

Janet watched Nessa fold the woman into her arms. As she was tall and heavily pregnant, and Nessa was short and bulky, it ought to have been a comical sight, but somehow it was anything but. Instead, it was deeply moving; as if Nessa and Sukai were mother and daughter, reunited after a long gap.

'Oh, Sukai, my dear. I'm so very happy to see you again.' The two women kissed, and then they both laughed, wiping the tears from their faces. Then Nessa turned to introduce Janet. 'Sukai, this is Janet. I've brought her with me so that she can experience the true Gambia.'

Sukai broke free from Nessa's arms to smile at Janet. 'You are welcome, Janet. A friend of Binta's is also a friend of ours. Binta is family.'

Fatu had let go of Janet's hand and was peering into the Land Rover. Janet wondered what she was looking for.

'Binta?' Fatu asked Nessa. 'Have you brought a bike for me? You say next time you come I get a bike, and then you don't come.'

The smile on Nessa's face became an expression of regret. She went over to put her hands on the girl's shoulders. 'I'm so sorry, Fatu. I haven't been able to bring any bikes with me this time. I haven't forgotten my promise to you, but things didn't work out. But I'll do everything I can to make sure you get one very soon. I promise. And in the meantime, can I depend on

137

you to take care of my friend Janet? Will you show her around the village?'

Fatu nodded. 'Yes, I will do that.' She turned to Janet. 'You can sleep in my bed with me.'

Janet, who was a little taken aback by this offer, found herself admiring the way the girl managed to put aside her disappointment about the bike straight away.

'Thank you, Fatu,' she said. 'That's very kind of you.'

The village, when they reached it, was as basic as Nessa had warned her it would be – a collection of thatched huts and ramshackle buildings with corrugated iron roofs.

'I'll introduce you to Yoro, Sukai's husband,' Nessa said breathlessly to Janet. 'Then Fatu can show you around.'

'Okay.'

They walked past several huts and an arrangement of cooking pots and a stove laid out on the ground, which Janet took to be an outside kitchen, until they reached a group of what looked like at least three generations of men, seated beneath some palm trees talking.

'Yoro,' Nessa said, moving forward into the group. 'How are you, my man? As you see, I have returned, and I've brought a friend with me. This is Janet.'

Yoro was dressed like the other men in a traditional white kaftan with a small skull cap edged in gold on his head. He had a ready smile, and greeted Nessa warmly, enquiring after her health. Then he did the same to Janet. Nessa gave him some kola nuts as a gift, and these were warmly received. Then, it appeared, the audience was over.

'See you later, Yoro,' Nessa said, with a smile and a little bow.

'He looks young to be Sukai's husband,' Janet observed as they walked away, and Nessa gave her an ironic little smile.

'The men often look younger than the women in The Gambia,' she explained. 'Their lives are very much easier, as you'll see. And speaking of work, I'll leave you in Fatu's capable hands while I catch up with Sukai and help her to make the meal.'

Fatu had been hovering while they spoke with Yoro, and now she clutched hold of Janet's hand to pull her along, obviously keen to show her everything that was home. First, they went into one of the dark, dusty-smelling huts. 'This is where I sleep with two of my sisters. You will sleep here with us tonight,' Fatu said.

Looking down, Janet saw that someone had brought her bag from the Land Rover. It was on the floor next to a straw-stuffed mattress. There was very little else inside the room, but squinting through the dimness, Janet could just about make out a large cut off tin can to one side.

'That is the toilet for night time,' Fatu told her, catching the direction of her gaze. 'I will show you the toilet for the day.'

'Thank you,' Janet said, making up her mind not to drink too much in the evenings so she wouldn't need to use the tin can. 'And is there somewhere I can wash? I'm very sticky after the journey.' Sticky wasn't all. She could also catch a faint whiff of sick coming from her clothes or her hair. Possibly both. The breeze on the boat must have blown it up onto her. Disgusting.

'I will show you,' Fatu said, leading her through a group of chickens that were roaming free, pecking at the red dirt.

'Do you feed them corn?' asked Janet, thinking how pretty and self-absorbed they looked.

Fatu shook her head. 'We never feed them. There are plenty of ants for them to eat.'

'Oh,' said Janet. 'That's good.'

A boy went past on a rusty old bike, loaded up with bags of what looked like cement. As Janet watched, wondering how the tyres could stand it, he gave her a cheery smile and a wave, which she returned. A girl walked by with a container of something balanced on top of her head. She also smiled.

'That is Fatu,' Fatu told Janet.

Janet frowned. 'She has the same name you do?'

Fatu nodded. 'She is a first-born girl like me. All the first-born girls in our compound are called Fatu.'

Janet thought that must get confusing, but kept the thought to herself. 'How many compounds are there in the village?' she asked.

'Twenty,' Fatu told her. 'Twenty compounds.'

A small group of boys were playing a game, throwing something towards a wall. 'What are they doing?' Janet asked, smiling at the group.

'They see who can get the nut closest to the wall,' Fatu told her with a shrug, as if this was a stupid occupation, worthy only of boys.

She led Janet on, past a pair of tethered goats. Their goat smell was strong, and suddenly overpowering, and Janet had to cover her nose with her hand. She really ought to have got over her sickness on the boat by now, but it seemed she hadn't.

But the smell of the goats was nothing compared with the stench from the pit latrine Fatu took her to next.

'This is the toilet for the day-time,' Fatu said, showing it to her, and Janet did her best not to blanch as she looked at the latrine. Could she really survive here for a week, using that? Already, with only one small peek at it, sweat was breaking out on her forehead, the smell was so strong. To have to come here many times a day … How did they survive it?

'I will show you where you can wash,' Fatu said now, and Janet allowed herself to be pulled away gratefully.

Janet hadn't imagined a power shower – after all, on the way here, Nessa had told her there was no electricity in the village – but somehow she had anticipated more than a large bowl, about the same size as a baby bath, behind a roughly-woven screen of twigs.

'You can fill the bath with water from here,' Fatu told her, indicating a large water container. 'I will see you later. I have to help with my little brothers and sisters now, while Mamma cooks.'

'Thank you, Fatu,' Janet said, and the girl smiled and left.

Alone, Janet looked at the bath tub doubtfully. Were you supposed to get into it? Or to have an all-over wash? It was so small. And if she did try to get into it, would she ever be able to get out again? And, since there was no way of locking herself in anywhere, would she get interrupted if she got undressed?

Oh, sod it. She stank, and she needed to wash. That was all there was to it. At least there was a screen of sorts. She was just going to have to go for it, even if someone did come in. Even if the whole damn village trooped past one by one.

The image made her giggle, albeit nervously, and she got busy, filling the bath with water from the heavy plastic water container and quickly stripping off her clothes. When she got in, there was so little space, her knees came up to her chin.

Hugging her legs, Janet rested her forehead on her knees, suddenly exhausted. What a few days it had been. She closed her eyes, the water lapping around her as she breathed in and out. Sounds drifted to her – the excited cries of the boys, still playing their cashew nut game. Birds tweeting in the nearby trees. One of the goats bleating, and another joining it. A chicken clucking nearby. And another.

Janet could tell they had come to join her in the wash area when she heard the sounds of pecking, close to the bath, and she smiled. But she didn't open her eyes. Was there anyone else in the whole world taking a bath surrounded by chickens at this moment in time? Very probably, somewhere. But it certainly wasn't anything she'd ever done, or expected to do.

'Knock, knock,' came a woman's voice. Nessa. Janet's head came quickly up, and she moved her knees even closer to her breasts.

'Only me,' Nessa said, moving around the screen as if it were the most natural thing in the world to interrupt someone while they were taking a bath. 'Thought I'd check you were okay. By the way, you might want to put a little less water in there next time. The women have to carry it from the well, at the other end of the village.'

Janet looked down guiltily at the dark patches on the ground where the water had slopped over the side of the bath. 'The women carry it?' And she remembered the other Fatu and the container she'd been carrying. Had that been water?

Nessa nodded. 'And the girls. The women do most of the work around here, as I told you. Anyway, I just wanted to tell you about dinner. They serve food in a communal bowl here; I don't know if you knew that? Everyone dips their hand in to eat. There's a bit of an art to it, but if you copy what I do, you'll soon get the hang of it.'

'Okay,' Janet said doubtfully, unsure whether she'd be able to eat anything anyway, with her stomach feeling the way it did.

Nessa seemed to read her mind. 'And, if you can, do try everything. Sukai might be offended otherwise.'

Janet's smile was wan. 'I'll do my best,' she said. It was the most she felt she could promise.

The huge white enamel dish with a blue rim was exactly the same as some her mother had possessed when Janet was a child, only a lot larger. But her mother's bowls had always been filled with vegetables or apple crumble, not a fragrant-smelling stew and rice like this one.

'Looks good, doesn't it?' Nessa said as they took their places on the floor cushions.

'Very good,' Janet said, and Sukai smiled at her.

'Please,' she said. 'Our guests should eat first.'

'You're very kind,' smiled Nessa.

Janet watched very carefully as Nessa reached towards the bowl with her right hand and took a handful of rice. Closing her palm around it, she appeared to squeeze it into a ball. Then she let it fall forward to her fingers and popped it into her mouth. Nessa made it look simple.

'Do you want a spoon, Janet?' Sukai asked with a smile, but Janet shook her head.

'Let me try first,' she said. 'Then we'll see.'

Her first attempt was a failure. Her second wasn't much better, but she sensed Sukai appreciated her efforts. And soon everyone was diving in to eat themselves, removing the spotlight from Janet.

In any case, her clumsy efforts meant Janet could hide how little she was eating. For, while the food was good, her stomach still felt churned up.

'Do you have children, Janet?' Sukai asked, and Janet nodded.

'Yes,' she said. 'One grown up daughter, Debbie. She's twenty-four now.'

'You only have one?'

'Yes. We would have had more, but it just didn't happen. You have lots.'

Sukai smiled. 'Seven.' She patted her belly. 'This one make it eight. It is a lot of work. But the girls, they help me. Your girl, she is married?'

'Not yet, no.'

Sukai's smile was sympathetic. 'Ah, she work? Career girl?'

'Yes, that's right.' It was simpler to agree, even though it wasn't really true, because Janet had an idea Sukai wouldn't understand Debbie or her life at all. Why would she? Janet hardly understood it herself. If Debbie had seemed happy, Janet wouldn't worry, but she didn't seem happy. Her daughter appeared to be drifting aimlessly along through life, and it made Janet feel as if she'd gone wrong somewhere as a parent.

'Binta, she doesn't have any children,' Sukai said. 'This is why she comes here, I think. So we can be her family. And yet she stay away from us for so long.'

'Oh, Sukai,' Nessa said. 'I told you. If I could possibly have been here, I would have been here. This village is where I love to be more than anywhere in the whole world.'

'Well, you are here now,' said Sukai, and Janet wondered what Nessa's health problems had been, and whether they were completely behind her now.

It was an enjoyable evening of talk and laughter, then singing and more laughter. Candles were lit, stories were told, and lives were put to rights.

A short distance away, Janet could hear the men doing exactly the same thing. It seemed strange to her that the sexes divided themselves up, but it was somehow nice too. Perhaps both groups could be truly themselves in this way.

The warmth and the company worked their magic, and by the end of it, when Janet emerged with Fatu into the darkness, she felt tired but relaxed. Above her stretched a huge star-filled sky.

'Isn't it beautiful?' Janet said, but the girl just shrugged.

'The stars are always there,' she said. 'If you remember to look up.'

Janet looked at Fatu, inexplicable tears suddenly filling her eyes. 'Yes,' she said. 'You're right.'

Fifteen

Shelthorpe-on-Sea

'So, what have you been doing with yourself lately? Have you got your flat how you want it now?'

Kate and Debbie were eating their sandwiches together in the college canteen. It was the first time they'd managed to meet up since Debbie had moved out, and Kate was worried about her. She looked as if she hadn't slept properly since she'd left them, and whenever Kate tried to meet her eyes, she looked away. Relaxed, she most definitely was not, and Kate's something's-wrong-but-they're-not-telling-you sensors – which she used on almost a daily basis in her job with the catering students – had switched into overdrive.

'Not really, no,' Debbie said, shaking her head, eyes still on her sandwiches. 'It's full of Gran's things. I can hardly move for them.'

Kate frowned. 'I thought Janet had dealt with all that. I know she cleared out lots of stuff before she sold the house.'

Debbie shrugged. 'If she did, then there's loads

more. Bags and bags of it. I started to try and sort them out, but I don't feel as if I can get rid of anything without asking Mum first.'

'And Janet's currently uncontactable in remotest Africa?'

Another nod. 'Yeah.'

Kate could clearly remember how low Janet had been when she'd been clearing out her mother's belongings. Since it had still been quite early on in their friendship, she hadn't offered to help her out the way she would have done now. 'I expect she shoved it all in the flat because she didn't know what to do with it either. It must be hard to get rid of everything.'

'I suppose,' Debbie agreed.

Kate drank some of her orange juice, reflecting that a cramped flat with your dead gran's crap wasn't much of a life for a young person. But there was more to it than that, she was sure of it. Something else was upsetting Debbie's world. 'So,' she asked casually, 'what have you been up to, if you haven't been doing up the flat?'

Debbie shrugged. 'Reading mostly.'

'Yeah? Torn yourself away from the Shelthorpe-on-Sea nightclubs then, have you?'

It was a relief when Debbie smiled. Kate had always believed in a good old piss take to show your feelings for somebody. And lighten things up. And yet ... 'You are all right in that flat, aren't you? It can be lonely living on your own. Make sure you get out now and then, won't you?'

'I do,' Debbie said, sounding slightly defensive, but Kate wasn't sure she believed it. Maybe she ought to tell Debbie she could come back to live with them if she wanted to? Because she could, obviously. Even though things between her and Geoff were pretty much the same as when she'd left. Between late courses and assessments, there never seemed to be enough time for a proper talk. Especially as Kate was scared of what a proper talk might lead to.

She sighed, then smiled brightly, forcing her own problems from her mind to concentrate on Debbie. 'Anyway, what have you been reading? Anything interesting?'

Now the girl looked downright embarrassed. 'Non-fiction, mostly,' she said with a shrug. 'About peoples' reactions when things go wrong, or when bad things happen in their lives.'

'Oh? And it's a book, is it? What's it called?'

'*Staying in Neutral - Responses to Change Your Life.*'

Kate frowned. That sounded familiar. Then she remembered. Of course, at her wedding – the strange-looking woman with the pink fascinator. 'I was given a copy of that as a wedding present. I'm not sure what happened to it. And you say it's all about reactions?'

Debbie nodded. 'Yes. Whether there's a set way of reacting or not. The theory is that every event in your life is neutral, and you can choose how to respond to it.' She looked up briefly. 'I thought it was rubbish at first, but then ... well, I've been thinking about it and wondering, you know, if it might be helpful if I could believe it, give it a try.'

Kate shook her head. For goodness sake; what utter bollocks people wrote. And if Debbie had latched onto it, as clearly she had, then there must be something particular in her life she was trying to deal with. If only she could come right out and ask her. But she knew from experience that young people only revealed stuff when they were good and ready to do so. Though surely it wasn't a good idea to have someone telling you your natural reactions were wrong? That somehow you weren't entitled to feel them?

'I'm not sure I buy it,' Kate said. 'After all, what about that woman in the news at the moment? The one whose daughter's gone missing in Great Yarmouth? Single parent, struggling to bring up two kids, but doing all right, just. Holding down a job.' As she spoke, Kate remembered how she'd felt, watching the woman on TV. Poor cow; she'd been desperate. 'Then the worst possible thing happens; her daughter disappears and everything gets blown out of the water. I don't suppose she thinks there's any choice about how to react to all of that, poor woman.'

She saw Debbie thinking about it. Neither of them were eating much of their lunch. 'No, I don't suppose so.'

Kate leant forward over the table, warming to her

theme. 'Sometimes, when bad things happen to you, you feel too much to hold it all in. All those emotions have to erupt out of you somehow. Vesuvius coming out of your ears and nostrils.' She paused for a moment, finding courage from somewhere because she sensed somehow that Debbie needed her to find it. 'Like when my husband cheated on me with my best friend.'

'You mean Geoff?' Debbie was looking straight at her now, obviously shocked to the core.

Kate laughed, feeling some of her tension slipping away. Whatever was happening between her and Geoff, at least it still seemed like an impossibility that he would ever be unfaithful to her.

'No, not Geoff, bless him. He'd never do anything like that to me. No, I meant my first husband, Ian. I caught him in bed with my best friend Jennifer, and believe me, there was no choice about how to react to that. I mean, how else can you react to a ton of bricks dropping on you from a great height? You just get squashed. And then you hate. With a passion. For a very long time.'

Debbie put her sandwich down, giving up all pretence of eating. 'Who did you hate the most?' she asked. 'Your husband or your friend?'

Kate thought about it. 'Both of them, obviously. But her, more.' She nodded. 'Yes, definitely her. All that sneaking around behind my back. Sitting there in the pub listening to me pour my heart out about Ian being so busy at work. When all the time, it was her keeping him busy.' She shook her head. 'Treachery like that takes some dealing with, I can tell you.'

Debbie was quiet, sipping at her Coke. Kate wondered if she was aware of how very like Janet she was, and wished suddenly that Janet were here. It ought to be her dealing with whatever was wrong with her daughter, not Kate.

'Do you ever see her now? Your friend?'

'Judas Jennifer?' Kate shook her head. 'No. Amazingly, I've never run into her since, thank God. They moved to Cromer, and she works in Norwich. Just as well. If I did see her, I'd probably still want to scratch her eyes out. You see? I've got a new life, a new husband, and a baby on the way, and I'm still bitter. Not that I'm saying you're wasting your time reading that book of yours or anything ...' Kate broke off, noticing the time. She'd have to go soon, but she was still worried about Debbie, even though she sensed it wouldn't help much, if she could stay longer. 'Listen, sorry, Debs, but I'm going to have to make a move now. But let's do this again soon though, yeah? It's been nice to catch up. And feel free to pop over and see me anytime you want, won't you?'

'I will. Thanks.'

Debbie's response was so lacking in energy, it made Kate feel more worried than ever. 'In fact, how about I come over and help you go through a few of those bin bags? I know you can't actually chuck anything away until you've spoken to your mum, but we could make a start at sorting it out. I can come round tonight, if you like? I'm not doing anything.' The sooner the better.

'All right. Thanks. I could get a pizza in, if you like. And you can meet my new kitten.'

Kate smiled. 'Kittens and pizza? How could I say no? About seven-thirty?'

'That's fine, yes. And ... well, thanks.'

'No problem.' Kate gave her a final wave and went on her way, wondering if Debbie were pregnant. She hadn't seen her with anyone, but that didn't mean anything. Young people didn't seem to actually date these days. It was all FaceTime, and hanging around in parks. Admittedly, Debbie was older than her GNVQ lot, but even so. Oh well, maybe she'd find out what the problem was tonight.

But, as Kate walked along the corridor towards the Catering Department, it wasn't easy to leave the conversation she'd had with Debbie behind. It had brought back too many bad memories, namely the afternoon she had returned home with fish and chips to find her husband in their bed with her best friend, his mouth clamped around her nipple.

A student suddenly burst around the corner, cannoning straight into her. 'Walk, Burrows!' she barked, putting a protective hand to her baby bump, just as Adam Bailey, the Deputy Principal, also rounded the corner.

'They never remember, do they?' he said, smiling

and shaking his head. 'Are you all right?'

'Yes, I'm fine,' she said, returning his smile with difficulty. She'd disliked the man ever since she'd seen him snogging a woman who most definitely wasn't his wife in an Ipswich nightclub. Kate had been there for her sister's hen party. He'd probably been there so he wouldn't run into anyone who knew him.

Bastard.

Sixteen

Shelthorpe-on-Sea

After Kate had left, Debbie sat on in the canteen for a minute, feeling stunned. Did her mum know about Kate's husband and her best friend? Yes, of course she would know. She hadn't mentioned it to Debbie, but they'd never had a gossipy kind of a relationship. Besides, Kate wouldn't thank anyone for spreading it around.

What if Kate ever found out about her and Adam? She'd hate her, and that would suck, because she really liked Kate. And the bummer was, that since she liked her so much, Kate was exactly the person she'd love to pour her heart out to about it all. She was easy to talk to, and always gave good, common sense advice.

Not like her mum. Janet was always so hesitant. Or at least, she'd always been that way with Debbie. So tentative in offering her opinions, always hovering in the background somewhere or doing her best to keep the peace. Growing up, it had been hard to respect someone who was so passive and easily walked over. And equally hard to accept that such a person could change so much and demand a divorce.

Janet's transformation had been bewildering; like suddenly being faced with a stranger. A stranger who'd changed overnight from a person who kept everything bottled up, to a person who wanted to express and analyse her each and every feeling. Debbie had run a mile.

No, much better to be like Kate. Kate was consistently outspoken. You always knew exactly where you were with her. And Debbie imagined what it must have been like, in that bedroom, face-to-face with evidence of her husband and her friend's treachery. She bet Kate had given them both hell.

For a moment, Debbie imagined how terrible it would be to be discovered in bed with Adam by his wife. But that should never happen, because they would never meet at his house. Still …

There was half an hour of Debbie's lunch break left. Maybe she'd finish her sandwiches in the nearby park, and phone her dad. To her knowledge, he still didn't know about Janet remarrying, and he probably should. Besides, it was better than half an hour of feeling guilty about her and Adam.

He answered on the second ring. 'Hi, sweetheart,' he said. 'How are you?'

'Fine,' she said, trying to gauge from his tone of voice whether it was a good time to call or not. 'You?'

'Busy, as usual. I'm heading into a meeting soon, but I've got five minutes. It's good to hear from you.'

It was different now, when she and her dad met up. Now that he'd moved into a riverside apartment in Norwich, she couldn't just pop round when she felt like it. Also, a part of his attention always seemed to be caught up with what his young neighbours were getting up to, or by the roar of the crowd from the nearby football stadium if there was a match on. Debbie was often left feeling that her and her father's roles had reversed; that it ought to be Debbie living in a trendy apartment close to the Norwich nightclubs, with her dad still in sleepy Shelthorpe-on-Sea.

'How are things with you?' he asked.

'Fine, thanks. I've moved.'

'Oh, again? Somewhere permanent now? That's good, give me the address.'

'Well, it's not exactly permanent, but it's good for now. I've moved into the flat above Mum's shop.'

'Oh, I see.' He sounded disappointed. 'Well, that's good. And what's she up to these days? Celebrating her new-found freedom by living as a goat herd in the Andes?' He laughed, amused by his own joke. 'Volunteering to save the lesser spotted ibis in the Pharaoh Islands? Or no, I've got a better one. Giving igloos an interior design makeover in Alaska.' He laughed again, pausing, and Debbie knew she was supposed to fill the gap with her own laughter.

It was a game they had often played in the past she and him, uniting against Janet and her 'eccentricities'. The two of them had laughed together about Janet's Dreams, her mother's idea for an interior design shop, and shaken their heads when Janet had mothballed the plan.

'It's a bit more extreme than goat-herding or saving the ibis,' she said. 'She's remarried.'

'What?' Her father sounded outraged. 'Not to that dickhead she swanned off with? I knew it! She swore blind that tosser wasn't on the scene before we split up, but I knew she was lying. Not even Janet would be mad enough to marry someone she's only known for a few months.'

While they spoke for a bit longer, the red mist of resentment which had engulfed Ray at the mention of Janet's marriage cancelled out any chance for them to speak meaningfully about anything else. Although, Debbie wasn't sure what that might be anyway. Corrinne Walker's neutral theory? No. Her relationship with Adam? Hardly. The decision she'd taken the previous Saturday to adopt Brutus after all? No, her father loathed cats. He'd have gone on about commitments, ties and cat hair. All of which were true of course, but Debbie was still happy about her change of heart.

Waking up on the Sunday morning after a lonely Saturday night, Debbie had remembered the kitten peeping out from the top of the red-laced boot and smiled. And somehow, after breakfast, she'd found herself driving over to the Cat Calls UK Rescue Centre to see how the kittens were doing.

'Ha! I knew you wouldn't be able to resist,' Paul said, smiling at her as she came in through the door. 'He got his claws into you, didn't he, the little charmer?'

'Literally,' she said, wondering if she was going crazy.

But Paul didn't give her the chance to change her mind. 'Come on, I'll take you to him,' he said. 'He's been pining for you.'

'I don't expect so,' she said. 'Not after such a brief acquaintance.' But she couldn't help smiling.

Paul led the way through several locked gates to where the cats waiting to be rescued were housed in a long, low brick building with lots of small windows facing outwards. Once inside, with the outer door carefully closed behind them, they walked along a central corridor with cat runs on either side. Most, Debbie saw, were occupied, and some of the occupants looked out at her hopefully. Others were fast asleep and ignored them.

Finally, they reached a run where the occupants were very vocal. This had to be it. It was. And there, his little face pressed up to the glass, was Brutus. And Debbie had been smitten all over again.

'Debbie, love, are you still there?' came her father's

voice down the phone, interrupting her thoughts.

'Yes, sorry, Dad. I'm still here.'

'Well, look, I've got to go to my meeting now anyway. We'll speak again soon, yes?'

'All right, Dad. Bye.'

'Bye, sweetheart.'

As she was putting her phone away, someone came through the park gate and started to walk towards her. Adam!

'Hello,' he said. 'I thought I might find you here.'

'Hello, you,' she smiled.

Adam often took a turn around the park to get some fresh air at lunch time. Which was precisely why Debbie was in the habit of eating her lunch here. Applying sun lotion when the weather was hot, and shivering in her hat and scarf when it was cold, getting glove fluff on her sandwiches.

Carefully, Adam looked around them to check that the coast was clear. Then he moved in for a quick, passionate kiss, one hand delving into her dress to cup her right breast.

She returned the kiss, her forgotten sandwiches falling to the ground. But all too soon it was over.

'I'm glad I saw you here,' he said. 'Good news. I can come round next Sunday afternoon. Caro's taking Liam to see her mother. If you're free of course.'

'That would be lovely.'

He moved in for another kiss, and she kissed him back, trying not to mind that it was only an afternoon when he'd promised they could spend a whole weekend together when Caroline took Liam to see her mother. At least she would be seeing him. And when they were lying together in the afterglow of some incredible sex, she'd remind him about the weekend away plan.

'You can meet my new kitten, Brutus.'

Adam frowned. 'You haven't got a cat, have you?' he said. 'I'm allergic.'

'Oh.'

The sound of a group of students reached them from round the corner. 'Hell, someone's coming,' he said. 'See you back at the office. I'm sorry about the cat. You'll have to take it somewhere if you want me to come round on Sunday.'

Seventeen

The Gambia

In the space of a couple of days, Janet had settled into village life. Much to her surprise, she slept well every night, despite the lumpy mattress and Fatu's slender body curled next to hers. The girl had been Janet's guide and constant companion ever since she'd arrived, introducing her to the routines and customs of the community, and gently teasing her when she did something wrong. Together they filled the water containers from the tap, with much giggling as Janet tried – with a spectacular lack of success – to carry the container back to the compound on her head.

They did domestic chores and looked after the younger children while Sukai was cooking, washing clothes, or resting her pregnant bulk over a cuppa and a good old catch-up chat with Nessa. Janet found since she – and Nessa – were so occupied, they didn't actually see much of each other. When they did spend time together, Nessa seemed to be obsessed with discussing Corrinne Walker's book – to the point that

Janet felt she knew the content of it off by heart. Yet she still didn't know what to make of the neutral event theory, which was mostly what the book was about, and when Nessa wasn't around, it wasn't in the forefront of her mind anyway. It was far more interesting to talk to Fatu.

As they worked together, side-by-side, Fatu asked Janet question after question about her life back in England, and about everything she'd seen on her travels. The girl was hungry for information – at times, it seemed as if it were *any* information. And Janet didn't miss the longing looks Fatu gave her three brothers as they cycled off to school every morning. What the girl wanted more than anything was an education, and Janet was more than happy to teach her what she could.

In only a few days they had become very fond of each other, and it was difficult for Janet not to compare their easy relationship with the prickly relationship she had with Debbie. Her daughter was so easily annoyed, it had got so that Janet was almost nervous to speak to her, which, she imagined, was irritating to Debbie.

Still, she wished she had been able to let her know she hadn't married Scott after all. She was pretty sure Debbie would be very pleased about that.

As Janet worked alongside Fatu, helping the girl with her chores, she couldn't remember when she had last felt so relaxed. It was immensely freeing somehow, not to have to think about what she was going to do; to let events unfold. To just be.

Then, on the third afternoon, everything changed. A vehicle drove up the track in a choking cloud of dust, sending scattering chickens in its wake, and the children went running out to greet the visitor – just as they had done when Janet and Nessa had arrived.

'David!' Janet heard Fatu shout. 'It is David!'

Janet, who had been following Fatu, stopped dead on the dirt road. David. Oh, hell. How had she managed to put the possibility of David from her mind? It was if she'd been in a bubble these past few days; a bubble where she had forgotten absolutely everything else.

Nessa came to join her. 'How lovely!' she said. 'It's Sukai's eldest son. It's years since I've seen him.'

The dust was beginning to settle. Janet watched as David – for it was most definitely he – picked up Fatu and swung her through the air, the girl's cries of delight reverberating around the compound.

Janet licked her lips, not looking forward to the moment when he recognised her. Why could nothing stay the same? She'd been happy enough, travelling the world with Scott until he'd decided to propose, and she'd been truly happy here these past few days, just bumbling along.

Beside her, Nessa smiled as she watched David with his sister, and Janet knew she must be completely unaware of the way David tried to make his living in Banjul. If she had known, then she would surely be extremely disappointed, since she had paid for his education.

Finally, David walked towards them, carrying one of his youngest brothers on his hip, with Fatu dancing along beside him. The rest of the children were like a noisy, excited froth around his legs.

'We've already met in Banjul,' Janet told Nessa before he reached them. 'The night before you and I set out.'

But Nessa was moving forward to meet David, her arms outstretched, and Janet wasn't sure she'd heard.

'How wonderful to see you again, David.'

David put his brother down to take Nessa into his arms. He was so very much taller than her, he had to bend right over to embrace her. 'I hear from my friends at the river ferry that you have come,' he told her. 'This is why I have returned home.'

Janet wanted to go and hide somewhere. To curl up in denial on the mattress she shared with Fatu. But it was too late.

'But who is this you have with you?' he was saying, smiling at Janet over Nessa's head.

Nessa moved out of his arms. 'This is my friend Janet, as I believe you know, David. She tells me the two of you met recently?'

David laughed. 'We did meet,' he agreed, speaking through the excited babble of the children, and came towards Janet with a huge smile, proceeding to look her up and down. 'I did not know you at first in these clothes, Jan-net.'

Janet looked down at the blue and green grandmuba she was wearing, taking a step back in case he tried to hug her. 'Your mother lent it to me while my clothes are being washed,' she explained, feeling suddenly self-conscious and stupid, like an adult caught in dressing up clothes. He hadn't seemed in the least bit surprised to see her, and she wondered if his ferry boat friends had given him some sort of clue she was here. Though perhaps it was a coincidence, and she was just being paranoid. After all, why should he seek her out? If he really wanted to form an attachment with a tourist, there were plenty more like her in Banjul without his having to travel all this way.

'It looks well on you,' David started to say, but just then his mother came out of the hut, and everything else was lost in her rapturous welcome.

'He's grown into a fine figure of a man,' Nessa said when David moved on to go and see his father. 'When I first met him, he was only a boy, but he knew what it wanted.' She smiled. 'He threw a note into my car asking me to help him get to school.'

Janet was still looking after David, and couldn't help smiling when she heard Yoro's shout of delight. 'Yes, he told me about that.'

'He told?' Nessa looked at her, sounding surprised.

'Yes. We had quite a long chat.' Somehow she didn't want to tell Nessa about David propositioning her. It seemed too cruel to disappoint her. 'He was seated at the table next to me in a restaurant.'

'Really?' Nessa said, eyebrows raised. 'Well, he must be getting some sort of work then, if he can afford to eat in restaurants. That's good.'

Janet was relieved when Nessa went off to find Sukai and didn't ask any further questions, although she felt a bit guilty about concealing the truth. Somehow, it felt as if David's arrival was going to change everything.

This proved to be the case. Even though life continued as normal, and Fatu and Janet resumed their normal activities together, Janet was constantly aware of David, with his loud laugh, and the happy-go-lucky tone of his voice. Even when there was relative silence, the air felt charged by his being in the village. It made Janet feel on edge. Like the visitor she really was.

Lying in bed early the next morning with Fatu's body spooned against hers, Janet decided she would ask Nessa when she planned to leave. To tell her that she must start to think about getting back to her family and her friends.

But when she went to look for her, she couldn't find her anywhere.

'Sukai?' she said, 'do you know where Nessa is?'

Sukai was busy making bread for breakfast, her hands white with flour. 'She has gone to visit her friends in the next village,' she told Janet, kneading the dough on a flour-covered board. 'She will be away for a few days. Maybe even a week.'

Janet was dismayed. 'A week?' she said. 'Why didn't she tell me she was going?'

Sukai looked up from her labours. 'She did not tell you of her plans?' she said. 'This is strange.'

Strange was the very least it was. 'Why would she just go off like that without even saying goodbye to me? Without any word of explanation. It's so … '

Sukai shrugged. 'It is so Binta, this is what it is. Nessa, she is a very dear friend of mine. I love her like a mother. Better than a mother, because it is not always possible to speak of everything to your mother. Binta, I speak of everything to her. Anything. But always she tells me little of herself. And I know that I must use my time with her well, because one day she will be gone. The last time it was for three years.'

Janet felt even more dismayed at that, and her feelings must have shown in her face, because Sukai laughed. 'Do not worry, Janet, Binta will not be gone for three years this time. She has only gone to Fana Kunda village to see some other friends. It is not so very far from here.'

At that moment, David came out of his hut dressed only in a pair of loose trousers, his naked torso gleaming in the early morning sunlight.

'Good morning, Mamma. Good morning, Jan-net,' he said, and when he yawned, stretching his arms up to the sky, Janet knew it was a deliberate action, designed to get her attention.

Or was she being paranoid? Sukai certainly didn't

seem put out about it. Either way, Janet sensed it was going to be a long week, while she waited for Nessa to return.

Eighteen

Shelthorpe-on-Sea

'Some of this stuff would be snapped up at a vintage fair, I should think,' Kate said after they'd eaten their pizza and begun looking through the Ask Mum pile of her gran's belongings.

Brutus, having been thoroughly played with and admired, was fast asleep on her pillow. 'It's a shame your gran was so tiny, really.'

Kate was holding up an eighties-style jacket complete with shoulder pads. Debbie could remember seeing something similar to it in an old film. What had it been? *Working Girl* that was it. When had Gran ever worn the jacket? It wasn't exactly the type of thing to wear shopping on the high street.

'Here's the skirt that goes with it,' Kate said, delving again. 'Quite high-powered looking, isn't it?'

Debbie nodded. 'I don't know why she had it. She didn't work.'

Kate laid the skirt on the bed, on top of the jacket. 'Maybe she bought it for when the Queen visited

Shelthorpe. You know, when she came to open the new lifeboat station?'

'Maybe.' Debbie could remember seeing footage of the royal visit on a school trip to the lifeboat station, and wanted suddenly to watch it again, in case she could catch a glimpse of her gran in the crowd, dressed in the suit, waving a Union Jack flag. Would Janet have been there? Yes, she remembered the narrator on the film saying that local school children had been given the afternoon off for the occasion.

Kate was bringing baby clothes out of the black sack now – booties and knitted matinée jackets and hats. 'I've got a feeling Geoff's gran is busy knitting this sort of stuff for Bradley, worst luck. I mean, I don't want to sound ungrateful, but it's not very practical, is it? Can't just sling knitted clothes in the washing machine when they get covered in baby sick, can you?'

Debbie reached out to take a soft, pink matinee jacket from Kate's hands. It had a complicated pattern on the front, which must have been extremely challenging to knit. 'I wonder if Gran made these for Mum, when she was a baby?'

'Could have,' Kate agreed. 'There's a little hand-sewn dress in here too, look.' And she pulled out a small white dress with a pattern of green leaves on it.

Debbie put the matinée jacket down to take the dress from her. 'I think I've seen a photo of Mum wearing this, somewhere.'

'There are more dresses about the same size,' Kate

said, pulling two or three of them from the sack and laying them down on the bed. 'D'you think that's what this is? A bag of memories? Look, here's a hat that must have gone with your gran's suit.'

'Yes, maybe it is a bag of memories,' Debbie said thoughtfully, imagining her no-nonsense gran secretly keeping all these things, and her mother discovering them after Gran's death. The two of them hadn't had the best relationship in the world. What must it have been like for Janet to have found all these carefully-preserved clothes? To have to go through them all on her own? And Debbie wished suddenly she had helped Janet with the job instead of … what? What had she been preoccupied with a year and a half ago? Grieving about Gran, certainly. But what else? Nigel, an old boyfriend, probably. They'd recently split up. Funny now, to think how upset she'd been about it. Adam had driven all thoughts about her ex-boyfriend from her mind forever.

'You all right, doing this, Deb?' Kate asked suddenly, and Debbie looked up, doing her best to smile.

'Yeah. It's not easy though, is it?'

Kate reached out to give her arm a quick squeeze. 'No. I can understand why Janet didn't get to finish it off before she left.'

Debbie put the little dress on the now crowded bed and turned to another black sack, untying the ties to peer inside. 'This one's full of fabric,' she said, lifting some of it out. 'Yes, that's all it is. Piles and piles of fabric.'

'For dress-making, maybe. There's some nice stuff.'

Inspiration suddenly struck. 'I know what this is,' Debbie exclaimed. 'It's Mum's material hoard! She was always collecting pieces of material. Dad moaned, because she never did anything with it. I thought she'd got rid of it years ago.'

Kate grinned. 'Kept it secret from your dad, by the look of it.'

Debbie nodded. 'Looks like it.'

Her phone began to ring. She picked it up and saw from the caller ID that it was Adam. 'Excuse me,' she said to Kate. 'I must take this.' And she took her phone out onto the landing, closing the door behind her.

'Hi.'

'Hi, I'm outside. I was just jogging past and saw your lights on. Don't suppose you've got rid of the cat yet?'

'No, sorry, and I've got someone here at the moment actually.'

'Oh.' He sounded disappointed, and her heart surged. She spoke quickly.

'But I could probably meet you somewhere in half an hour or so, if you don't mind hanging around?'

'No, I've got to get back. It'll keep. I'll see you in the morning, okay? Bye.'

'Bye ...' But Adam had already gone.

When she went back into the room, Kate had her

jacket on. 'Listen, I'll get going, if you don't mind. I'm bushed, and it doesn't really feel we can achieve much here without speaking to Janet.' She began to walk to the door, pausing when she got there to give Debbie a wicked smile. 'Besides, I wouldn't want to get in the way of any last-minute impulsive assignations. Go on, ring him back and say you're free after all.'

'Oh, I ...' began Debbie, but Kate only laughed.

'It's all right, I wasn't ear-wigging. These walls are a bit on the thin side, that's all. I'll see you soon, okay?'

'Yes,' answered Debbie vaguely, worrying about the possibility of Kate running into Adam outside the shop. 'And thanks for coming round. I'll let you out.'

'That's all right, I'll make sure the door's properly closed. See you soon.'

'Bye.'

The minute she heard Kate clumping down the stairs, Debbie called Adam, who answered straight away.

'Had a change of heart?'

'Well, I'm just phoning to warn you. Kate Bramling's on her way out of the shop in case you're still nearby.'

'Thanks,' he said. 'But don't worry, I'm already miles away. Champion jogger, me.'

Of course he was. 'Okay. I just thought –'

'Yes, very sensible. Look, see you tomorrow, okay? Sleep well.'

Once again, he ended the call before she could answer, and Debbie sighed, putting her phone back into her pocket and turning to face the mess of clothes on the bed. Brutus woke up and gave a huge yawn, digging his claws into the pillow to stretch his stripy legs.

'It's all your fault, monster,' she told him, but he didn't seem to appreciate the seriousness of the situation, instantly beginning to purr at the sound of her voice, then meowing to be picked up.

She smiled and held him close to her face. 'Well,' she said. 'I'll let you off this time, but you've got to go somewhere on Sunday, all right?' Cradling the purring animal to her cheek, Debbie stroked him while she tried to think of a solution. Then it came to her. Paul. He'd have Brutus back. Especially if she offered him some help in exchange.

He was in the middle of the catteries, sweeping up, when she arrived on the Sunday. As soon as he saw her, he straightened, smiling. There was sawdust in his hair, and his jumper had claw snags on it. He smelt – quite strongly – of cat food.

'Hiya,' he greeted her. 'You know, when you called the other night, I thought you were going to say you wanted to bring Brutus back.'

'No, just a visitor with a cat allergy.' Debbie felt her cheeks redden, and turned away to pick up the cat carrier, annoyed with herself. It wasn't as if she was lying. Adam did have a cat allergy. The fact that she'd let Paul believe on the phone it was a female friend with a cat allergy was irrelevant. It was her business who she invited to her flat and what she did there. She paid her rent. 'Brutus is settling in very well, actually.'

'Glad to hear it. Come on, bring him along here. I've finished cleaning out pen number four. He can have that one. And once he's settled, I'll fetch you a broom. I was glad of your offer of help, actually. My last volunteer moved away recently, and I've been too busy keeping the place going to do much about getting anyone else in.'

He opened the door to the cat run, and Debbie went in and began to unfasten the straps on the carrier.

'I can knock up a flyer asking for volunteers if it would help?' she offered, watching as Brutus took a tentative step out into the run.

'That would be great, thanks. I'd really appreciate it. That's it, Brutus, go and explore.'

They stood and watched the kitten sniff his way around the run, then scoot up the ramp to the upper quarters.

'Want to come out? He looks settled.'

'Thanks.' She left the cat run, and Paul closed and bolted the door after her.

'If you ever fancy volunteering on a permanent basis, let me know. We're always on the lookout for new recruits. And you could bring Brutus here any time your friend's visiting, provided we've got the space.'

'Can I think about it?' she asked. 'My life isn't always completely predictable at the moment.' As she spoke, she realised it was the second time she'd made such a statement to him, and wasn't surprised when he looked at her curiously.

'No?' he said, waiting for her to say more, just as he'd done the first time. When Debbie didn't fill the silence, he turned away to reach for a broom.

'Here,' he said, handing it to her. 'You can start on the run next to Brutus's. I'll do the one next to that.'

The runs were divided by solid walls, but she could still hear the sound of Paul sweeping because both the front doors were open. It was companionable, working alongside him, and Debbie thought she might actually like to volunteer here, provided it didn't take up too much of the time when she could be with Adam. It was such a worthwhile charity. Besides, she liked Paul.

'Have you always done this kind of work?' she asked, speaking loudly to make sure he would hear her.

He laughed, popping his head round the door to look at her, leaning on his broom for a moment. 'Oh, no. Believe it or not, I used to have a high-powered job in the city; commuted in every day like a good boy, mowed the lawn and washed the car at weekends.'

Debbie straightened, surprised. 'What made you give it up?'

'My friend dropped down dead one day on a tube train. That changed everything.' He gave her a grim smile and retreated back into his run to continue sweeping.

'That must have been dreadful,' she said.

'It was. I immediately took voluntary redundancy, got rid of my power suits and tried to persuade my wife that down-sizing was a good idea. Turned out she didn't agree. Also turned out that my long commute had suited her down to the ground because she was carrying on with a local estate agent.'

Debbie stopped sweeping and went out to look into his run. 'I'm so sorry.'

He straightened with a shrug. 'Not half as sorry as the estate agent's wife. She'd just had twins when the pair of them decided to run off together.'

'That's tough.'

He nodded, turning his back on her to sweep out the furthest corner, and she returned to her own run, her broom moving vigorously as her thoughts flickered with unwelcome inevitability to Adam's wife. Normally, she avoided thinking about Caroline at all. She was Adam's responsibility. It was up to him to worry about whether she would be hurt if she found out about their relationship.

Finally, the sweeping was finished, and they both emerged from their runs.

'What about you?' Debbie asked. 'Have you got children?'

He nodded. 'One; Jonah. He's six. I normally have him Saturday afternoon to Sunday lunchtime. He's just gone home, actually. Jonah's the reason I could do with a bit of extra help on weekend mornings. I hate my job having to cut into our time together too much.'

His hair was sticking up on one side; probably where he'd slept on it. There was a hole in the elbow of his claw-snagged jumper. He couldn't look any less like an ex high-powered executive type. Her mother would love him. Much more than she would ever like Adam, if she were to meet him.

What was Janet doing right now? And when would she be back? Not that it would make much difference, because Debbie couldn't imagine going round to see her with Scott there, dominating everything.

'All right?' Paul asked her.

'Yes, thanks.'

He nodded. 'Not the work or the company making you scowl then?'

'No,' she said. 'They're both fine.'

'Good. I'll put the kettle on soon. When you've cleaned out another couple of runs.'

She smiled at that. 'Slave driver.'

He laughed. 'Call it a hangover from my big business days.'

Nineteen

Extract from Staying in Neutral, Responses to Change Your Life by Corrinne Walker.

Every single thought you have can be changed. The proof for this is all around you.

When you were young, perhaps you had a teddy bear you would never be parted from. Let's call him Harry. Harry Bear. Harry Bear was grubby, and he'd lost one ear, but that didn't matter to you. You loved him, and you couldn't sleep without him. Then, one terrible day, you arrived home from a shopping trip with your parents, and Harry Bear wasn't in the buggy next to you. He was missing. You were devastated, unable to accept his loss. You lay down on the hall floor and you screamed and kicked your legs about, completely and utterly inconsolable, and your parents went through hell and high water in their efforts to get him back.

But imagine if Harry Bear never got lost. Imagine you

grew up into an adult, and Harry Bear ended up in a box in your attic with other items from your past. Then one day you move house, and the box accidentally gets forgotten. You only remember it after a two hundred mile journey to your new home, when you start unpacking. I may be wrong, but I don't think you would lay down in your new hallway and begin to scream and kick your legs in the air. You'd be more likely to think, *Ah, poor Harry Bear*, and move on. The loss of the bear is an event, and your reaction to the event has changed as you have changed.

Another example. You're driving along a country road on your way to a well-needed holiday. Work has been pressured, and you're exhausted, in need of a complete break. It's a rural area, and there's a slow-moving tractor ahead, with a long queue of traffic behind it. Behind the tractor is an unconfident driver who doesn't like overtaking on country roads. They're not going to attempt to get past, even when there's an opportunity to do so. This is their right. No law exists in the Road Traffic Act that states that, should a driver be caught behind a slow-moving vehicle, it is their duty to overtake as soon as it is safe to do so. Similarly, there is no law that states that, in overtaking a slow-moving vehicle, we are contravening Section bla, of bla.

There is nothing to tell us that we should always get angry and stressed when we are stuck behind a tractor or an unconfident driver on a rural road, and there is nothing to tell us that we should always feel calm in such a situation either.

Whether we choose to resign ourselves to our arriving at our holiday cottage thirty minutes later than we'd planned to do, or turn into an enraged, horn-beeping tailgater, is entirely up to us. The tractor and the decision of the unconfident driver not to overtake are both neutral events.

Twenty

Shelthorpe-on-Sea

It was the first session of Kate and Geoff's ante-natal classes, and it was a rush to get there on time because Geoff had a late-finishing bakery class.

Then, when they did finally arrive at the church hall, Kate just sat there, not moving to get out of the car straight away. There was a fluttering sensation in her belly, and she put her hands over her bump, analysing it.

'All right?' asked Geoff. 'Bradley at the disco again, is he?' And he reached out a hand to push her hair up at the back, away from her neck, the way he liked to do.

Kate smiled and pushed her head back against his hand. It had been a tense few weeks one way or another, and she was relieved that his recent preoccupied mood seemed to have passed, at least for now. She wanted everything to be perfect tonight; the two of them learning and preparing for Bradley's arrival together. And suddenly she knew what the fluttering in her belly was – not their son working on his jive moves after all, but excitement.

'I've just been looking forward to this. Makes it all feel more real somehow. Though I must admit, it seems strange coming back to this place to do the class.' She shook her head, remembering the course about sensuality she'd attended at the hall. *A Woman's Harvest of Delight*, it had been called, and it was where she'd first met Estelle, Janet and Reenie. 'I certainly never imagined I'd be pregnant within a year of finishing those classes.'

Geoff took his hand from her neck and opened the car door. 'Well, do me a favour and don't get confused about what course you're on tonight, eh? Be a bit embarrassing if you start going on about your G-spot.'

Kate snorted with laughter and took his arm. 'Let's hope I've still got a G-spot after I've popped Bradley out,' she said.

Inside the hall, there was a sign for the class, pointing upstairs.

'You all right?' Geoff asked her. 'Need any help?'

'No, I'm good,' she said, although the truth was, she almost did need help. What was it going to be like when she was almost ready to pop? 'Good idea having the session upstairs, eh? Not.'

'Welcome, welcome,' an earth mother type with her blonde hair piled up on top of her head beamed at them as they entered the room. 'I'm Heidi, your course leader. And you are?'

'Mr and Mrs Bramling,' Geoff told her. 'Kate and Geoff.'

'You're very welcome, Kate and Geoff. Do find yourself a seat. We'll make a start as soon as you're settled.'

They took the last two seats, next to a smiling couple who looked to be in their late thirties. He was bald, with a sunburnt head, she was decked out in Laura Ashley and looked as if she needed a flower-trimmed hat. Kate smiled back at them, and Geoff stuck his hand out. 'How do? I'm Geoff, and this is Kate.'

'Mary and Dave,' said the man, shaking Geoff's hand, and Kate smiled again, her gaze sweeping round the room, analysing the women's baby bumps. Everyone looked about the same amount gone as her, although that was pretty much where the similarities ended, because some of the women were stick thin and looked as if they'd strapped their baby bump on, and others were more lardy, with water-thickened ankles. Most of the women were wearing make-up, and just for a second, Kate wished she'd made more of an effort with her appearance. Then she mentally shook her head. Sod it. She'd barely worn any make up for her wedding, let alone to come here. They could flipping well take her or leave her.

Heidi gave a little cough to get their attention, her

smile embracing them all. 'Good evening, everyone! I can't tell you what an honour and a privilege it is to have you in my class as you prepare for what must surely be the most exciting event of your lives – the arrival of your first child! This evening, we'll be getting to know one another and learning some basic facts about giving birth and caring for your baby. But for now, I'd be grateful if each couple could complete this form so we can get a few extra details about you, if that's okay? Here you are. Could you pass them around, please?'

The forms were duly passed around together with pens and clipboards to lean on, and Kate started to fill it out. Next to her, Geoff was shifting uncomfortably on his seat. 'You all right?' she asked him, without looking up.

'Yeah, fine,' he said, and she got on with filling out her medical details on the form.

After the forms were handed in, the group introduced themselves in small groups, and Kate discovered that Dave and Mary owned a bed and breakfast on the seafront.

'It's overlooking the pier, with lots of hanging baskets outside. Mon Repose, it's called.'

'Oh yes,' Kate said. 'I know it. My friend's got an apartment near there.' She remembered how she and Estelle had laughed once about the B & B's pretentious name. Still, Dave and Mary seemed nice enough.

Introductions over, Heidi produced a plastic model

and placed it on a table out the front. 'This is a one hundred percent accurate model of a woman's pelvis,' she told them with what, Kate was beginning to realise, was her trademark smile. Kind of benevolent. Earth-mother with a touch of Mother Superior.

Heidi was reaching for something in a shopping bag now, and Kate saw it was a doll; one of those dolls that is so life-like, it's a little disturbing, because it doesn't move. A dead baby in all but colour. Hideous.

'The birth canal measures ten centimetres across,' Heidi continued, pointing to the appropriate place on the model. 'And the baby's head is ten centimetres too.' As the class watched, Heidi proceeded to tug the baby through the model head-first, 'giving birth' to it. 'See; it's a perfect fit. Isn't nature wonderful?'

Geoff's hand shot up.

'Yes?' Heidi said. 'It's Geoff, isn't it?'

'That's right.'

'Did you have a question, Geoff?'

'Not really. I just wanted to say, wouldn't nature be a bit more wonderful if the baby's head was eight centimetres, or the birth canal was twelve centimetres? Easier on the woman that way, I should think.'

A ripple of laughter went round the room. 'Good point,' Kate whispered to her husband, noticing that he was a bit red in the face.

At the front, Heidi's smile was unwavering. She was cradling the dead-looking baby in her arms now, and Kate winced. The thing was positively macabre.

'I take your point, Geoff,' she said, 'but believe me, nature makes sure everything works exactly as it's intended to.'

Much to Kate's relief, Heidi put the baby back into the shopping bag and moved the model away. While she was doing this, Geoff told Kate, 'Just popping to the gents,' and left the room.

'Your husband makes me laugh,' Mary said as they waited for Heidi to continue.

'He said what everyone else was thinking,' Dave added.

Kate smiled, feeling a surge of pride. 'He usually does say what he thinks.'

'Okay,' said Heidi. 'I've got a fun and informative activity for you to do in small groups now, if you'd like to work with the couple next to you. One thing you're going to be doing a lot of after your baby is born is, of course, changing nappies.' She fished into one of the carrier bags and held up a disposable nappy in one hand, and a terry nappy in the other. 'In another session, we'll be looking at the pros and cons of disposable versus washable nappies, but for the moment, we're going to concentrate on what goes in the nappy; namely poo.'

What was taking Geoff so long? This was essential stuff, since he would be doing as much of the nappy changing as she, once Bradley arrived.

'You may be surprised to know that a baby can produce several different types of poo in the first few days of life, and that the nature and quality of this poo gives us a clear indication of how things are going with him or her.'

Beside Kate, Mary was diligently writing everything Heidi said in her notebook. Kate wished she'd thought to bring one and hoped there would be a handout.

'In a moment, I'm going to pass round some filled nappies for your group to look at. Don't worry, the nappies won't contain real poo!'

'That's a relief,' Dave said to Mary and Kate. 'Otherwise it could get a bit stinky in here.'

Where *was* Geoff? This was priceless.

'Along with the nappies, I have four written statements. Your job is to try to match the nappies with the correct statement. I'll read them to you.' Fumbling slightly while still holding the nappies and the slips of paper, Heidi reached for a pair of glasses and perched them on her nose. 'Number One: I am six hours old and this is my first nappy. Number Two: I am five days old, breastfeeding well and do six nappies like this every day. Number Three: I am two days old and not very good at breastfeeding yet. My mum might need some help with feeding. And Number Four, I am three days old and breastfeeding well. My mum's milk has just come in.' Heidi took her glasses off to smile at them all again. 'Okay? All clear? Right, I'll go round and distribute your nappies.'

Soon each table had four nappies – one with a dark brown substance on it, one with a pale green substance, another with a yellowish-brown, and a final one with dabs of reddish pink.

Dave picked up the green one. 'Is that pesto, d'you think?'

'It smells like it,' Mary agreed.

'This is molasses, I think,' said Kate, picking up the nappy with the dark brown filling and giving it a sniff.

'I can't say I know what molasses is like,' said Mary.

'You do realise how wrong it looks to sniff it like that?' laughed Dave.

'Yes.' Kate smiled. 'I don't think I'd be doing it if it was the real thing somehow.'

Geoff returned.

'There you are mate!' said Dave. 'You've been missing all the fun.'

Kate looked at Geoff carefully. He'd been red-faced when he left, but now he looked pale. 'Sure you're all right?'

He nodded. 'Yeah, fine. What are you up to?'

'We've got to match these nappies with the right statements,' Mary told him. 'Look, what about this one? "My mum might need some help with feeding".'

'Well,' said her husband. 'I don't think it's the curry one.'

'No. How about this one, with the red? It looks worrying that one. At least, I think I'd be worried if I saw a nappy like that. Is that supposed to be blood?'

Heidi, who was travelling from group to group,

overheard Mary's comment and stopped at their table. 'We'll go through all this in detail with everyone in a moment, but no, the red colour represents urate crystals, not blood. A show like this can indicate that baby may be dehydrated, and although they're usually nothing to worry about, they're certainly an indicator that Mum needs to talk to her doctor or midwife to make sure there are no issues with feeding.' She broke off. 'Oh, excuse me, it looks as if we have some visitors.'

Kate was busy trying to match the molasses-filled nappy with the correct statement and didn't look up. 'D'you think it's this one?' she asked the group. 'Six hours old?'

Geoff was pulling at her sleeve. 'I think you'd better take a look,' he said, staring towards the front of the class.

Kate looked. And nearly died of shock to see her ex-husband, Ian, speaking to Heidi. And, standing bold as brass beside him, with a baby bump to rival any in the room, her ex-best friend, the bitch traitor Jennifer.

Holy shit.

As Kate looked, suddenly trembling, she saw Ian notice her. Watched as he broke the news to Jennifer with a poke of his elbow and an urgent whisper. Saw Jennifer look over at her with big, shocked eyes and a protective hand on her belly.

Their gazes locked. Kate breathed quickly, teeth clenched, torn between a strong desire to tear to the front of the class to expose Jennifer for the husband-stealing bitch she was, and an equally strong sense of sadness that she and Jennifer, who had once joyfully shared so much of their lives, were not now sharing their pregnancies in the same way.

So many firsts. First loves. First lovers and lost virginities. First jobs. First flats. A whole history of firsts, until Jennifer had brought their friendship to an end with a first to end all firsts. First betrayal.

Jennifer's gaze slipped away from Kate's as she turned to speak to Ian. Would they leave? By rights, they bloody well ought to. They didn't even sodding well live round here. As Kate watched, Ian's arm slipped round Jennifer's shoulders. Jennifer gave a nod. Then Kate saw her shoulders move back as Ian handed her a chair. She sat down on it, shooting Kate a brief, defiant glance before shifting the chair ever-so-slightly to block Kate out with her back.

At their table, Mary and Dave were getting on with the nappy task, blissfully unaware anything was wrong. 'So, we're definitely saying the curry paste is five days old and breastfeeding well, are we?'

Kate closed her eyes and took a deep breath. She had a sudden memory of Debbie talking about that book she was reading; about people having the freedom to choose their reactions when bad things happened in their lives. Yeah, right. Maybe if the choice was whether to take Jennifer's head in a head lock, or to spit in her face in front of the whole class.

'Is Kate okay?'

Geoff's hand was holding hers tight. He gave it a squeeze. 'Yeah,' he said to Dave. 'Just give her a moment.' Geoff's voice was calm, the pressure of his hand consistently loving. Both helped Kate to contemplate the unpalatable truth. She was going to be a mother very soon, and, if she wanted to be a good one, then she couldn't go around spitting or putting people in head locks.

Impossible as it felt, she was going to have to rise above it, turn the other cheek, and hope that every cloud had a silver lining. Not kill two fucking birds with one stone the way she'd like to. One bird called Ian, and the other called Jennifer.

'It'll be easier after Bradley's born, you'll see,' Geoff whispered, and instantly tears filled Kate's eyes. Every time she thought she couldn't love him any more than she already did, he said or did something to make her realise she could.

'Are you sure you're all right, Kate?' Mary asked, and Kate wiped her eyes on the back of her hands, somehow managing to dredge a smile from somewhere.

'It's the pesto,' she said. 'I always get emotional when I smell pesto.'

Beside her, Geoff gave a snort of laughter. 'Our first date was a meal out in an Italian restaurant,' he lied.

'Ah,' said Mary. 'That's so romantic!'

And, with a giant effort, Kate returned her attention

to the entirely unromantic subject of filled nappies.

Twenty-One

Extract from Staying in Neutral, Responses to Change Your Life by Corrinne Walker.

When something happens – an event – that rocks your world, don't respond immediately. Give yourself time to think before you act. In time, with practice, this will become a quick process, over in the blink of an eye. But at first, you may need to leave the room, find some space. Go for a walk, or simply shut yourself in the toilet. (Note: if the event happens to be a tsunami wave heading in your direction, run for high ground as far as your legs will carry you.)

When you have found your sanctuary, relax your mind and your body thoroughly using the exercise on page 78 of this book. Then, once you have achieved a relaxed, receptive state, imagine that you are placing the event you are currently dealing with into a large, empty cardboard box.

The box is a magical box. Once it is sealed with the

special tape provided with it, it cannot be opened unless you decide to open it. It may rattle and shake, but trust that it will not burst open without your help.

Now, turn your back on the box and settle yourself comfortably as you work through the following steps.

1) Ask yourself what "everyone" (i.e. society) thinks about the event in the box. Is there an "accepted" "normal" or "traditional" way of thinking about the event? If there is, ask yourself whether this is influencing the way you instinctively want to react to the event, and remind yourself that you are your own person, with your own free will. You do not need to react in any prescribed way. You possess the freedom to react in the way you choose to.

2) Imagine two people with completely opposing reactions to the event you are dealing with. Doing this will emphasize the event's neutrality to you.

3) Think of the highest possible thought you can think of in relation to the event in the box. Feel the power of this thought like glowing energy in the very centre of your mind. Allow the glow to move down through your face and into your neck. Imagine it feeding into your veins, sending its healing light into your blood. See it begin to circulate right around your body, moving faster and faster until you are filled entirely with glowing, positive light.

4) Whilst you are in this supremely powerful, altered state, allow the event you have contained in the box to enter your

mind once again. Imagine yourself responding to the event with the highest possible thought you identified in the previous step.

Picture, in detail, the smile on your face as you respond to the event with this higher thought. Feel the relaxed state of your body as you do so – your hands unclenched, your shoulders wonder-fully loose.

Accept that this event is but one stitched panel of life's rich tapestry, and that you have complete freedom of choice when you go into a shop to buy tapestry silk.

Make the decision today to stitch a beautiful tapestry for your life. See it, with its bright colours and awe-inspiring handiwork, displayed for all to see. Make the decision to be inspirational.

Then, and only then, when you are feeling truly replenished and filled with the light of these higher thoughts, begin to unpeel the tape on the box containing the event you must respond to.

Twenty-Two

Shelthorpe-on-Sea

Debbie was sitting at a table by the window having a cup of coffee in the Cupcake Café across the road from the shop. It was Saturday, and almost whole week had passed since the disaster of her so-called special afternoon with Adam while his wife was away.

Not that it felt like a week. Every time Debbie remembered herself opening the shop door to let Adam out only to find Paul on the doorstep, she wanted to die.

'Oh!' Debbie had squealed when she saw him. She was dressed only in an extremely flimsy dressing gown, and knew that it must be only too obvious how she had spent the afternoon. 'Paul! I didn't expect to see you. This is … my friend Adam. Adam, this is Paul. He … he's sort of my landlord.'

Her 'sort of landlord' was holding a box. The scrabbling sounds and plaintive mewing coming from within told her it contained Brutus. 'Hello,' he said to Adam, his accusing look clearly saying, 'this isn't a female friend.'

198

'Sorry, but I've just had a call from my ex-wife,' he said, handing the box over to her. 'Something's come up and she needs me to have Jonah back this evening. I've got to go and collect him. I did try to call, but you weren't answering your phone.'

Debbie felt herself flush at his cool, polite tone of voice. Her mobile had rung at a highly inconvenient moment. She'd ignored it.

'Oh, sorry about that. And thank you so much for …'

'No problem,' Paul said, giving her a brief – and to her mind fake – smile before striding quickly back to his car without another word.

'Rude man,' Adam observed, then promptly sneezed. 'God, I thought you'd got rid of the kitten.'

'I did. Well, for the afternoon, anyway,' Debbie said miserably, clutching hold of the box.

'Well,' Adam said, shrugging his jacket on. 'If I'm going to keep coming here, you're going to have to do something about it on a permanent basis. I'm sorry, darling, I really am. But I can't help being allergic, can I?'

And he'd left without even kissing her goodbye, because to do so would bring him into greater proximity to Brutus. Since then, for the whole week at work, there hadn't been an opportunity for them to be alone together. Usually Debbie contrived some reason to be alone with Adam, but this week she hadn't, because she hadn't wanted to give him the opportunity to ask her if she'd done anything about Brutus. And the truth was, she still hadn't made a decision about what to do about Brutus. The little ginger kitten had completely claimed her heart with his tendency to disappear behind cupboards and terrify the life out of her by jumping out. Not to mention his habit of curling up on her pillow when she went to sleep at night, and being there when she woke up in the morning.

Also, she kept remembering the expression on Paul's face. He'd been disappointed in her, and while it was true that he was only her landlord, and that in theory she could have five lovers over in one afternoon if she chose to, she liked him. He was a nice man, and she enjoyed his company. It didn't feel good to have semi lied to him.

So, coming out for a coffee had felt like a good idea – she already spent too much time in her flat as it was. Having Brutus meant she wasn't completely alone, but it wasn't the same as human company. Her gran's stuff reminded her of happier times for one thing. And so she had come to the Cupcake Café to read her book.

The café was packed – Debbie only managed to get a table because somebody happened to be leaving as she arrived – and she soon saw she was the only person in there alone. Oh well, never mind. Maybe Corrinne Walker could help her to get over her blues. She'd got to the part about how to deal with a crisis.

When something happens she read – *an event – that rocks your world, don't just respond. Give yourself time to think before you act.* Debbie had only been reading for a few minutes when someone pulled out the vacant chair at her table, scraping it unpleasantly on the stone floor tiles. 'Would you mind very much if I joined you? Only there aren't any other free seats.'

Debbie looked up. 'Of course not,' she replied, because she could hardly say anything else. Then she frowned, recognising the woman who was now arranging her jacket on the back of the free seat.

'Oh, hello, dear,' said the woman, looking across at her. 'We've met before, haven't we? Across the road.'

It was the woman who'd put *Staying in Neutral* down on the table in the charity shop.

'Yes,' said Debbie. 'That's right.'

The woman looked down at Debbie's book. 'And I see you bought a book when you were in there. An excellent choice, if I may say so. I really enjoyed it myself. I'll just get myself a cup of tea, and we can have a good chat about it.'

'Oh,' said Debbie, taken aback. 'All right.'

But the woman had already swept off without waiting for her answer, and Debbie sipped some more of her coffee, shaking her head. Some people were so totally convinced their company and opinions would be welcome to everybody. Adam was a bit like that. Perhaps it came with getting older? She'd never thought everyone would find what she had to say interesting, that was for sure.

The woman returned with her tea and settled herself

down opposite Debbie. 'I'm not sure I ought to have taken my jacket off,' she said. 'I've only recently returned from Africa, you see, and I'm still getting used to the change of temperature.'

'Do you go there often?' asked Debbie.

'As often as I possibly can,' the woman said, taking a big breath and exhaling it with a dreamy smile. 'It's where I feel most at home. My name's Nessa, by the way.'

'Debbie.'

'Good to meet you, Debbie,' Nessa said, taking a sip of her tea. 'Now, tell me, are you enjoying the book?'

Debbie looked down at her copy of *Staying in Neutral.* 'I haven't had the chance to read that much of it yet. But I think the author must be some sort of a super woman if she really manages to stop herself blowing up when something major goes wrong.'

Nessa took a large bite of cake and nodded as if she quite understood. 'Where have you got up to?' she asked, spraying cake crumbs onto the table as she did so.

Debbie bent her head, turning the pages of the book. 'I'm at the beginning of Chapter Three.'

Nessa nodded. 'Ah. Tapestries and golden light,' she said.

Debbie scanned the text. 'Yes, that's right. You sound very familiar with it.'

Nessa nodded, slipping a piece of cake into her mouth. 'I've made a point of studying it. It's essential reading for my line of work.'

'Oh?' said Debbie, interested. 'What do you do?'

Nessa wiped her mouth with her napkin, and took another sip of her tea. 'It's quite difficult to explain,' she said finally. 'Let's just say I rescue people. When they're in danger of getting their toes burnt.' She laughed and nodded. 'Yes, that about sums my job up. I help people to move forward on to a better track.'

Debbie frowned. 'Like a sort of social worker?'

Nessa shrugged, eating more cake. 'That kind of thing, yes.'

The woman was like no other social worker Debbie had encountered before, and she'd met quite a few in a previous temp assignment for the Children's Services Department. She was intrigued, and wanted to know more. But before she could ask Nessa anything else, she looked up and froze, her coffee cup half way to her mouth. Adam was walking past the café. Had he come to see her? Had he been over to the shop only to find she was out?

With her heart suddenly hammering, Debbie half got out her chair, about to run out of the café to stop him, before he vanished. But then, with a horrible sick feeling in her stomach, she realised he wasn't alone. He was with his family – with Caro and Liam. And they were laughing together. Sharing a special family moment.

Debbie sank back into her seat with one hand lifted protectively to her chest. Suddenly there didn't seem to be enough air in the room. Outside, still smiling, Adam glanced into the café. Saw her. Looked quickly away. Seconds later, he was gone.

Nessa's hand reached across the table towards her. 'Shh, dear, it's all right,' she said. 'You're all right. Breathe. That's it. And again. I know it's hard, but this is exactly the sort of situation Corrinne's advice is designed for. Come on, try it out now. I'll help you. I'll talk you through it, one step at a time. Okay?'

'What …?' Still in shock, Debbie didn't know what Nessa was on about. Hardly even knew where she was. Why would Adam bring his family here when he knew there would be a risk of running into her? It didn't make sense. And they had looked so happy together.

'By the looks of things, I reckon the beach is too far away,' Nessa was saying. 'And the toilet's already occupied. I just saw someone go in there. So, you'll have to stay where you are. That's okay. Corrinne does say that bit about a tsunami, and I can tell this is your own personal tsunami happening right now. Okay, so starting by breathing.'

'What?' Debbie said again. 'I … I have to go. I have to …' And she began reaching for her bag, tears suddenly filling her eyes.

Stupid, so stupid. She'd known all along about his family. It really shouldn't hurt to see the evidence of them. But it did. Oh, how it did.

'No,' said Nessa, taking her hand. 'Going anywhere isn't a good idea right now. Sit. Breathe. Close your eyes.'

Debbie didn't have the strength to protest. She wasn't at all sure her legs were strong enough to support her, even if she did stand up. So she closed her eyes, making a sound that was half sob, half sigh.

'Now,' said Nessa in a calm, soft voice. 'Imagine there's a white light above your head. Make it the moon, if that's easier. A big, bright full moon. Picture it pouring its light into the top of your head. Feel it spreading right through your body.'

Debbie opened her eyes.

'You're right,' Nessa agreed. 'There isn't time for moons and lights in a crisis. Okay then, think about a box instead. A big empty cardboard box.'

'A box?'

Nessa nodded enthusiastically. 'Yes. What happened out there; what you saw. It's an event, and you know what Corrinne says – all events are neutral. So, just for a moment, while you sort your head out, you're going to put that event into your cardboard box – the one you've just been reading about. And then you're going to seal it down with special tape. Go on, do it. Imagine yourself doing it.'

Debbie felt mesmerised. She wanted to leave, but something about Nessa's voice was fixing her to the spot. She closed her eyes again, and did her best to imagine stuffing all the images of Adam walking past the window with his family into a box.

'I bet it's a big box, isn't it?' Nessa said, seeming to

read her mind. 'It needs to be to stuff all of that inside it. Better get yourself a step ladder so you can make sure the tape's fixed down properly.'

Debbie's eyes opened again. It was almost as if Nessa knew what had just happened to her. But how could she?

'Box all taped up?' Nessa asked, and the kindness of her smile made Debbie's lip tremble. She nodded.

'Good,' said Nessa, handing Debbie a napkin to blow her nose on.

Debbie blew.

'Right,' said Nessa, 'now Corrinne says you need to ask yourself whether there's a "normal" way society has of looking at the event that's just happened, so I'll leave you to think about that for a few minutes.'

A man walks with his family along the high street, and his lover sees them as they go past the café she's in. That was the event. And society would be one hundred percent on the side of the deceived wife. But then, she'd always known that, hadn't she? And knowing it didn't help one bit.

'Next,' Nessa said, still in that kind voice, 'If I remember correctly, Corrinne says you should remember that you're your own person, with your own free will. That you don't need to respond to that event you stuffed into the box in any prescribed way. You're free to react in the way you choose to, not in the way everyone says you ought to.'

Still with her eyes closed, Debbie frowned. What

did that mean exactly? That she could say to hell with what society thought about women having affairs with married men? That she had the right to run out there and force a showdown in front of Adam's wife and family?

'Look,' she said, opening her eyes. 'This is very kind of you, but I don't think I … '

'It'll be okay, dear,' Nessa encouraged her again. 'You'll see. It will all turn out the way it's supposed to.'

Tears filled Debbie's eyes. 'Will it?'

'Of course. Now, next, Corrinne says you should think of two people with opposite views of your event.'

There wasn't an opposite view. How could there be an opposite view? There was only one way to view what had just happened, and that was as a flesh-ripping, stomach-acid churning disaster.

Debbie's shoulders began to shake. Any moment now, she knew she was going to let out a howl of anguish so loud it would blast people's coffee cups up to the ceiling, containing as it would, six months' worth of pent-up stress and angst. Six months of being the other – less important – woman to a man she adored.

She had to get out of here. Now. 'I'm sorry, I have to go,' she said again, this time managing to act on her words. Picking up her bag. Pushing her chair back. Evading Nessa's outstretched hand.

The sounds of the café echoed around her ears and her brain, fragments of different conversations coming at her in an intermittent pulse. None of them sufficient to distract her from a gathering panic and despair as she pushed herself through the crowded clutter of tables and chairs.

'Don't do that, darling, it's not nice.'

'My nephew's going to hire one for me.'

'I love that lipstick on you.'

'You forgot your book!'

At last, at last, she was at the door. Pulling it open. Free to run. She was sobbing openly now, and turned her face away from people's sympathy. But where to go? She'd have to face more curious glances and well-intentioned questions if she went through the shop to get to her flat.

The car. She could sit in the car. At least there, she could lock herself in. But her Corsa was parked on a nearby street, right where a group of kids were playing a game of football on the pavement. All the talk there was about kids shutting themselves away to play computer games, and this lot had to be out here with their loud voices and their curious glances.

Feeling hunted, Debbie let herself into her car and sat there for a moment, gripping the steering wheel. A meltdown, this was what this was. One of those words that people casually bander about, but which are five hundred times worse in reality. She couldn't stop her hands from shaking. Or her pulse from racing. Her mind was on a video loop, replaying that happy family scene over and over again. The smiles. The carefree, we don't need the world smiles. A team. Us.

Shit. She had to get a grip. Had to go somewhere. Do something.

Debbie started the engine, drawing in a few deep, jagged breaths as she did so, a car beeping at her angrily as she pulled out from her parking space without looking first. 'Sorry, sorry!'

She took a left, then a right, with no clear idea of where she was going. Until she saw the sign for the cat sanctuary.

Parking the car, she switched the engine off and sat there, looking out at the low huddle of buildings. Why had she come here of all places? She could hardly go in, could she? Not in this state, and not after the way Paul had looked at her last week, caught out in that lie.

A sudden knock on the window made her jump. It was Paul himself, looking in at her, tear-wrecked face and all. Reluctantly, she wound the window down. As usual, his hair was sticking out all over the place, like a little boy's.

'Have you come to volunteer?' he asked at last. 'Only I could do with some help this afternoon, if you have.'

She wiped her eyes with the backs of her hands. 'Why not?' she said jaggedly. 'If … if it would help you out?'

He nodded. 'It really would, yes. We've had a crisis case come in today, and I've been so busy dealing with her I haven't been able to clean all the runs. Come inside when you're ready, and I'll introduce you.'

And he turned away, clumping towards the entrance to the cattery in his big green wellington boots, his complete acceptance of her state causing her mouth to tremble all over again. Shakily, Debbie reached for a well-used tissue and blew her nose. A crisis case, he'd said. Well, she was a crisis case too. So perhaps she could be of use. One crisis case to another. At least she would have some empathy.

'The poor little thing was found shut away on her own in a small, dark room,' Paul told her when she ventured inside. 'Whether she was abandoned or forgotten when her family moved on, isn't clear. Goodness only knows how long she'd been there like that.'

The cat's body was fragile a bag of bones beneath Debbie's hands, and yet the animal began to purr loudly, arching her back to press her head against Debbie's hand. The affectionate gesture was intolerably moving. She wanted to cry all over again.

'It's funny,' Paul said gently, once again ignoring her tears, 'in the bad cases like this one, I've noticed that cats react in two different ways when they're rescued. Either they hide themselves away and scratch and spit at you if you so much as try to get near them, or they're like this one, and can't get enough human warmth and comfort.'

He paused, watching Debbie stroke the cat, which had now settled herself comfortably in her arms. 'I think we can safely see which category this little girl falls into.' He reached out to stroke the cat's head. 'I think it can be pretty similar with humans when something bad happens too, don't you? At least for a while. I know when I split up with my wife I shut everyone out at first – didn't want to talk about it, refused all offers of help or a listening ear. Drank too much. Which is probably the human equivalent of hiding, scratching and spitting.'

Debbie manoeuvred one arm so that she could wipe her wet face with her sleeve.

'It was Jonah who made the difference,' Paul said. 'My son. Having to pull myself together for him.' He pulled up his own sleeve to take a look at his watch. 'Speaking of Jonah, he'll be here quite soon, so I'd better crack on with things if you're okay here? I'll bring you some food for her in a little while. As she hasn't eaten for so long, she can only eat small amounts at a time for now. But she needs those fairly often.'

He had let himself out of the run while he was speaking, and now he looked at her through the bars. 'Okay?'

Debbie nodded, somehow managing to croak an 'Okay,' in response.

Paul nodded, then clumped off in his wellies. Seconds later, she heard a radio go on at the far end of the corridor, and the sound of sweeping.

The cat was asleep in her arms now, relaxed enough to give in to the exhaustion of the trauma she had suffered. Debbie leant back against the wall, closing her own eyes, aware of the animal's fragile body moving gently as it breathed. She let out her own breath in a deep, ragged sigh, wishing she too could sleep. It seemed like such a very long time since she had, properly. Her churning mind kept her awake, searching for answers that were never forthcoming.

Suddenly she thought of Nessa, in the café; of what a strange coincidence it had been to meet her again like that. For them to have been talking about Corrinne Walker's book just before she'd seen Adam with his family. Nessa had seemed to know exactly what Debbie was going through. Why was that? Presumably because she'd looked shocked. But for some reason, it felt like more than that; as if Nessa had known exactly what had happened. Which she couldn't do, obviously. What had Nessa just asked her, before she'd blundered from the coffee shop? Something about the two different extremes of reacting to an event.

Debbie bent her face to smooth the cat's fur with her cheek. If the abandonment of this poor creature was an event, which she supposed it was, then what were the two extremes of reacting to that? The first reaction was easy. The owners were despicable people who deserved to be hunted down and punished for what they had done to their cat. Publicly brought to shame. Banned from keeping pets for life.

But what about a so-called higher thought about the event of the cat's abandonment? Debbie frowned, unable to think of anything but the horror for whoever had opened up that stinking room to find the half-starved, terrified animal.

Then the cat moved suddenly in her arms, opening deep amber eyes to look straight up at Debbie, her purr starting up again. And suddenly the higher thought came to her. 'Of course,' she said, stroking the cat's head. 'You've got a new chance now, haven't you? A new chance for happiness.'

The cat meowed softly, as if to agree, then closed her eyes again, settling back down to sleep, and Debbie sighed, shifting to get more comfortable herself, thinking about other possible causes and reactions to the cat being abandoned. What if the cat's owner hadn't been cruel after all, but simply ill – either mentally or physically? Public shaming wouldn't be appropriate then, would it? Compassion would.

Debbie's head ached, a reaction to the emotional turmoil of the morning. She sighed and closed her eyes, wanting very much to relax and to forget about Corrinne Walker and her neutral event theory. But somehow she couldn't. Something was urging her to do what Nessa had asked her to do back in the café – to look at the two extremes of reaction to her own event. The event of Adam walking past the café with his family, the three of them a picture of a happy unit.

Well, the first extreme of reaction was very easy to come up with, because she'd just lived it, complete with a pain like a thousand stab wounds all over her

213

body. But the other extreme? That was a great deal harder to think of. Maybe if she were some kind of selfless super woman, which she wasn't, she'd be able to think, *How nice to see such a happy family.* Or perhaps she'd feel grateful to have been presented with the reality of his marriage and his family life. To have been handed a potential catalyst to break free from their affair to start a new, hopefully happier, life.

Just like the cat.

What would the cat do if her former owner were to turn up now? Stay here, in the safety of Debbie's arms? Or spring up to greet her old owner? And what would Debbie herself do on Monday morning? Pull a sickie? Or go in to work and face Adam?

'Are you sad about the pussy cat?' a young voice asked suddenly, and Debbie opened her eyes to see a small boy looking at her through the meshed door.

She sat up, somehow managing to smile at him, knowing he had to be Paul's son. 'Yes,' she said, 'I am sad about what's happened to her.'

Paul himself strode up, bending to place his hands on his son's shoulders. 'Don't bother Debbie, Jonah,' he said. 'She's helping the cat to work some things out at the moment.'

Jonah nodded, as if he quite understood that. 'Ellie,' he said. 'The cat's name is Ellie.'

Paul smiled. 'Good choice. What do you think, Debbie?'

The cat began to purr again. 'I think it's perfect.

And listen, she agrees. She likes it too.'

Paul smiled at her over his son's head. 'Right,' he said. 'It's time for Ellie to have something to eat. D'you want to help me get her food ready, Jonah?'

'Yes.' Jonah nodded simply, and off they went.

When Debbie got home later that afternoon, Sheila, the volunteer, was getting ready to shut the shop. 'A lady left you something, Debs,' she said. 'A book. Said you'd left it in the café?'

Nessa.

Debbie took the copy of *Staying in Neutral.* 'Thanks.'

'Oh, and a gentleman came in, asking for Janet.'

Sheila reached under the counter for a piece of paper and put her glasses on to read it. 'A Mr George. John George. Asked to be remembered to your mum. Looked most put out when I told him she was abroad with her new husband. I hope I didn't put my foot in it?'

John George; the name meant nothing to Debbie. Though, even if she'd heard it before, the chances are she wouldn't remember it right now. 'I'm sure you haven't, but I'll pass the message on when I speak to Mum. Thanks, and have a good evening. Do you want me to lock up for you?'

'Thanks, love. Have a good evening yourself.'

Sheila went on her way with a final wave, and Debbie locked the shop door then walked wearily back through the shop, clutching the book to her chest. What a day. Like a day that gave you four seasons of weather in the space of a few hours. Only for her, it had been emotions, not weather – a maelstrom of them. Still there couldn't be anything left to feel, could there?

But she had forgotten Brutus.

At first, when she let herself into the flat, she couldn't see him. And he didn't come when she called him either; not even when she rattled his box of cat biscuits.

'Oh, Brutus,' she sighed, resigned to an evening of hunting for him among the contents of the black sacks. Which was exactly when he jumped out at her, taking her completely by surprise.

'You little devil!' She laughed, clutching his squirming body to her face. 'You gorgeous little devil you.'

And right then, as her laughter turned into tears, she knew she could never give him up. He was one of the few really good things to have happened to her lately, and because of that, he had to stay in her life. Whatever consequences may come with that decision.

Twenty-Three

The Gambia

'Are you going to marry my brother, Janet?'

Janet looked quickly up from her bowl of washing to check whether Fatu was joking or not. 'No, of course not!' she said. 'Why on earth would you think such a thing?'

'He likes you,' Fatu told her with a smile, pummelling the clothes in her own bowl. 'I see him looking at you all the time.'

Janet had noticed this too – a lot more often than made her comfortable. Fortunately, she and Fatu had been extremely busy, which had made it relatively easy to avoid having many direct conversations with David, what with him taking his meals with the men. Sukai had been feeling extremely tired lately so, with Nessa gone, Janet and Fatu had taken on pretty much everything but the cooking, including looking after the children and doing the washing.

'You are always very busy, Jan-net,' said a deep voice now, and Janet looked up to find David leaning against a nearby tree. Watching her again. Next moment, Fatu was hopping off somewhere, abandoning her tub of washing, deliberately leaving them alone.

Janet sighed, vowing to murder the girl later, and glanced warily up at David. 'There's a lot to do,' she said. 'Haven't you noticed how much your mother needs to rest at the moment? Her baby's almost due.'

David shrugged. 'Innaji has given birth many times,' he said, using the Gambian word for mother. 'This is her ninth baby. It is you who needs to rest, I think, Jan-net. You look tired.'

Janet frowned. Ninth? She'd thought it was eight. But he was right about one thing, she was tired; bone tired. At night, she practically crawled into bed to cuddle up to Fatu. Nobody had told her she had to do all this work, but if she didn't do it, then who would? Fatu already worked alongside her; she couldn't do any more. And even if she could, then how could Janet comfortably sit around reading her book while Fatu worked?

'Perhaps you could help out,' she suggested to David, but regretted it straight away when he immediately took Fatu's place at the neighbouring washing tub, his body too close for comfort as he squatted right next to Janet and his male scent filled her nostrils.

David's efforts with the washing made Janet laugh. 'I can tell you haven't done that before,' she said. 'The clothes won't get clean by you tickling them.'

He nudged her with his elbow, almost making her fall over. 'You are an expert in washing clothes in this way, Jan-net? You do it like this at home?'

'Well, no,' she admitted, righting herself again. 'I have a washing machine. Or at least, I did have a washing machine …' When she'd had a home.

David flicked water in her direction. It went down the back of her neck. Janet squealed. 'What did you do that for?' she asked.

'Because it is fun,' he said.

'Life is about more than fun,' she said, rubbing herself dry.

He flicked more water at her. 'You are too serious, Jan-net. You are on holiday. You should have fun.'

'Maybe when the washing's done,' she said, and he laughed.

Fatu was giggling somewhere too nearby. Janet could hear her. 'Hey, missy, come back here!' she called out, smiling.

'No,' the girl answered. 'I do not want to get wet.' And she squealed and ran off as her brother began to chase her.

Janet watched them, shaking her head. David thought he was so grown up, and in some ways he was. But most of the time he behaved like a child. A child with a well-toned man's body. A body he persistently

219

tried to flaunt at her, despite her giving him absolutely no encouragement. David was certainly an attractive young man, but young was the operative word. He was younger than Debbie and acted even younger than that. Janet wasn't sure what Jade or her friends would think about the situation. It was possible they would encourage her to explore her sensuality while she had the opportunity. But she couldn't do it. It just didn't feel right.

When, a few days later, Janet discovered two sisters in one of the other village compounds who made the most wonderful batik material, David arranged for her to spend some time learning the craft from them.

'Why?' Janet wanted to know as they walked slowly along towards the batik maker's compound. 'Why have you done this for me?' Although she had her suspicions.

David smiled his now very familiar smile. 'Because I can. Because I like you. Because I want to make you happy. How many reasons do you like me to give you, Jan-net?'

She laughed, unable to help herself. She didn't trust him, but that didn't seem to matter. 'That's enough. And thank you.'

The air was filled, as usual, with bird song and the chatter of those children who were not at school. Janet breathed in the hot, dusty scent of the air and wondered what it would smell like during the rainy season. And she remembered a trip to London's Kew Gardens on a school trip as a child, how the wet, earthy smell in the tropical rainforest glasshouse had filled her with deep pleasure. So much so, she hadn't wanted to leave it, her imagination captured by the story of the gardener Joseph Paxton who placed his seven-year-old daughter on the Victoria Regia water lily he had cultivated, to show the world how strong it was.

London. Kew Gardens or not, it was a far cry from this village, where life went on, very much the same, day after day. Janet herself had spent the morning as usual, helping out with domestic chores. As the days passed, she was finding all the tasks easier now, even lighting the charcoal stove. Although she still hadn't managed to balance a water jar on her head. She wasn't sure she would bother trying to perfect that any longer. It was clearly a lost cause.

'You like that I help you with the water this morning, Jan-net?' David said now, and Janet smiled to herself, because Gambian or not, he was only a man, and in her experience men could rarely help you out without reminding you that they'd done so.

'Yes,' she said. 'I did like that.'

It had been a surprise at first, when David had broken with tradition to help her out with what were usually women's jobs. She knew it was probably all part of his campaign to get her to see him in a different light, but if that was what he'd set his heart on, then he was going to be disappointed.

She still liked it in the village though, even though she did wish Nessa would come back. And that Fatu could have an education. Home felt so far away from here; Janet was completely involved in village life. But that didn't mean she didn't think about Shelthorpe-on-Sea, or wonder whether everyone was thinking about her. Probably not, as they thought she was still on her honeymoon with Scott. And even if they had started to worry about her, what could she do about it? It was best – at least for now – to just accept the situation she found herself in.

What good would worrying do, after all? It was best to view things as Corrinne Walker would do. As neutral events. To simply be. And actually, it was relaxing not to be constantly thinking of the next thing; to listen to the clucking of the chickens, to be aware of the breeze on one side of her face and the warmth of the sun on the other. Although, she had to admit, that too much 'just being' might become boring without the sheer amount of work it took to keep everything in the village going.

'I will collect you later, after your lesson is finished,' David told her when they arrived at the sisters' compound.

'You don't have to do that. I can find my own way,' she said, but he shook his head.

'I come, Jan-net. In two hours.'

She shrugged. 'It's up to you.'

Walking into the compound, she found the sisters

smiling at her. 'I'm Janet,' she said. 'Thank you so much for showing me how to make batiks. I love your material.'

The pair smiled and led her inside, where Janet was greeted by the smell of hot wax, which was melting in a pan on a stove.

'David, he is your boyfriend?' asked one.

Oh, no, did everyone think that? 'No,' she said firmly. 'He's not. He's too young for me, and anyway, I don't want to have a boyfriend.'

The sisters looked at each other and giggled.

'It's true,' she said. 'Why don't you believe me?'

But they just laughed again and began to show her how to paint the wax onto a piece of thin white cotton.

'Show me what you have done,' David said what seemed like ten minutes later, after the impromptu lesson was over, and Janet showed him the pieces of dyed cloth she'd pegged out onto the line.

'I'm going to come back tomorrow to put the second coat of wax on,' she told him excitedly. 'I can't wait. I loved this afternoon!'

David laughed. 'You know that today is Saturday?' he said. 'In Gambia we believe that the things you do on Saturday you will do again many times in your life. This is why, if a person is ill, or a person dies, we do not visit the family on a Saturday. We do not want this bad thing to happen again.'

'I see. Well, that's okay, in fact, it's good, because I want to do batik again.'

'I think that it means more than this, Jan-net, that you learn batik on a Saturday. I think it means that batik will be important in your life. Perhaps you will sell these materials in your shop.'

Janet had mentioned her plans for her shop in one of their conversations, and it had seemed to immediately capture his imagination.

She thought about it now, as they walked back to the family compound, imagining the shop window filled with a display of striking African fabrics and batiks. Would they sell in Shelthorpe-on-Sea? Possibly, if she could find a way to let the weekenders from London know about it.

'I have many contacts,' David said. 'I can help you. We can do good business together.'

Janet's attention snapped quickly back from Janet's Dreams. 'We?'

His smile was big and innocent, and now he moved to stand in front of her on the trail, blocking the way and forcing her to stop. 'Yes,' he said. 'I think we should be partners, you and I.'

'Business partners?'

He laughed, the sound a deep rumble in his throat. 'What other partners do you like us to be, Jan-net?' he asked cheekily. 'Partners who kiss and share their dreams? Hmm. I like that idea very much too. But I told you this in Banjul, I think. My thoughts on this matter have not changed. I like you, and I wish for you to be happy. I am not like your horrible Ray who leaves you alone in a country you do not know, and I am not like Scott, who is so cold and unfaithful all through your marriage.'

There had been one night when the village had been celebrating Yoro's birthday, and a secret supply of homemade alcohol had been brought out. Drinking always had made Janet talk too much. She'd ended up talking at great length about her lonely marriage and how Ray had sapped every bit of her self-confidence with his infidelity and domineering ways.

'It's the other way round,' she said now with a sigh. 'It was Ray who was cold and unfaithful, and Scott who left me here.'

David batted the correction aside with a large, expressive hand. 'Scott, Ray; it does not matter. They are both like irritating flies that buzz around a goat's arse.'

Janet burst out laughing – a great, undignified splutter of sound that had David joining in. Then, while she was still weak with it, he took her firmly by the shoulders to draw her close.

'You are a lovely woman, my Jan-net,' he said, looking down into her face. 'You should have better in your life than those goat's arse flies. You should have the love of a real man; a man who knows how to make your body sing. A man like me.' And, bending down, he kissed her on the lips.

As quickly as she could, Janet pulled away, wiping her mouth with the back of her hand. 'No, David. You mustn't do that. It's not right.'

But he only shrugged, not looking in the least bit put out. 'Remember what I told you,' he said with a wicked smile. 'It is Saturday today. And what happens on a Saturday will happen again.'

She shook her head. 'I've told you before; you're too young for me. And, more than likely, you just want to marry me to get a visa.'

If she'd expected him to look hurt, then he was anything but. In fact, the wicked smile grew. 'Jan-net,' he said, 'it is you who has mentioned marriage, not I. But I like this idea.' And he nodded, as if giving it serious contemplation. 'Yes, I like this idea very much.'

She shook her head again, determined to get through to him. 'David, this isn't funny. What would your mother say if she knew? And Nessa? She'd be so disappointed in you, after supporting your education the way she did. You need to aim higher in your life.'

But David only smiled and walked ahead. Sighing, she followed him.

Twenty-Four

Shelthorpe-on-Sea

By Sunday morning, Debbie had pretty much convinced herself it was time to create an event called Breaking up With Adam. Her higher thought about this event was that she got to keep Brutus, with all the fun and unconditional love he came with.

The only trouble was, whenever she thought about actually speaking the words to set this event in motion, she couldn't stop crying. And tomorrow, Brutus and his winning ways wouldn't be with her, and Adam with his expensive suit and sexy aftershave would.

Still, she could always replay the video clip that had been on repeat inside her head all weekend – the one of him walking past the café with Caro and Liam.

And there she was, crying again. Sod it.

At ten o'clock, the doorbell rang. Still not dressed, Debbie went down to answer it and there was Adam, dressed in running clothes and holding the biggest

bouquet of flowers Debbie had ever seen in her life.

'I haven't got rid of Brutus,' she told him defiantly.

He frowned. 'Brutus?'

'My cat. I haven't got rid of my cat. And I'm not going to either. This is his home.'

'That's okay,' Adam said in an annoyingly casual tone of voice. 'I dosed myself up with antihistamines this morning. Now, are you going to let me in or not?' And he pressed the flowers into her arms.

Feeling vaguely stunned, Debbie found herself stepping back to let him inside. Closing and locking the door after him. Leading the way upstairs.

Inside the flat, he took the flowers from her and placed them on top of one of the bulging black sacks. 'I'm glad you're in. I so wanted to see you today,' he said, and began to kiss the side of her neck.

'You did?' Passively, she allowed herself to be pushed down onto the bed. Soon Adam's hands were sliding over her body, finding all her responsive places.

Debbie struggled against a familiar fog of desire, trying to keep her mind clear for a little longer. Brutus helped, meowing to get her attention somewhere across the room, and Debbie pulled herself away from Adam and went to pick the kitten up.

Adam sighed and propped himself up on one elbow. 'I'm sorry about yesterday,' he said. 'Caro wanted to go to the antiques market, and I couldn't think of a way to get out of it.'

Debbie kept her head down, avoiding his gaze.

Brutus slipped out of her hands and plopped onto the bed. He began to walk towards Adam, who eyed him warily. 'I'm sorry,' he said again. 'I realise how much it must have hurt you to see me with them.'

She turned away from him to look out of the window, swallowing hard. 'It did hurt, yes,' she agreed. She took a deep breath before continuing. 'It made me decide that ... '

There was a movement behind her as Adam got off the bed. Next moment, he wrapped his arms around her, his chin nestling against the side of her neck.

'It made me decide something too,' he said, interrupting her before she could finish, his voice vibrating against her the way Brutus's purr did.

The fog turned into a tingle. 'I want to be with you,' he said. 'All the time.'

'What?' She turned in his arms to look at him, unable to believe what she'd just heard.

He was smiling, pleased with himself. 'I want to be with you, Debs,' he told her again, reaching out to stroke the side of her face. 'Always; not for a snatched hour or two. I'm going to leave Caro.'

There was a roaring sound inside Debbie's head. This was all in such contrast to what she had been imagining she couldn't think straight; couldn't register properly what she was feeling. But in any case, any response she might have made was cut off before she could open her mouth. Brutus, having grown bored of being ignored, suddenly catapulted himself from the bed to cling to Adam's back, where he swung, suspended by his claws.

'Argh!' Adam screamed. 'Get him off me! Argh! Get the little fucker off me!'

After Adam had gone, Debbie went out for a walk, too churned up and restless to stay in the flat. As always when she needed to think, she headed for the seafront with its cliff wall and Victorian lampposts. Normally, she walked along the promenade, but today she needed the tide's edge and some crashing waves.

Going down the nearest steps, she crunched her way across the pebbles, the sound instantly transporting her back to her childhood. Summer days down here with her mum, just the two of them while her dad was at work, picking their way over the stones with their bags of swimming things, towels and sandwiches. Debbie running, eager to reach the sand, Janet treading more carefully.

'Watch out for oil spills, Debbie. You don't want to ruin your new sandals.'

Janet had always seemed to be worried about something, though Debbie had no idea why she was even thinking about all this stuff at a time like this. Maybe it was easier than thinking about what had just happened? Adam wanting to leave his wife; wanting the two of them to be together. The fact that he had dosed himself up with antihistamines so he could come and tell her.

It was time to celebrate. To break open a bottle of wine. Except that none of it seemed real somehow, and she wished suddenly that she had someone to share it all with. Someone she could speak the words out loud to so it felt more real. But there wasn't anyone. She'd lost touch with most of her friends when she'd gone to university, and the few she still had would disapprove of her affair with Adam. And of course, she had never told Janet about him.

Debbie sighed, leaning against a break water to gaze out to sea. She wouldn't be able to tell her now either, even if she were here. Janet would worry too much about it all. About where she and Adam were going to live. Whether or not they were going to marry. Whether Adam's wife would go out of her way to make the divorce process as difficult as possible. How Debbie would cope as a stepmother to Adam's son.

How would she manage as a stepmother? She'd never had much contact with kids. Would she know what to do? Suppose Liam hated her?

But why was she having all these negative thoughts when the very thing she'd longed for was finally happening? She ought to be filled with hope, not doom. Sighing again, Debbie looked out to sea, her hands in her pockets. There was a fishing boat on the horizon, silhouetted against the pink sky. The sun was starting to set, and the view was the epitome of peace.

Peace. If only.

Perhaps it would help to try to act on Corrinne

Walker's advice in *Staying in Neutral.* To think of the highest response to the event of Adam Deciding to Leave His Wife. Yes, it was worth a try.

But before she could, someone called to her from further up the beach. 'Debbie?'

She looked up quickly, immediately recognising the voice, her heart giving a lurch of excitement. 'Scott!' she said. 'You're back. Why didn't Mum tell me?'

He frowned, walking towards her, his hands in his jacket pockets. 'You mean you haven't seen Janet? She isn't back?'

'No,' Debbie said, suddenly worried. 'I've not seen her. Should I have done? Scott? What's wrong?'

Shit, shit, shit. Debbie took her worry out on Kate's door knocker, then stood impatiently, waiting for the door to be answered.

'Hi, Deb. Blimey, what on earth's wrong?'

Kate was in her pyjamas and dressing gown. The dressing gown was belted up, but didn't quite meet at the front over her baby belly.

'It's Mum,' Debbie said, and promptly burst into tears. 'She's gone missing!'

'What? What d'you mean, gone missing? Come on, come in. Tell me what's happened.'

So Debbie went in and explained what Scott had told her.

'So, Janet decided not to marry the fucker after all? That's great!' Kate said after she'd finished.

'I know, yes. But she's all on her own there. Scott was so furious he got on the first flight out of The Gambia and left her there on her own with hardly any money! Then he had an attack of conscience and came here to make sure she was all right. Oh, Kate, why d'you think she hasn't been in touch with me?'

'Maybe she just needed some space.'

Debbie walked about Kate's living room, unable to keep still. 'I can't believe he left her alone like that.'

'I can, the little shit,' said Kate grimly.

'He couldn't believe I hadn't heard anything from her. I'm really worried. What can we do? I've tried ringing her, but it goes straight to voicemail.'

'Well, listen, we mustn't automatically think the worst. I don't expect the phone reception's that good where she is. It could be she's just decided to do what they were going to do anyway. Didn't you say they were going to travel around some of the more remote parts of the country?'

Debbie nodded. 'Yes, they were. I suppose she could have. It seems a bit brave of her to do it on her own though.'

'Well, it was brave of her to realise she was making a mistake with Scott and to act on it, wasn't it? Your mother is brave, Debs.'

Debbie thought about that, and felt even more emotional. Kate was right. It had been brave of her mum to dump Scott. Why was she always so quick to believe the worst of her?

'Have you been reading that book?' she asked Kate now. '*Staying in Neutral*? Only that's a great example of thinking the highest thought about an event.'

Kate shook her head, giving her a small smile. 'No, that was one hundred percent Kate Bramling. I never did find my copy.'

She came over to give Debbie a hug. 'Look, your mum will be all right, don't worry. I'm sure she'll get in touch very soon. And if she doesn't, then we'll just have to organise a trip out there to find her.'

Debbie watched as Kate suddenly winced, reaching round to rub her back. 'I don't somehow think you'll be dashing to Africa to organise a search party any time soon.'

Kate grimaced. 'Maybe not. But Estelle'd go with you if you needed her to, I'm sure. In fact, maybe we better give her a call now. Tell her what's happened. She'll know what to do.'

'Thank you.'

Debbie was very glad she'd come to see Kate. It was so good not to feel she had to deal with this on her own.

Kate gave her another hug before reaching for her phone. 'No problem.'

Twenty-Five

Shelthorpe-on-Sea

As Kate arrived at work on Monday morning, she was thinking about Janet. Estelle had been reassuring the previous day, voicing the same possibilities for Janet's silence that Kate had suggested to Debbie herself. But it had been obvious to Kate that her friend was worried, and so was she. For all she'd said to Debbie about Janet being brave, Kate knew she could be also be inclined to panic.

Turning up the corridor which led to the Catering Department, Kate sighed. Debbie was right; at eight months pregnant, there was very little she could do to help out. Bradley was due in a month, and she was getting so tired now, she was almost asleep on her feet by the end of a day at work. Which was a shame, because it was the night for the antenatal class. Two hours in a room with sodding Ian and Jennifer. Great.

Still, Estelle had immediately offered to go to The Gambia with Debbie should she want her to, just as Kate had suspected she would, and Kate was relieved about that. It still sometimes surprised Kate that she had a friend like Estelle. She'd thought she was such a stuck-up bitch when they'd first met in Jade's classes, with her superior attitude and company director snobbery. Only it had turned out that all that was a colossal front, and inside, Estelle was about as secure as a sink hole. Just like the rest of them.

But Estelle would certainly be useful if Debbie did need her help in The Gambia. Although, remembering the phone call Debbie had been so secretive about when Kate had been round at her flat, maybe she had someone else to ask?

Reaching the Catering Department, Kate glanced at her watch again. Was there time to call Debbie before the session started, see if she was all right today? Not really. It was almost nine forty-five, and the session started at ten. Even taking into account the fact that half of the lazy shower she was expecting today would be late for class, she still had to get the room prepared, ready to start. And experience told her this would take her longer than she expected it to, because somehow it always did. She'd have to give Debbie a ring later.

Pushing the classroom door open, Kate manoeuvred her bulky body through the entrance, holding her register and her teaching folder on top of her bump, then came up short with surprise. A woman was sitting on one of the high stools at the teaching benches; a woman who was so short and dumpy, Kate couldn't imagine how she'd managed to get up onto it. She looked to be in her sixties, dressed in a flouncy floral dress. Kate knew her straight away. It was the woman from her wedding reception. The one wearing the pink fascinator who had left the book.

'Hello, are you sure you're in the right place?' Kate asked, advancing into the room. 'This is NVQ Level 2 Hospitality and Catering.'

The woman's skin was almost as white as the flour Geoff's bakery students always got all over the bakery floor. But there was nothing fragile-looking about her smile. 'Yes, that's right,' she said. 'That's what I'm here for.'

'Okay,' said Kate, putting her file down on the worktop and reaching for her register. 'What's your name?'

'Nessa O'Brien.'

Nessa O'Brien. Kate was pretty certain that name hadn't been on her register when she'd scanned it this morning; that there'd only been the same old names she'd seen all term. And yet there it was, between Kieron Morton and Jaeden Peters. *Nessa O'Brien.* How strange. She couldn't think how she'd missed it earlier on. And what a funny time of year to start. Since this was a day release course, all the students needed to have a job in catering to join it. They worked in their job four days a week, and came here for the day on

Mondays. Wherever Nessa worked, they must have made some sort of special arrangement with the Head of Department for her to start at this late stage.

Still, it wasn't for Kate to wonder about the whys and wherefores. It was just her job to teach, and only that until Friday, when her maternity leave kicked in.

'Am I on the list?' asked Nessa, still smiling.

'Yes, you are,' Kate said, closing the register. 'Which restaurant do you work in?'

'The Cupcake Café, on the High Street,' Nessa told her.

The café near Janet's shop. Kate frowned. 'I didn't know they served hot food there,' she said. 'I thought it was all drop scones and lemon drizzle cakes.'

'Don't forget the cupcakes,' Nessa smiled. 'Actually, they've only just started offering meals. Hence employing me.'

Kate smiled, wondering whether she ought to bring up their previous meeting or not, but just then a noisy group of seventeen-year-olds – who were the normal staple of the course – turned up, complete with banter, dodgy haircuts and suspect hand cleanliness. Kate turned her attention to kicking them into touch, and the moment passed.

She didn't get the chance to speak to Nessa alone again until the end of the class, when, predictably, all the other students streamed out on the dot of five.

'Thank you for today, dear,' Nessa said. 'I did enjoy it.'

Kate smiled. 'The Cupcake Café are lucky to have found you,' she said. 'Your cooking skills are excellent. I'm not sure you need to do this qualification.'

'Oh, it's always best to have everything backed up. You never know what's going to happen in life, do you?'

It was an interesting reply, but Kate didn't pursue it. She still felt a bit awkward about not mentioning their previous meeting.

Nessa seemed to read her mind. 'I saw you at your wedding, didn't I?' she said, slipping down from her high stool with more ease than should have been possible, given her bulk and height challenge.

'Yes.' Kate smiled.

'You looked so wonderful in your red.'

'Thank you.'

'And your husband of course; he looked very dashing too.'

'Yes.'

Nessa's gaze dropped to Kate's ballooning waistline. 'And you must be expecting your happy event very soon?'

Bradley chose that very moment to give her a sharp kick in the ribs, and Kate clutched her belly with a little gasp. 'Yes, only four weeks now. I go on maternity leave on Friday. It can't come too soon, I can tell you.'

'I'm sure,' Nessa said sympathetically. She was standing in front of Kate. There was something very strong about her, somehow, for someone so short. Even the lads in the class had seemed to be in awe of her. Or at least, they hadn't mucked around as much as they usually did, with Nessa in the class, anyway.

'And tell me, did you find the book helpful?'

'Actually,' Kate said, feeling hugely embarrassed, 'I don't think we ended up taking it home. In fact, I've got to be honest, I don't know what happened to it. I'm so sorry.'

Nessa's smile didn't falter. In fact, she laughed. 'Oh, don't worry about it,' she said. 'These things happen. You were a bit preoccupied. Please, allow me to give you my copy.' And she reached into her bag to pull out a book, holding it out to Kate.

'Oh, really,' said Kate, regarding the book doubtfully. 'You don't have to do that.'

'Oh, but I want to.' Nessa smiled. 'And now I really must be going. Thank you so much for today. I thoroughly enjoyed it.'

'Good, I'm glad. We'll see you next week then. And thank you for the book ... '

Nessa stopped at the door to smile at her, looking a bit like the Queen with her white handbag hanging from her arm.

'You're most welcome. I hope you find it useful. Bye for now.'

Kate shook her head. What a mysterious woman. She looked down at the book cover, reading the title. *Staying in Neutral - Responses to Change Your Life*.

Cynically, Kate turned the book over to look at the picture of its author with her perfect- toothed smile. She didn't fancy the author's chances of staying serene when the GNVQs were arsing around. Still, it took all sorts.

Putting the book down on the worktop, Kate toured the room, checking for left-on cookers, re-wiping some of the surfaces where some students had been more than a little slap-dash with their cleaning efforts. She was almost finished when something caught her eye out of the window. A police car was parked in the car park. Only it wasn't any old police car. It was sodding Ian's police car. And what's more, Ian was standing next to it, staring straight into the room she was in.

What the fuck did he want?

Snatching up her bag and files, Kate switched the lights off and stormed out.

'What's the matter?' she called to him when she got near. 'Not enough criminals for you to arrest in town? Got to try and nab some students?'

Ian was leaning against the driver's door of his police car with his arms folded, waiting for her. He shook his head. 'Are we ever going to be able to have a conversation that isn't a slanging match, Kate?' he asked.

'I sincerely doubt it,' she said, walking past him to get to her own car.

He sighed, following her. 'Look, I just came to talk about the ante-natal classes.'

'What about them?'

'Well, I realise it's unfortunate that we've ended up in the same group –'

Kate zapped the car open and chucked the files onto the back seat. 'Er, yeah,' she agreed sarcastically, 'just a bit.'

It still didn't seem possible that Jennifer could be eight months pregnant and Kate not know about it. And it was so fucking typical. The bitch had ruined Kate's marriage, and now she had to try and take the gloss off her pregnancy too. Of all the ante-natal classes in all of Norfolk, she'd had to pick the same one as them. Geoff had said they could leave, but why the hell should they? They needed the classes, and they'd joined first. It should be Ponce Face and Loose Knickers who left.

'I just wanted to remind you that, as an expectant couple, Jennifer and I have got every bit as much right as you and whatisface to be there.'

'Geoff,' she said, opening the driver's door. 'His name is Geoff.'

'Oh, yes,' he said, reaching over to hold the door open. 'We've got as much right as you and *Geoff* to be there. It's our first child, as it's yours. We need to learn everything as much as you do.' He sighed, looking at her mutinous expression. 'So, please, Kate, could we just try to declare peace for the duration? It's only a few weeks, and there's no need for us to wash our dirty linen in public, is there?'

Kate's laugh was one hundred percent humourless.

'Wash our dirty linen in public!' she mocked. 'Do you realise what you sound like? Nobody says that these days.'

He sighed again. 'Whether they do or whether they don't, you know exactly what I mean. Why do you always have to be so difficult? Surely what happened between us should be water under the bridge now? I know we're never going to be best mates, the four of us, but can't we go along to the classes and be civilised with each other?'

Kate yanked the door from his grasp and climbed into the driver's seat. 'I expect so,' she said. 'If civilised includes ignoring people. Because I can tell you right now, I've got no intention of getting into a cosy chat with your bitch wife about post-natal incontinence and tears to my perineum. Or anything else for that matter.'

And she closed the car door on him, started the engine, and sped off.

'So those are the various options for pain relief, and, as I've said, which option you choose is very much a personal choice.' At that evening's class, Heidi was as relentlessly smiley as before. 'Some women go for a natural birth, not only because they want to be fully present during every moment while their child is making an entrance into the world, but also because they fear that drugs will cause their baby to be sleepy and less responsive. There is some indication that a less responsive baby can prolong labour, and lead to greater difficulty with breast-feeding after birth. But, to a certain extent, as I say, pain relief is every woman's individual choice. Something to be decided alongside your midwife and your husband.'

Blimey. An unbiased opinion then, thought Kate, shifting uncomfortably in her seat. Her back was killing her – probably as a result of standing for most of the day – and Bradley was doing his usual Zumba session inside her. If he was going to be this energetic once he was born, they were going to be in for a lively time.

For a second Kate tried – and failed – to imagine a day that consisted of dealing with GNVQ Hospitality and Catering students before picking up Bradley from the nursery. Still, at least the combination of her bad back and Bradley's Zumba session were an effective distraction from Ian and Jennifer over on the other side of the room.

She was still fuming about their conversation in the college car park, and Geoff hadn't been much help. 'You know he's a total tit, Katie,' he'd said. You shouldn't let him wind you up.' Which had done very little to calm her down. In fact, it had just left her feeling annoyed with Geoff too.

'Okay, everyone,' Heidi was saying now. 'Very much bearing in mind what I said about pain relief choices being, to a large extent, a personal choice, I'm going to divide you into two groups, and I'd like you to share your views and goals regarding pain relief with your group. So, we'll divide the class in two down the middle here, if you could turn your chairs round to face each other?'

Geoff helped Kate up, and moved their chairs. From her new position, she was relieved to find that she had absolutely no view of either Ian or Jennifer. Not that this did anything to block out Jennifer's voice. She'd always been a fog horn. At school, the teachers had picked her for important roles in school plays because she could project her voice so well. Though, come to think of it, the bitch must have had excellent acting skills too, bearing in mind the way she'd so completely nailed the part of Kate's loyal, loving friend, when all the while she'd been shagging Ian in Kate's bed.

Listen to her droning on now, drowning everyone out as usual. 'Well, I think a completely natural birth must always be the ultimate aim, mustn't it? Women have been giving birth for millennia, after all.'

'Yes,' Kate heard Ian pipe up. 'In parts of the undeveloped world, they work in the fields until the very last minute, don't they? Then they just move to the side to have their baby when it's time.'

Kate closed her eyes and prayed for strength. Beside her, Geoff felt for her hand and gave it a squeeze, whispering, 'Total tit' in her ear.

Kate repeated a mantra to herself. *All for Bradley. This is all for Bradley. Keep strong for Bradley. You'd better be worth it, Bradley ...*

'The way I see it,' a woman in Kate's group was

saying, 'pain relief can't really be something you decide on as a couple. It's the woman who's experiencing the pain. It's her body. It's not exactly the same as deciding on the colour scheme of your nursery or the style of buggy you're going to buy, is it?'

'You didn't let me help decide those either,' said her husband, and a ripple of laughter went round the group, including Geoff's booming belly laugh.

Kate smiled. It was good to hear him laugh. He hadn't done much of that lately.

'We went for yellow for the nursery in the end,' one of the other women said. 'We decided not to find out the sex of the baby, you see, because we wanted it to be a surprise. But we didn't want to be completely unprepared when he or she arrives. Do you all know the sex of your babies?'

'Yes, we're having a boy.'

'A girl.'

'A girl for us too.'

'A boy,' answered Geoff. 'Bradley.'

'Oh, that's so sweet! He's got a name already.'

It was more than sweet, thought Kate, closing her eyes again. It was what made all of this possible, Bradley's having a well-defined identity for her. If he were something less tangible, then Kate didn't feel she'd be able to restrain herself from shouting something offensive across the room at Foghorn Jennifer. The stupid bitch was proclaiming now, as if anybody cared, 'It's definitely going to be a drug-free birth for us. We're both completely agreed on that.'

'Are you tired tonight, Kate?' Mary asked, and Kate opened her eyes again. 'Yes,' she said, 'I am tired. Tired of a lot of things. But as for pain relief, I just don't see how you can make a decision about it in advance. After all, you don't know in advance what your labour's going to be like, do you?'

'That's so true,' said the woman with the yellow nursery. 'My sister was all no drugs, completely natural birth, and then she was grabbing for the gas and air and demanding an epidural after the very first contraction.'

'And was her baby all right?' Mary asked. 'Did it feed okay?'

'Oh, yes, it all went absolutely fine. In fact, she's only recently stopped breast-feeding, and he's four now.'

Now it was Kate's turn to find Geoff's hand for a squeeze. He squeezed hers back, then dropped it to fumble for his extra-large man-sized handkerchief, ostensibly dealing with a coughing fit, but really, she knew, to stifle his laughter.

Twenty-Six

The Gambia

Janet was sweeping up outside one morning when she heard Sukai calling from the main hut.

'Fatu? Fatu, come in here.'

Janet looked around but couldn't see Fatu anywhere, so she went to see what Sukai wanted herself. 'Fatu isn't around at the moment, Sukai. I'm not sure where she's gone.'

'Oh, Janet.' Sukai was lying on the bed. Janet was alarmed to see that she was clutching her belly. She hurried over. 'Are you all right?'

Sukai smiled, despite being in obvious pain. 'Yes, I am all right. But this baby is no good at telling the time. He comes now. Please, can you ask David to fetch the midwife?'

'Of course,' said Janet, doing her best to stay calm. 'Yes. Of course. Straight away. Stay there, I won't be long.'

Sukai laughed. 'Believe it, Janet,' she said, 'I do not plan to go anywhere.'

But as Janet hurried away, she heard Sukai groaning with pain again.

'Fatu!' she called, running along the track, looking around as she went. 'David! Have you seen Fatu or David?' she asked everyone she passed, but nobody had.

Eventually, she found the girl at the water taps, with her brother.

'What is it?' David asked when Janet ran up to them breathlessly. 'What has happened?'

'You've got to come quickly,' she said. 'It's your mother. The baby's coming!'

Immediately Fatu ran off, back towards the compound. David walked with Janet, his long strides easily keeping up with her half run. 'She wants you to go and fetch the midwife,' she told him. 'Where is she?'

'Fana Kunda, the next village,' he told her calmly. 'I will go on the bike. Do not worry, Jan-net. Everything will be all right.' And he bent to give her a quick kiss on the cheek before striding ahead. She saw him take the rusty old bike from the tumble-down picket fence marking the boundary of the compound, mount it and push himself off with one elegant movement.

Janet's hand was still on her cheek, where he'd kissed her. It was the first time he'd kissed her since the time after the batik workshop. She wished it had felt like the kiss of a friend, but it hadn't. Clearly he still hadn't got the message.

'David,' she called after him. 'Tell Nessa to come back. Tell her I need her.'

David was already a long way up the dusty track, but she saw him put a hand in the air to acknowledge that he'd heard her. 'If I see her, I will tell her,' he called back, and then he went around a bend, out of sight.

When Janet got back to Sukai's hut, Sukai was on her feet, pacing, her hands on her distended belly, her face clenched with pain. Fatu was watching her anxiously.

'What can we do for you?' Janet asked, feeling helpless.

Sukai waited for the pain to subside before answering. 'You can go and get my friends,' she said. 'It will be nice to have them with me.'

'Your friends?'

'Yes, the ladies in the other compounds. Fatu can go with you.'

'Of course,' said Janet, holding out her hand to Fatu. 'We can do that. Will you be all right on your own?'

Sukai laughed. 'Yes, I will be all right. I am having a baby. It is a natural thing. You know this already, because you have a daughter.'

'Yes,' agreed Janet doubtfully, because Debbie's birth had been just about as unnatural as it was possible for a birth to be.

'Come,' said Fatu, pulling her out of the door. 'I will go this way, you go that way.'

'All right.'

Fatu ran off to the left, and Janet did as Fatu had bid, turning to the right, back down the dirt track through avenues of tall maize plants, until she reached the first compound and called out, standing in the entrance, sweating and panting.

Here they baked bread for the whole village, and at her call, the baker and his wife emerged, their hands white with flour. 'How is it?' they asked her, using the traditional Gambian way of greeting, their wary expressions telling Janet how wild she must look.

'Sukai's having her baby,' she told them. 'It's coming early. She wants her friends with her.'

The woman said something in reply, and began to strip off her apron, and Janet left her to it to run off to the next compound. Then the next. By the time she and Fatu returned to the village, the baker's wife and two other village women had already arrived, and were inside with Sukai. Soon others came, many of them with their young children, until the compound was a mass of people, resembling a party more than a birth gathering. Everyone was smiling and talking, and the children were running around together, chasing the animals.

Now and then, Janet heard Sukai give a low moan of pain, but between times, she sometimes thought she could hear her laughing or chatting with her friends too. Fatu had disappeared somewhere – Janet wasn't sure if she had joined in with the children's game, or whether she was inside with her mother. Janet missed her company, and felt somewhat redundant, so she sat down on an upturned oil drum, a fixed smile on her face. The wealth of human warmth and camaraderie towards Sukai had made her think about her own friends again. How was Kate getting on? It must almost be time for her to go on maternity leave. And was Debbie still living with her and Geoff?

Oh, Debbie.

Janet heard Sukai cry out again and sighed, remembering her own experience of giving birth. There had been pain such as she had never imagined possible; pain she would surely die from. How frightened and alone she'd felt, with her feet up in stirrups, the obstetrician bearing down on her with a frightening pair of forceps. Then, finally, Debbie had emerged in a terrible temper, staring at Janet crossly, as if she resented having been born, the bruising from the forceps already livid on her head.

Ray, arriving from work when it was all over, had looked thoroughly disappointed by his first sight of his daughter. Not that Debbie seemed to notice. From the very first moment she saw her father, the baby had been entranced, all signs of anger smoothing immediately from her face. It only returned again after Ray had departed to 'wet the baby's head' at the pub with his friends, leaving Janet and the baby alone again.

Sadly, Janet remembered those first desperate months of Debbie's childhood. Trying, and miserably failing to breast feed. The colic that had kept her up with the baby all night. Nothing she'd done had seemed right. It was as if her daughter had decided to dislike her from the moment she had been born.

Things had improved, with time. But Debbie had always remained a Daddy's girl.

One of Sukai's friends began to sing. Another began to dance. And suddenly, the whole compound was a mass of brightly-dressed singing, dancing women. Someone caught hold of Janet's hand to pull her up. She did her best to go along with it; to join in and to banish bad thoughts of the past. To become a part of the magic.

Time passed. Then suddenly, in the depths of the celebration of community and life, the clear sound of a baby crying pierced the excitement. Sukai's baby had arrived, and the singing gave way to cheering and excited chatter.

'It's a boy!' someone announced from inside the hut, and immediately the singing and the dancing recommenced, rising in volume as the women celebrated the new life.

And in the middle of all this, David arrived with the midwife on the bicycle. She was sitting on the saddle, and he was standing to push down on the pedals. It didn't look possible for the pair of them to have covered so much ground in that way, and yet here they were.

The midwife was a large grey-haired woman with a huge smile. Despite her size, she dismounted the bike much as David had got on it – with easy grace – and went straight inside to Sukai, calling a few greetings on her way.

'She's too late,' Janet went over to tell David as he propped the bike back against the fence. 'Your brother has just been born.'

'A brother, huh?' said David, standing with his hands on his hips. 'And he is well?'

Janet nodded. 'I haven't seen him, but I think so, yes,' she said.

'My last brother died,' David said, and Janet caught her breath, remembering Fatu's earlier tension.

'That's awful.'

Despite the singing, the baby's loud cries could clearly be heard coming from inside the hut, and David laughed. 'But I can already tell that this little brother is very healthy,' he said.

Just then, the midwife came out carrying a small, protesting bundle, and there was a babble of excited chatter as she began to tour the yard to show the baby to everyone.

'I will go and tell my father the baby is born,' David said, and began to walk away.

'David,' she called after him, 'did you see Nessa?'

'No,' he said. 'I did not see Nessa. I found the midwife and then I came back.'

There was no chance for Janet to reply to this, because the midwife had reached her with the baby, and was holding him out for her to see.

Janet looked down at the bundle and smiled. The baby was perfect, absolutely perfect, the resemblance to both David and Fatu plain to see. 'Oh, he's beautiful,' she said. 'Really beautiful.'

She looked up to share her pleasure with the midwife, only to find the woman staring at her with a strange intensity. Goodness, how strange. It was almost as if the woman were looking right into her soul.

Feeling claustrophobic, Janet might have taken a step back if there had been room for her to do so, but there wasn't, with all the village women crowding around to take their first look at the baby. So, when the midwife suddenly lifted her hand to stroke Janet's cheek, the baby cradled safely in one arm, Janet was helpless to do anything about it.

Then the midwife spoke, her words were both clear and shocking. 'You will have a child like this boy very soon.'

'What?' Had she heard right? Surely not. The woman was crazy.

But Janet found she couldn't look away from that all-seeing gaze, and she licked her lips. 'Oh, no,' she said with a fake laugh. 'My daughter's all grown up now.'

As if she hadn't spoken, the midwife's hand moved disconcertingly from Janet's face and down to her belly, giving it two firm strokes. 'Your son,' she said. 'He is in here. A brother for your daughter.'

Janet wanted to push the woman and her words away, but was too afraid of hurting the baby to do so. 'That's not possible,' she said. 'I'm far too old.'

But the midwife shook her head and laughed, returning both her hands and her attention to the baby. 'You are pregnant,' she insisted. 'It is God's will.' And then she moved on with the baby, leaving Janet reeling.

Pregnant? How ridiculous. The woman couldn't possibly know it just by looking at her. Could she? And anyway, she was forty-four years old. Her periods had been irregular for a while now, and she and Scott … Frantically, Janet thought of the times they had used contraception, but could remember a few times when they had not.

And then she began to remember how she had been off her food for weeks now; certainly ever since she'd come here, to the village. Of how she'd thought her stomach was still adapting to the different food, or getting over that appalling travel sickness in the boat. But travel sickness didn't last that long. What if the woman were right? What if she was really pregnant with Scott's child at her age?

Oh, God, she had to know for sure; she just had to. As soon as possible. Which meant leaving here and getting back to civilisation. Somewhere she could buy a pregnancy testing kit. Even if that did mean puking her guts up on that awful ferry again. But she'd have to reach the ferry first. And how on earth was she going to do that?

Oh, where the hell was Nessa? How dare she just abandon Janet here like this? And why, oh why, had she so stupidly tagged along with the woman in the first place?

The bike David had used to get to Fana Kunda was still leaning against the picket fence. Nobody noticed as Janet wheeled it away.

Nessa had got her into this, so Nessa must get her out. She would cycle to Fana Kunda village to find her. Sukai needed her friend back here anyway. And the fact that David hadn't been able to see Nessa meant nothing at all. He'd been thinking about his mother and searching for the midwife. With such an urgent task, naturally he hadn't had time to search for Nessa.

It was years since Janet had ridden a bike. Probably thirty years. The front wheel wobbled alarmingly in the red dirt as she climbed on and pressed down on the pedal, clutching the handlebars for dear life. But soon she was out on the track, and a few minutes later she passed the spot where the Land Rover had stopped when she'd first arrived here with Nessa from Kachikally.

Kachikally. The sacred crocodile pool. Women went to that place for a blessing if they wanted to get pregnant. And she had received a blessing.

The track was heading very slightly uphill, the red dust sent up by the wheels choking her throat. Janet coughed, wishing she had some water with her. Thoughts of water brought memories of the sudden shock of cold water on her head and body at the blessing. No, this was silly. If she was pregnant, and surely she couldn't be, then she must have already been pregnant when she went to Kachikally. Mystical as things sometimes seemed in The Gambia, you couldn't get pregnant without having sex, and she hadn't had sex since the eve of her almost wedding to Scott.

She pedalled on for a while, trying to calm her thoughts, but finally had to stop when she reached a crossroads. Which way was the village? She had no idea. They hadn't passed a village when they'd driven here, or at least, not one that David could have ridden to and from in the time it had taken him. But that didn't mean the turning on the left was the right way to go. There could be another turning, up ahead.

Janet looked around, shading her eyes from the sun. There was nothing to see but scrubland, bush and red dirt. And, back in the direction she'd come from, a cloud of red dust.

Someone was coming after her, and she had a pretty good idea who. David.

Making a decision, Janet turned the bike to the left and pressed down hard on the pedal to get going. Straight away, there was a snapping sound and the pedal fell off, almost taking Janet with it.

Within a few minutes, he was at her side on a rickety-looking borrowed bike.

'Jan-net,' he said. 'Where are you going? That is not the way to Fana Kunda, and anyway, we are celebrating the arrival of my new baby brother. Come on, let me take you home.'

'But I want …' she started, but he put his arm around her shoulders, and finally she gave up and wheeled her borrowed bike back to the village with him, because there seemed to be nothing else to do.

But somehow, everything felt different now. For the first time, it really occurred to Janet how truly alone she was here. Surrounded by friendly people who wished her well, but completely alone.

Nessa had abandoned her, and there was no way for Janet to leave. She barely had any money, and no phone.

And even if she'd had either, they would be useless. There was nothing to pay for here, and no phone signal. She couldn't get a taxi or hire a car. There was no way to get back to the river to catch a ferry back to Banjul. No way to leave at all. She was entirely helpless.

Almost as if she had been very affectionately kidnapped.

Twenty-Seven

Shelthorpe-on-Sea

'Well done, Katie,' Geoff said at the end of the antenatal class. 'I award you the Geoff Bramling Award for Self-control Kept Under Severe Provocation 2017.'

Geoff, having only eaten a hasty sausage roll before the class began, had expressed a desire for chips from the shop down on the seafront, and now, with the chips eaten, they were strolling hand-in-hand along the street-lit promenade because Kate wanted to see where the goats slept at night. The local council had introduced the goats onto the sloping grassland along the cliffs at Shelthorpe-on-Sea a few months previously for scrub control, and they'd proved to be quite a tourist attraction.

'Weren't they the sodding end?' said Kate, referring to Ian and Jennifer, wiping her greasy lips with a tissue.

'Aren't they always?' said Geoff. 'Anyway, let's forget about them and find these goats. I reckon they must huddle down under the steps at night. That's where I'd go. Must be a bit more sheltered there. It can get chilly down here at night.'

'You're probably right,' Kate said, wincing at a sudden pain in her back.

Geoff noticed. 'Want me to give your back a quick rub?'

'Yeah, please,' she said, grimacing as she wiggled her shoulders.

'Come on then, get under this street light so I can see what I'm doing.'

They moved on until they were directly beneath a street light, and Kate turned in the direction of the pier as Geoff got stuck in. With hands accustomed to kneading dough, Geoff gave a bloody good massage. It was one of the things she loved about him. One of the many things.

'It was funny tonight though, wasn't it? When whatsherface said about her sister breast feeding?'

Geoff giggled. 'The kid'll need a pair of steps soon.'

'Special breaks in the school day for titty.'

'Ha! Hope she didn't realise I was pissing myself laughing.'

'Don't think so. Though, I have to admit, I was amazed to be laughing at anything with the unmentionable pair irritating the heck out of me across the room.'

'What they do well, isn't it?' Geoff said easily, stopping his massage to take her hand and kiss it. 'That better?'

'Yeah, lots. Ta, love.'

They moved on companionably, towards the steps. 'Think it's going to be too dark to see any goats?'

'No, I reckon their eyes will gleam under the street light,' said Geoff. 'Went to the Isle of Skye once, and all the sheep were lined up alongside the road on the way to the pub. It was like a line of gem stones, lighting the way to the whisky.'

Kate laughed. 'You are funny,' she said, then paused. She was reluctant to say anything to spoil the moment, because there hadn't been many moments like this lately. Which was precisely why she needed to speak up.

'What?' Geoff asked, as usual, instantly picking up on her mood.

She sighed. 'You're like *you* tonight,' she said. 'Or more like you.'

'Like me? How can I be anything else but me?'

'I don't know, love,' she said. 'You tell me. But it's true. In fact, I don't think you've been quite you since the wedding.'

He sighed. 'Not that again.'

'Look, don't be cross. I know you don't want me to go on about it, and I've tried not to. In fact, what with getting ready for Bradley and work and now Janet going missing, well, I haven't had time to think about it much, let alone talk to you about it.'

'About what?'

'About what's wrong with you. And don't say "nothing" or try to tell me it's all in my imagination, because I know it's not.'

Geoff began to walk up the first flight of steps, then stopped to peer through the hand rails. He was silent for so long, she thought at first that he wasn't going to answer her. But then he said, 'I don't suppose I can distract you with some gleaming-eyed goats?' and he sounded so miserable, Kate was suddenly really worried all over again.

'I'll marvel at them afterwards,' she said, joining him. 'Come on, love. Spill.'

Geoff looked away from her and began to fumble with his beard. Suddenly Kate realised he was trying not to cry. Bloody hell. What on earth was wrong?

She grabbed his hand. 'Come on, Geoff, what is it? You're scaring me now.'

He sniffed and blew his nose on an outsized handkerchief. 'That's why I didn't want to talk about it. Because I ... I didn't want to scare you, not with Bradley and everything. Because ... because it might turn out to be something and nothing, you know?'

Her grip tightened on his arm. She gave it a little shake. '*What* might? Tell me!'

He shuffled his foot. 'Well,' he said at last. 'I had a sort of funny ... do at the wedding.'

'A funny do?' she said. 'What do you mean a funny

do?'

'A pain. In my chest. A bad one.'

'Shit, Geoff!' Kate suddenly felt chilled to the bone. She reached out to take hold of his jacket lapels, forcing him round to face her, remembering how he'd disappeared during the wedding reception. How she'd finally found him out on the balcony. 'And you just kept quiet about this? Why?'

'Because I didn't want it to spoil our lovely day,' he said, sounding utterly miserable.

'Our lovely day was weeks ago,' she reminded him. 'You've had ages to mention it since then. Please tell me you've been to see a doctor.'

His foot was kicking at the base of the wall beneath the handrail now, and he shook his head. 'Not yet. I have made an appointment now, but at the time I thought … well, I don't know what I thought.'

Suddenly Kate was so angry she wanted to spit. Angry and scared. Why? Why did this have to happen to them? What had she done that was so wrong in life that the shit just kept getting shovelled on and on?

'Bloody hell, Geoff,' she said, pulling him close, terror making her angry with him too. 'This is *us*, not … not bloody Ian and Jennifer or Tarquin and Pigmy or whatever their names are in the class. We don't do big secrets from each other, do we? Especially not secrets like this. When's your appointment?'

'In a couple of weeks. They couldn't fit me in sooner. Lots of flu about apparently.'

'Look, we'll go to the doctors together tomorrow, okay? I'll insist they see you. We'll get it sorted.'

He looked at her with frightened eyes, and she imagined how tortured the past few weeks must have been for him, keeping this secret to himself. 'But what if it's something that can't be sorted though, Katie?' he said. 'What then?'

Somehow she held his gaze and stopped her mouth trembling. 'Then we'll deal with it. But we'll deal with it together. All right?'

Kate couldn't sleep that night. She hadn't been sleeping particularly well for weeks, but this time it wasn't because of Bradley's usual restlessness, or the fact that no position she lay down in seemed to be comfortable.

Silly sod.

Why hadn't he told her? All right, maybe she could understand why he hadn't said anything at the wedding. But all the days afterwards? She'd been a complete bitch to him, moaning on about their lack of sex life and him being boring wanting to look at gardens. And all the time the poor man had been terrified that, if he gave in to her demands for sex, he'd have a heart attack.

The thought of Geoff gone, of him dying, was inconceivable. He was hers; part of the very fabric of her life. The person she got up for in the morning and went to bed with at night. They needed him, her and

Bradley. He would be all right. He had to be. She'd tried to get him to go to Accident & Emergency, unwilling suddenly even to wait until the next day to go to the doctors as she'd first suggested, but he had refused. 'No, Katie, not now. It's late, and you need to rest. We'll go to the doctor's in the morning, like you say. I've waited this long.'

She'd begun to cry then, and he'd said, 'Oh, shh, Katie; this isn't doing Bradley any good, is it?' and gathered her into his arms.

It was where she felt the safest, in his arms. Where she'd felt the safest ever since she'd had that blinding realisation that what she wanted from her big, burly, drinking mate of a friend was, well, more than friendship. Very luckily, he'd been feeling exactly the same thing for months, and the rest was history. Within weeks they'd moved in together, and within days, as it turned out, Bradley had been conceived. And now this. It wasn't fair. It just wasn't bloody fair.

Giving up on sleep for now, Kate went to the loo and then padded downstairs to make herself a mug of hot milk. Then she took it into the living room and went to the window, pulling back the curtain aside to look out. There was nothing to see, except the street. Their little terraced house was one of the new builds up the hill from the Morrison superstore. The estate agent's details had hinted at a sea view, but you'd have to stand a step ladder on the roof to catch it. Kate didn't care. They'd made it their own, she and Geoff, complete with clutter and a kitchen bursting at its seams with cooking and baking equipment.

For some unknown reason, the woman in her class popped into Kate's mind. Nessa. She thought of the book she'd given her, realising she'd left it behind in the classroom when she'd seen Ian in the car park. Funny, she was fated not to read that book somehow. Not that it mattered. Not that anything mattered except for Geoff being all right.

Sighing, Kate dropped the curtain and turned back into the room. How insignificant and unimportant even her anger about Ian and Jennifer seemed now. She'd go to those classes with them for a whole year if it made any difference to Geoff. For sodding eternity.

Perhaps it would only be a small op. One of those key-hole procedures. He'd go in, they'd do it straight away, and he'd be in the clear before Bradley was born. Because he had to be there when Bradley was born. He just had to be. He *would* be. He would, he would, he bloody well would!

Oh, it was useless, useless, thinking like this. It wouldn't change anything. Wouldn't make tomorrow come any quicker. Stubborn, stubborn man, refusing to go to Accident and Emergency. All right for him, snoring away upstairs. Completely flipping ironic, really, him not wanting to go because she needed rest, only for him to be sound asleep and her wide awake. At least they both had the day off tomorrow, so they'd be able to see a doctor without any bother. And maybe, when they got home, she'd be able to get some sleep then.

But what if there was something badly wrong? You didn't get that kind of pain for no reason, did you? Fearfully, abandoning the positive thinking, Kate made herself contemplate the very worst outcome of tomorrow's doctor's appointment instead. A woeful expression on the doctor's face. Emergency surgery. Geoff dying.

If the worse came to the worse, would they manage on their own, she and Bradley?

Twenty-Eight

Shelthorpe-on-Sea

Debbie had wanted to tell Adam about her mum's disappearance on Monday morning, but he'd been out all day at a conference. So when Tuesday came round, after another twenty-four hours of silence and still no answer from Janet's phone, she arrived early for work so she could speak to him about it before Rosemary arrived.

It had been agony, not being able to call him to tell him about it before. They'd always had an agreement that she would leave him to make any telephone calls, so, although she had his number, she didn't like to ring it. Of course, soon all of that would be over once he'd left his wife and they could finally be open about their relationship.

Arriving at the college, Debbie saw, to her annoyance and immense frustration that Rosemary's perfectly-maintained Peugeot was already parked next to Adam's Audi in the car park. For goodness' sake. The stupid woman didn't start work until nine, and it was only eight-fifteen. How ridiculous. The woman was the Principal's PA, not Adam's, but she still acted like Adam's slave when she could, anticipating his every need. She probably got in this early every day just so she could make his cup of coffee when he arrived.

Quickly, Debbie hurried up the stairs to the office. Dumping her bag on her desk, she crossed straight to Adam's office door, giving only the briefest of knocks before going in.

Rosemary and Adam looked up with identical startled expressions. Both were holding coffee mugs, and were obviously in the middle of a cosy chat.

'Are you all right, Debbie?' Rosemary asked. 'You look a bit stressed.'

She nodded. 'I'm worried sick about my mum, to be honest. She's gone missing in The Gambia. She was supposed to be getting married out there, but she changed her mind, and the man she was supposed to be marrying stormed off in a temper without leaving her with any money, and now she isn't answering her phone. What do you think I should do?'

They both gaped at her.

'Oh, dear,' said Rosemary at last. 'I am sorry to hear that.'

As Rosemary spoke, Debbie saw Adam's gaze slide

apprehensively towards Rosemary and back to Debbie again, and it was enough, just that tiny movement of his eyes, for Debbie to realise that nothing had changed. Or was likely to change. Saturday afternoon and his announcement, their celebratory love-making; it had all meant nothing. Here she was, being open and vulnerable about her mum being missing abroad, and all he cared about was whether Rosemary might realise that he and Debbie were more than work colleagues.

He was never going to leave his wife.

He might keep saying he was going to. Might even convince himself he was going to. But somehow he would never quite get round to it. And while Debbie continued to wait and to hope, living in a crappy flat and working in a crappy job, she would somehow allow herself to be persuaded to find a new home for Brutus. And lose all her self-esteem in the process.

For nothing.

'How very worrying for you,' Rosemary added politely.

Adam still hadn't said a word. Now he said just one, in agreement with Rosemary. 'Yes.'

Debbie swallowed, controlling herself with an effort. 'I've decided to go to The Gambia to look for her,' she said, discovering that it was still possible to speak when your heart was breaking. When an era was passing like a spiny sea urchin through your guts. 'I came in to tell you.'

'Oh,' said Rosemary, looking concerned. 'I think

you'd better wait until nine o'clock to okay it with HR. I'm not sure it will count as compassionate leave. And where are you up to with typing Adam's marketing report? If you're not able to finish it in time, I'll have to do it myself, or ask HR to get a temp in.'

Heartless bitch.

'I'll just go and check.' With her cheeks flaring red, Debbie turned away to boot up her computer, even though she knew exactly how much more of the report she had left to type. About six pages. Around two thousand words. Easily achievable before nine a.m. for a fast typist like her. Almost as easy as deleting the whole bloody document altogether.

Debbie sat at her desk and closed her eyes. Then she took a series of deep breaths, reminding herself that the end of her relationship with Adam was a neutral event, and, as such, she could choose how to react to it. She didn't *have* to take her revenge by obliterating every word of his stupid, boring marketing report forever.

Oh, but it would feel so good to do so. She'd only need to hold her fingers down on the Alt and the A keys to highlight it all. Then press delete.

Twenty-Nine

Shelthorpe-on-Sea

Kate had fallen asleep on the sofa. At about nine a.m., she was woken by a sudden cry from upstairs and struggled to her feet, instantly awake.

'Geoff? Geoff! I'm coming!'

He was in bed, clutching his chest in obvious agony, his face deathly pale.

Kate felt sick. 'I'm going to phone for an ambulance. Hold on. Please, Geoff, hold on!'

Her phone was downstairs. Of course it was bloody well downstairs.

'Don't –' he gasped, but she ignored him, and as she hurried she slipped, falling onto her bum and beginning to slide. Managing to stop herself after bumping down two or three steps, Kate whimpered slightly as she got carefully to her feet.

Don't hurry, that was what Geoff had been trying to

say. Even desperately ill, he'd been trying to take care of her. But how could she not hurry? When he may be dying upstairs?

Somehow, clinging on to the handrail for dear life, she got safely to the bottom of the stairs, found her phone and tapped out nine, nine, nine; relieved to receive, as she did so, a reassuring kick from Bradley against her ribs.

'Ambulance. I think my husband's having a heart attack. Please, come quickly.'

She gave her address, and the calming voice reassured her the ambulance would be with them soon and told her what to do in the meantime. Then she unlatched the door and returned to Geoff, to find him sweating and still clutching his chest, but mercifully still alive.

'Don't go dying on us, d'you hear?' she told him fiercely. 'Bradley and I need you. We all need you. How would the world survive without your stupid record-breaking desserts, eh?'

She helped him to lay on his side, then held his hand, knowing she should be strong for him, but completely powerless to stop the tears streaming down her face. Her mind was filled with an image of Geoff, before they had become a couple, complete with a clip board, supervising the construction of a record-breaking trifle the previous summer. Completely crazy. Completely wonderful. He was her Geoff; one in four billion, or however many people there were on the planet. She couldn't lose him.

At last, at last, the dim bedroom was filled with flashing blue, signalling the arrival of the ambulance, swiftly followed by someone calling out and the clump of footsteps up the stairs.

'They're here, love,' she told him. 'Hold on, d'you hear me?'

His eyes were screwed tight shut, but his hand gave hers the tiniest squeeze, and then the paramedics were there and taking over, and soon they were driving through the morning rush hour streets towards the hospital. And all Kate could do was sit there and watch the paramedics working on her husband and wonder if he would ever return to their little home alive.

At the hospital, everything was a blur of lights and corridors and faces. People saying things to her. Her giving answers to questions she instantly forgot. Geoff lying back on a trolley, moaning with pain. A million and one thoughts going through her mind. *You should have insisted on coming last night. As soon as he told you, you should have got him down here. Why didn't you spot the signs before? You're the one who sees him the most. You're his wife. If he dies, it will be down to you. To your negligence.*

'Please wait here, Mrs Bramling. We'll bring you news as soon as we have any for you.' And off they went, leaving her there, taking the love of her life away.

Almost frozen with terror, Kate forced herself down

onto a chair to wait, but soon got up again. She badly needed a wee, and no matter how ridiculously inappropriate and badly-timed the bodily function seemed, it was not going to be denied. Better get it over with now, while they were working on Geoff. Before they came out to give her an update.

But where was the sodding, bloody toilet?

Frustrated and panicking, Kate walked along the corridor, searching frantically for signs or somebody to ask. She was still looking when a voice hailed her. A voice she instantly knew was Ian's.

'Come to gloat, have you?'

'What?' Hazily, dragged from her own predicament, she focussed on him. Saw him standing in front of her, face pale and hollow-eyed, mouth twisted with bitter dislike.

'What are you talking about?' she asked, shaking her head to try and clear it.

'You and your hatred, that's what I'm talking about. You sending your fucking bad Karma because you're still so screwed up about me and Jen.'

It was too much to handle. 'Look, Ian, I –'

He drew closer, jabbing one hand aggressively towards the empty corridor. 'They're up there, fighting for their lives. Both of them.'

'Jennifer's had her baby?' she said. 'But it's too early, isn't it?'

Ian erupted into noisy sobs, putting an arm up in front of his face. 'Of course it's too fucking early,' he said. 'That's the whole fucking point. The cord was wrapped around the baby's neck, and then Jennifer began to … she began to haemorrhage. And I blame you and your hatred. You wished this on us. You.'

He was deranged by grief, she knew that. But he was also so utterly convincing that Kate, in her already vulnerable state, almost felt she was guilty of his accusations. That perhaps the loathing she'd felt towards Jennifer had been responsible for this. That hatred as strong as the hatred she had felt for her former friend developed a life and a will of its own.

But she had never asked Jennifer to steal her husband, had she? Just as she hadn't asked Geoff to get ill the moment she'd finally found true happiness.

Geoff. She had to get back to Geoff.

'Look, I've got to go,' she told Ian, finally spotting a sign for the toilet up ahead. 'I hope they both get through. I really do.' And she turned and hurried on her way, leaving him there, broken and bitter.

Inside the toilet cubicle, Kate relieved herself, remembering all the times she'd wished for Ian to suffer in some way since their break up. For him to experience the same amount of heartbreak she had experienced herself. But now that he was doing exactly that, it gave her no satisfaction at all. All she felt was a deep pity. For both of them.

And she wondered if Ian would feel the same way for her, should Geoff die today. But no, she couldn't think about that. She couldn't contemplate that. She had to stay positive. To believe that, when she got back, someone would come out to tell her that this had been a bit of a warning. Geoff would be fine if he lost a bit of weight and did more exercise. Lack of food and enforced exercise would make him a grumpy bugger, but she could handle grumpy a lot better than she could handle dead.

No, positive. She was thinking positive.

Suddenly, a fluttering sensation started up inside her. It felt as if Bradley were swimming breast stroke. Or running his tiny fingers over the inside of her ribs. Communicating with her. *I don't want my dad to die before I've met him,* he seemed to be saying, *but if it happens, we'll be fine, you and I.*

Tears began to spill down Kate's cheeks. Because she knew that her unborn child was right. By just being there, inside her, a part of her, Bradley had given her a purpose in life. He was also a part of Geoff, a result of their love. And he was his own person too. But to become that person, he needed her.

Tearfully, Kate reached for some toilet paper to wipe herself, taking a deep, calming breath as she flushed the toilet.

'Listen, Bradley,' she said out loud. 'Don't write your dad off yet, okay? *He's* the one you'll be able to wrap around your little finger, not me. His classes are always chaotic. The students are crazy about him, but it's like baking bread in a football stadium. At least I manage to maintain some order in my classes. We'll be like good cop and bad cop, me and him, and believe me, you're going to need both of us.'

The fluttering sensations had paused, almost as if Bradley was listening. Kate nodded, took another deep breath and made for the door to face whatever she had to face.

When she got back to the waiting area, there was still nobody there to give her any news. Just a woman, sitting reading a book.

'Excuse me,' Kate asked her. 'Has anyone come out here to look for me in the last few minutes?'

The woman looked up with a smile. To her complete surprise, Kate saw it was the woman from her class. Nessa.

'You!' Kate said. 'What are you doing here?'

'Oh, I'm just waiting,' Nessa replied, still with that smile. 'Why don't you sit down, dear?'

Kate sat.

'Is someone you care for ill?' Nessa asked, and Kate nodded.

'My husband. He's had a heart attack.'

'I'm so sorry. That must be very worrying for you.'

Kate's lip trembled. 'Yes. And yet … and yet, in a funny sort of a way, I know that whatever happens, it's going to be all right. *We'll* be all right.' She placed a hand on her belly to indicate Bradley, and then much to her surprise, she found herself sharing her epiphany moment in the toilet with Nessa.

'It was almost as if I could see that I was in control

of how I react to all this,' she finished up. 'I mean, of course I want Geoff to pull through, more than anything in the world. But I don't have to be all panicky and out of control about it, because I know if the worst happens, I'll be all right. Me and Bradley, my baby, we'll manage. So I ... I suppose I'm choosing to be strong. I'm choosing, well, to believe.'

There was a short silence after she finished, and Kate gave a nervous laugh. 'I expect you think I'm either crazy or heartless,' she said, looking up.

But Nessa's smile was brighter than ever. She shook her head. 'Not at all. In fact, I think you've applied Corrinne Walker's wisdom to brilliant effect.'

Kate frowned. 'Corrinne Walker?' she said. 'Who's she?'

Nessa's smile seemed to falter slightly. 'Well, she's the author of *Staying in Neutral - Responses to Change Your Life.* The book I gave you.'

'Oh,' said Kate. 'I'm so sorry, but I accidentally left your book at work. So, I haven't had the chance to ...' She broke off, suddenly becoming aware of a wet sensation in the crotch of her maternity jeans. For a second she wondered whether she'd wet herself, but then, as the water kept coming, she knew exactly what it was.

'Shit,' she said, 'I think my waters have just broken.'

Thirty

Shelthorpe-on-Sea

Debbie closed her eyes tightly, imagining a huge full moon suspended above her head.

For a few months at university, she'd had a crush on a boy in the Astronomical Society. Week after week, she'd traipsed along to look through telescopes in the freezing cold until she'd discovered that the boy already had a girlfriend, and she'd dropped out of the group. But the close-up images of the moon had always stayed with her, and now she imagined every crater, picturing all that glowing, silvery light in a frosty winter sky.

'Deborah? Are you asleep?'

With an effort, Debbie ignored Rosemary's voice, busy visualising all that pooled silver light haloing onto the crown of her head, penetrating her mind as it made its way down her neck and into her veins.

Relaxed. She was relaxed.

'Do you think she's all right?'

With her eyes still closed, Debbie saw herself sitting at her computer. Adam's report was up on her screen, with every word highlighted. Her finger was raised. Slowly, it pressed down on the delete key, and the report disappeared.

Very carefully, taking her time, Debbie absorbed the feelings and reactions this visualised action gave her. Then, she mentally restored the report, and imagined herself taking a completely different action.

'Debbie!' Rosemary said again, but once more, Debbie ignored her, breathing deeply, keeping her posture upright and relaxed.

A hand came to rest on one of her shoulders, shaking her slightly. She ignored that too. Took another deep breath. Then, finally, she was ready. She opened her eyes and made a new Word document. Then she began to type.

After she was finished – and it didn't take long – Debbie sent two copies of the resignation letter she had typed to the printer. Then she shut her computer down and went to retrieve the sheets from the printer. Crossing to the pigeon holes by the photocopier, she placed one sheet in the pigeon hole marked HR, and the other in the pigeon hole labelled Adam Bailey, Deputy Principal.

Then she went back to her desk, retrieved her bag and turned to smile at Rosemary and Adam, who were both looking at her as if she'd lost her mind.

'Goodbye,' she said. And then she walked away, making sure to keep her pace slow and steady. In control.

Only when she reached the bottom of the staircase did she allow herself to speed up. It wasn't that she was afraid Adam would come after her; more that she didn't want to know whether he decided to come after her or not. She didn't know which would hurt the most, just as she didn't know what she was going to do next. It was as if her life was unfolding of its own accord, and she was allowing it to do just that.

But somehow it wasn't too much of a surprise when her car turned into the Cat Calls UK Rescue Centre. Or that Paul was out in the car park, almost as if he'd been expecting her to come.

'Hi,' he said. 'Shouldn't you be at work?'

'I just resigned,' she told him, and her voice began to tremble in sudden reaction to what she'd done.

Paul took her arm, leading her inside. 'Trouble?'

'Yes,' she said, answering a different question. 'My mother's gone missing.'

He stopped, looking down at her with concern. 'Janet's missing?'

She nodded. 'Yes,' she said, and explained what had happened.

He took her into the office and made them both a cup of tea. They sat together amongst the clutter, drinking it.

'So, I've decided to go to The Gambia to look for her, and I wondered if I could bring Brutus here for you to look after while I'm gone?'

To her surprise, he shook his head. 'No, I'm sorry, I won't be able to do that,' he said, but he was smiling, which made her feel confused.

'Oh,' she said, and he laughed.

'*I* won't be able to look after Brutus, but my relief manager will.'

'Your relief manager?' she repeated. 'Are you going somewhere?'

He laughed again, but this time his laugh had a rueful kind of a tone to it. 'Well, yes, apparently, I am, if you'll have me.'

'What?' She felt as if she were being stupid. As if she ought to understand what he meant. But she didn't. 'I'm not following you.'

Paul reached over to take her mug from her and set it down on the table. Then he took her hands lightly in his, the way she could imagine him holding a nervous animal, so as not to frighten it.

'This is going to sound completely strange,' he said, 'but I had a dream last night. A totally ridiculous, surreal dream. It started off with …' He broke off to laugh, sounding embarrassed. 'Well, there was this old man with a long white beard, and he was dressed in – of all things – a duck suit.'

'A duck suit?'

Paul shook his head. 'I know, right? Completely

wacko. It had this orange felt beak and everything. Anyway, there was this woman talking to him; a short white woman wearing brightly-coloured African clothes. She had the palest face of anyone I've ever seen, and, in my dream, I'm watching them, while they have their conversation. Then the old man nods and waddles away, and the woman, the one in the African outfit, she turns round to beckon to me. So, I go over to her. And she says, 'Tomorrow, someone will come to you; someone who needs your help. They might not ask for it, but they'll need it. You must help this person. Drop everything and go with them. Don't ask for anything in return, only know deep in your heart that this is the right thing to do.'

Debbie stared at him. Nessa. The woman he'd described had sounded a lot like Nessa.

Paul laughed, shaking his head. 'I told you it was crazy. I've never had a dream like it before.'

Hazily, Debbie shook her head. 'The duck outfit bit was crazy, perhaps,' she said.

He laughed. 'More than a bit! But anyway, I haven't finished. I mean, that's the end of the dream, but believe it or not, things get stranger. This morning, when I got in, there was an email from Head Office, telling me I was overdue annual leave. That they've arranged for a relief manager to arrive this afternoon – *this afternoon*, can you believe that? Well, I sat and read the email and I thought, what the hell are they playing at? But now, don't you see, with you turning up like this, it feels …' Again, he broke off, looking embarrassed.

'Meant?' Debbie said.

He smiled, nodding. 'Yes, exactly. So, what do you think? Shall we get on the internet and book two flights to The Gambia?' He saw her face. 'Don't worry, I'll put it on my credit card. You can repay me by cleaning out cat runs.' He looked at his watch. 'The relief manager should be here very soon.'

There was a knock on the office door. A woman waved at them through the glass. Paul got up to open it.

'Hi there,' the woman said. 'I'm Karen Watson. The relief manager? I can't wait to get started. Want to show me around before you go?'

Paul looked at Debbie. They both smiled.

'What?' asked Karen good-naturedly. 'Did I say something wrong?'

'No,' Paul said. 'The very opposite. Come on, I'll show you everything. And then you can help me get ready for a very special guest. Debbie's kitten Brutus is coming to stay.'

Thirty-One

Extract from Staying in Neutral, Responses to Change Your Life by Corrinne Walker.

So, you have a decision to make in your life. Maybe it's along the lines of which suit to wear to work, or whether to go to see a girlie film with your friend Rita, or an action movie with your new boyfriend.

Or perhaps it's on a different level entirely, like whether to ask your husband for a divorce, or if you should have a baby or not.

But whether it's a small thing like the film or a big thing like a baby, I've got news for you. It really doesn't matter.

What? I hear you cry. Divorce and babies don't matter! Are you crazy? The way I decide is going to affect the whole course of my life!

The thing is, if you believe that, then you're looking at the whole decision-making process the wrong way round. And who can blame you? From the very earliest age, we're trained to believe that we can only make good or bad decisions.

We don't tell a boy we've secretly admired for months we like him, and have to watch him smooching in Anita Nixon's arms all night at the school disco. Bad decision. We spend all our pocket money on binge-eating ice cream until we throw up. Bad decision.

What we've forgotten in these scenarios is the vital importance of learning from our so-called mistakes. Next time we like a boy, we're going to speak up. Next time we buy ice cream, we're going to eat just enough to keep it a treat.

The simple truth is, our decisions aren't as vital as we like to think they are.

If you don't have a baby, you'll be free to live an independent life, if that's what you want to do. If you do have a baby, you'll learn about a whole new nurturing side of yourself.

They're just different paths, with different good things along the way.

The more we can reduce the pressure from our decision-making processes the better. Trust your gut. It's almost always right.

Thirty-Two

The Gambia

If there was a baby, she would be connected to Scott for the rest of her life, the way she was connected to Ray because of Debbie. She would have to consult him about everything to do with their child. Consider his opinion. Accommodate him. Keep the peace. Make sure their child didn't do this, that or the other to annoy him. And didn't that sound familiar? Exactly like a repeat of her marriage to Ray.

Unless she didn't tell Scott about the baby?

But then how would she answer the child's questions about its father when they came? And what about earning an income after it was born? There was childcare, but that had to be paid for, and self-employment was notoriously unreliable. Would she be forced to get a proper job? If so, what? She wasn't qualified for anything but shop work, and that didn't pay much. Live on benefits then? Like a teenage mother but thirty years older? People would think she was the child's grandmother.

And Debbie. What would she think of having a brother or a sister who was twenty-four years younger than she was? She wasn't going to like it, that was for sure.

No.

This wasn't the only way to react to this situation. She'd finished Corrinne Walker's book, so she really ought to know better now. The situation – the event of her pregnancy – was neutral. She could choose how to react to it, and it didn't have to be with a feeling of doom and blind panic. What had the book said about decisions? They were just different paths, with different good things along the way.

So, what would be good about having a baby at the age of forty-four?

Well, it would be a new chance for her. A clean sheet. The baby would be someone to love; someone to love her. She could introduce it to the wonders of the world. The small, precious things, like the exquisite softness of moss growing on a wall, or the suck of wet sand underfoot as the tide goes out.

And she would be in sync with Kate; their babies would grow up together. How lovely. Janet smiled, imagining the four of them going on outings; sprawling on picnic blankets and eating delicious treats while the children splashed about in streams or played in the mud.

She could be a different kind of mother this time – the type who lets nothing stop her. Travelling the world with the baby strapped to her back, Gambian style. She could bring the baby to visit Fatu, so she could make sure the girl got an education. The baby could live an amazing, fearless life full of experiences it would never forget. It could bring her joy, instead of worry, and she could encourage it to fly instead of constantly urging it to be careful. Together, they could take on the world. She could learn from all the mistakes she had made bringing up Debbie, and make sure she made none of them again, this time around.

Yes. If that was the path she had to follow, then it would be all right. And in the meantime, since there appeared to be no way to get away from the village, she would stay calm and wait to see what happened. Which, for the moment at least, seemed to be pretty much all there was to do. If she was pregnant, her body would soon offer its own proof.

As for Nessa, she would either return soon or she would not. If she didn't, then Janet would need, at some point, to take some action. But for now, she would keep herself busy as she had been doing, and wait and see.

It was, in fact, quite a busy, if simple life, helping Fatu and Sukai with the baby and with domestic chores. Making more batiks. Talking to David while keeping him at arm's length. And, one night, gazing up at the myriad of stars before going inside to bed, Janet realised that she was, actually, pretty content. The people here were so poor, and yet, for the most part, they were happy. Perhaps there was freedom in not knowing what else life could contain, and in being pleased with simple things. And she knew, as she watched David laughing with his father and the other men from the village, that as much as he thought he wanted to leave this place to make a new life in another country, he would lose so very much were he ever to do so.

And then, one morning, as Janet held the baby while his mother cooked, she saw a cloud of dust on the horizon, getting closer and closer. Was it Nessa at last?

Thirty-Three

The Gambia

Paul had been so confident as they travelled to The Gambia. Dressed in a pale blue shirt and khaki cargo trousers, he even looked different to usual, and, as he effortlessly negotiated their way around Gatwick Airport, Debbie knew she was seeing the man who had been an executive in London.

'What?' he asked, becoming aware of her scrutiny as they waited at the departure gate.

'I'm so glad you're here with me, that's all.'

He smiled. 'Don't underestimate yourself. You'd have been fine on your own.'

'Well, I'm glad I'm not.' So much had happened in the last few hours, Debbie felt as if she were floating somehow. Nothing seemed quite real, as if she were here and not here at the same time, inside a waking dream. The reality that she'd broken up with Adam was somehow just out of reach, inside a bubble that would surely pop at any moment, sending shards of lethal pain showering down on her.

'When we arrive, I suggest we book into the same hotel your mum was staying at and take it from there. The staff are bound to remember a wedding that didn't take place as planned.'

They did. They also remembered that Janet had befriended something of a local celebrity; a woman they called Binta, whom everyone seemed to love. And that Binta had been bound for a village Upriver, by means of the ferry. Debbie and Paul duly went to the landing station used by the ferry, and when they questioned the staff, and showed them Janet's photograph, they received confirmation that Janet had indeed travelled on the ferry with Binta a few weeks previously. And that she had been badly travel sick.

'That definitely sounds like Mum,' Debbie said, feeling hopeful and somewhat reassured by what they'd found out.

Paul asked further questions, and soon they were in possession of the name of the person Binta had hired to drive them on from where the ferry had docked.

And now, five hours later, after a slow journey on the ferry and a bumpy ride across country, they were just arriving in the village.

'Well,' Paul said. 'I think this is it.'

'I hope she's here.' Debbie felt suddenly nervous that the information they'd been given could be wrong.

'We'll soon find out.'

'Yes.' She opened the car door and saw a gang of children running towards them, shouting excitedly.

'We seem to have caused quite a stir,' Paul said, joining her by the side of the car.

'Hello,' Debbie greeted the children. 'I'm Debbie, and this is Paul. We're looking for my mother, Janet.' But suddenly Paul nudged her arm, and she broke off to look in the direction he was pointing. To where a white woman was standing cradling a baby.

'Mum!' she called, her voice catching on a sob. 'Mum!' And, accompanied by the excited children, she began to run.

Thirty-Four

Shelthorpe-on-Sea

The doctor straightened from her internal examination. 'You're about four centimetres dilated, Mrs Bramling.'

'Is that good? Shouldn't I be feeling any pain yet?'

The doctor scanned her notes, then looked up and smiled. 'I see your baby is due in four weeks?'

Numb with fear, Kate nodded. 'Yes. It's too early, isn't it?'

'It is a little early, but we're fully equipped to deal with this kind of thing. The biggest danger once the waters have broken is infection, so if things don't start happening soon, we'll induce your labour. For now, if you feel like it, it might help to move around.'

'We can go for a walk, if you like,' Nessa suggested.

Kate wasn't at all sure how Nessa had ended up in the examination room with her. Presumably the staff thought she was a relative or a friend. But somehow Kate didn't mind her being there. It was very good not to be on her own.

'That sounds like an excellent idea.' The doctor

smiled, and went on her way.

'D'you need some help to get up?' Nessa asked, but Kate shook her head.

'No, I'm all right.'

'Come along then. We can walk up and down the corridor.'

But the corridor wasn't the destination Kate had in mind. 'I've got to see Geoff,' she told Nessa as soon as they were alone. 'To make sure he's all right. Will you help me?'

'Of course,' Nessa agreed, and Kate smiled gratefully.

'Can you remember the way?' She couldn't remember much herself; three shocks in a row – Geoff's heart attack, meeting Ian in the corridor and her waters breaking – seemed to have addled her brain.

'Yes, I remember. We're on the right floor. The Maternity Unit and the Coronary Care Unit are just on different wings.'

A wing for life to start, and a wing for life to end, separated by a long corridor. Only Geoff wasn't going to die. He couldn't.

Nessa pressed the button to open the ward doors, and waited for Kate to move through. 'Are you all right?'

She nodded. 'Yes, I'm fine,' she said, even though a pain like a period pain had started up in her lower back, and she had to pause for a moment to rock her body from side-to-side to ease it.

'Are you sure?'

'Yes.' Kate stopped rocking and began to move forward, but as she did so, the pain in her back suddenly intensified, as if somebody had quickly attached a vice to her. She couldn't help gasping out loud.

'Come on, dear, we'll have to go back again,' Nessa said, but Kate shook her head.

'No, I've got to see Geoff.' But the pain wasn't showing any sign of going away, and secretly, she suspected Nessa was right. She wasn't giving up yet though.

'It will be all right,' Nessa reassured her. 'You'll see. And once you're settled in the delivery suite, I can go and see if there's any news about your husband.'

'I want to see him,' Kate insisted stubbornly, but before she could move forward, she was struck by a pain so intense she cried out, gripping Nessa's shoulders hard, her head slumping forward as she gritted her teeth.

Nessa held her. 'Ready to go back now?' she asked gently, and as soon as the pain had subsided a little, Kate nodded, feeling like a failure, her clothes drenched with sweat.

'You win,' she said, and they turned back towards the ward.

A little later, in the delivery room, Kate got into a warm bath. The midwife had suggested it would relax her and ease the pain a little, and had promised she would try to find some news about Geoff. Nessa was still there with her, and somehow, goodness knows why, it didn't seem strange to have her there. On the contrary, it felt good.

'Have you ever had a baby, Nessa?'

'Sadly, no. I would have liked to, but it never happened. But then lots of adopted children passed through my life, so that made me more fortunate than some, I suppose.'

Kate closed her eyes, wondering if anything ever rattled Nessa. She had to be about the calmest person she'd ever met. Another contraction was on its way, making her wish with all her heart that Geoff were there with her. He'd be inadequate. He'd inevitably say the wrong thing and make her shout at him. Get in everyone's way and sob his heart out when the baby was born. Be generally larger than life the way he always was.

Oh, please, let him be okay. Please.

'Try not to be sad, Kate,' Nessa said. 'For Bradley. I know it's hard, but try to choose hope.'

Choose hope … The pain came, the vice squeezing her front and back this time, giving a little twist for good measure. *Choose hope. Choose hope.* Kate repeated the words like a mantra in her mind until the pain passed, and then she sat up in the bath panting and exhausted.

Until Nessa spoke four words that had her eyes

flying open. 'Kate, look who's here.'

Wearily, she looked up, her heart pounding. 'Geoff!'

He was in a wheelchair, pushed by a nurse, and his face looked grey. But he was here, and he was alive.

'Katie,' he said. 'Sorry I missed the first act. Came for the final one though … '

When Kate burst into noisy sobs, the nurse pushed Geoff's chair closer so he could take her hand. 'It's all right. Shh, love. It's all right. Turns out it wasn't a heart attack at all.'

She looked up. 'It … it wasn't?'

'No. It's cos … cos something.'

'Costochondritis,' said the nurse.

'Yeah,' said Geoff. 'That's the one. Something to do with my ribs.'

'It's a condition that causes inflammation of the cartilage connecting the ribs to the sternum, or breast bone,' the nurse continued. 'While it's an extremely painful and unpleasant condition, it's not life-threatening.'

Turned out she'd been right to choose hope then. 'Oh, Geoff,' she sobbed, the floodgates opening, 'that's so good.' And she reached out clumsily to hold him, causing him to cry out with pain.

'Sorry, sorry!' Instantly she moved back again, smiling at him through her tears, but then another contraction arrived, and it was her turn to scream.

'Bloody hell, Katie,' Geoff said, after the contraction had eased off. 'Are you all right?'

She lay there panting, her hand in his. 'Not really. Got to get out of this bath; the water's gone stone cold. Where's Nessa?'

Geoff shook his head. 'Nessa? Who's she? The midwife?'

'No, she's …' But Kate broke off, realising it would sound too daft to try to explain why one of her catering students had attended the early part of her labour. 'Don't worry,' she said. 'It doesn't matter. Besides, you're here now.'

He grabbed her hand and kissed it. 'Now and forever. Just so long as you don't grab my ribs again.'

Thirty-Five

The Gambia

Debbie was here. Had come out to Africa deliberately to find her. It was so thrilling the tips of Janet's fingers were tingling. If it weren't for the secret about the baby she would have been absolutely over the moon with joy. It felt so wrong to keep her possible pregnancy a secret after her daughter had gone to all this trouble to track her down, but it would be even more wrong to foist the news of it on her before it was definitely confirmed.

'We thought it might be difficult to track you down, but they particularly remembered you because you were travelling with … Binta, was it? Everybody seems to know her. Is she here?'

Nessa. 'No, she's away at the moment. I'm not sure when she'll be back.'

Janet noticed her daughter's gaze drifting over to

where Paul stood at the edge of the compound. He was laughing at something David had just said to him, his head thrown back, his expression relaxed. What a nice man he was. Attractive too.

'Are you and Paul …?' she asked, and Debbie flushed.

'Mum,' she complained, as she'd done as a teenager when Janet had tried to find out about her love life.

'Sorry, none of my business.'

'I've moved into the flat above your shop, actually. That's how we met. It was Estelle's idea.'

'And it was a good idea too. It will be nice for you to have a place of your own.' Janet smiled, remembering how she had had the same idea herself. Then her gaze moved on to the Land Rover, her passage to Banjul and a pregnancy test. If only she could grab her stuff right now and insist they get going, but that would be rude. Debbie and Paul had only just arrived after a tiring journey. And besides, she'd been living here for several weeks now, and had become almost a part of the family. She couldn't take off without tying up loose ends, and certainly not without speaking to Fatu to make sure they could keep in touch with each other.

'Let me show you around the village,' she said brightly, and Debbie smiled.

'Thanks, I'd like that.'

Janet took her arm. 'Well, this is the outdoor kitchen, and mostly Sukai's realm.'

Sukai, with the newborn baby strapped to her back, was busy stirring a fragrant-smelling cooking pot. She looked up, her smile broad. 'Janet, your daughter, she is so beautiful. She look just like you.'

'Ah, Sukai,' Janet smiled. 'Thank you. I don't know about me, but you're right about Debbie. She is beautiful. Just as Fatu is. I wanted to introduce them actually, but she's vanished. D'you know where she is?'

'I do not, Janet. But I think that she gives you some space now that your daughter is here. I think that she doesn't want to get in the way.'

'I see,' said Janet, and felt sad, knowing that Sukai was probably right. 'Oh well, I'm sure we'll find her as we walk around.'

They moved on, and Janet told Debbie about the difficulty Fatu and the other girls had getting an education in rural Gambia.

'You should sponsor her, Mum,' Debbie told her simply, and Janet stopped to stare at her.

'You wouldn't mind?'

Debbie frowned, shaking her head. 'Of course not. Why would I?'

As simple as that. Janet smiled, wondering whether perhaps she made a habit of over-complicating things, and suddenly she spotted Fatu peeping out at them from behind the bath screen and called to her, filled with a sudden surge of love. 'Fatu! Come here and meet my other favourite girl.'

As Fatu came shyly forward, Janet suddenly knew everything would be all right if she did turn out to be pregnant. There wasn't a limit on love, after all. Her heart would expand, as it had expanded to encompass Fatu. She could love Debbie, Fatu and the baby equally, and all would be well.

'Fatu, this is Debbie, my daughter. I want to show her everything in the village. Will you come with us?'

'Yes, I will come.' Fatu smiled, taking the hand Janet proffered, and together the three of them left the family compound to walk down the red dirt path, the sound of the men's laughter following them on the breeze.

Thirty-Six

The Gambia

Debbie was impressed. In a few short weeks, her mother had obviously made herself completely at home in this village and with these people.

As they walked along and Janet showed her this and that, people waved and called out friendly greetings. And Fatu was glued to her side, clutching Janet's hand. Afraid she was going to lose her maybe? Poor girl; Debbie could certainly empathise with that feeling, after the last few days.

'I ought to have let you know straight away that I wasn't going to marry Scott,' Janet said now. 'I'm so sorry to have caused you all this worry.' Her mother's tone was slightly placating; the one she often used when she spoke to her. Debbie could feel it having its usual effect of irritation. No, she didn't want that. It was time for things to change between them.

'It's not your fault you lost your phone, is it? And if Scott hadn't turned up the way he did, I wouldn't even have thought about it.' She smiled cheekily. 'Not until you'd been gone for six months or so, anyway. Then I might have started to wonder.'

Janet laughed. 'Oh, you don't know how good it is to see you,' she said. 'And I can't wait to show you the material I've printed. I've been learning how to do batik, while I've been here. I really enjoy it. Actually, I was thinking I might be able to set up a bit of a business connected to it, importing some of the local fabrics to the UK. You should see them, Debbie. They're exquisite.'

'That sounds like a great idea, Mum. Exciting. And by the way, Kate and I found your fabric collection the other week. You know, all those offcuts you'd never throw away? Kate came round to help me sort through some of Gran's things, and there they all were. Did you know it was all at the flat?'

Janet's eyes had lit up. 'No, I had no idea where it had gone. Oh, thank you! That's wonderful. I'd have been so sad if it had been lost.'

Debbie smiled, happy to have brought her mother so much pleasure so simply. 'Oh, and another thing,' she said. 'Someone called John George called into the shop asking for you?'

'Did he?' Now Janet's face had gone bright red. 'Well, well. Good old John. I was only thinking about him the other day. Is he okay?'

'I don't know, I wasn't there at the time. Sheila, the lady who works at the shop took a message. I think she might have told him you'd just got married.'

'Oh, did she?'

Debbie nodded. 'You'll have to look him up when we get home. Put him right about things.'

'Yes.' Janet's face seemed to look strained suddenly. 'Darling,' she said, 'did you find out the times of the ferries back to Banjul when you came here? Only there's something urgent I have to do. Actually, I'd like to leave as soon as possible, if that's okay with you and Paul? Oh, don't worry Fatu. I'll be back, very soon. And I'll make sure you get that bike you were promised very soon.' Debbie saw her squeeze Fatu's hand.

'Paul wrote the boat times down,' she said, wondering what could be so urgent. Her mother seemed suddenly almost feverish in her haste to be gone.

'Can we go and ask him? See if it's at all possible to get back to Banjul today?'

'Of course.'

With the village tour apparently over, they turned round to make their way over to where the group of men were still chatting and laughing. Paul, Debbie thought, looked entirely at ease; a part of the group, fitting in easily.

For a moment, she tried to imagine Adam in his place, but couldn't quite do it. The group dynamics would be completely different. Adam would still be talking and laughing with everyone, but it would be more like he was holding court. And he certainly wouldn't have found a dusty-coated tabby cat from somewhere to stroke.

Debbie was still smiling at the stripy brown cat weaving around Paul's legs when her phone began to ring in the depths of her bag, its shrill, insistent sound silencing everyone.

'Sorry,' she said, searching for it frantically, aware of David and his father saying something to each other.

Then Janet said, 'I don't understand, Debbie. How is your phone ringing? There's no mobile reception out here. Absolutely none at all.'

Finally, Debbie's fingers found the phone and pulled it out. 'I don't know,' she said, looking at the caller ID before she pressed accept. 'But it's Kate. Hi, Kate. Yes, I'm in Africa, with Mum. Yes, she's fine.'

Debbie smiled at Janet, then listened for a while, her smile growing by the second. 'Mum,' she said, 'Kate's had the baby! Bradley's arrived!'

Thirty-Seven

The Gambia

Debbie and Paul were drinking cocktails on the veranda of the hotel bar. For the first time since hearing the news from Scott about her mother going missing, Debbie felt relaxed. It had been an exhausting twenty-four hours. Almost as if life had speeded up after a long period of being on a go-slow.

'Thank you for coming with me,' she said, smiling at the man seated opposite her.

'My pleasure. I'm only disappointed it's been such a whistle-stop tour. I'd have been quite happy to stay in that village for a few days, and really experience their culture.'

'Me too. But Mum really wanted to get away, didn't she? I wonder what she wanted to buy so urgently in town?'

'I can't imagine. I think that boy was sorry to see her go, don't you?'

'David? Yes, he did seem a bit down about it. You don't suppose he wanted to have a relationship with Mum?'

Paul smiled. 'If he did, it looked to me as if she put him right. Oh, isn't that Janet now?'

'Where?' Debbie looked over, and was in time to see Janet half running past the entrance to the bar. 'Mum!' she called out, but Janet didn't seem to hear her. 'That's funny. Maybe I ought to go to her. Check she's all right.'

She was already half out of her seat, but Paul reached out a hand to detain her.

'I should wait a bit,' he said. 'She looked as if she needed a moment to herself, for whatever reason.'

Debbie was extremely aware of the warmth of Paul's hand on hers, and was disappointed when he removed it to pick up his drink. 'Perhaps you're right,' she said, picking up her own glass and savouring the blend of tastes on her tongue. How surreal it was to be here in such luxury after the basic nature of the village. And if it felt like that for her, what must it feel like for her mother after having stayed in the village for several weeks? Perhaps she'd just gone to buy herself some bubble bath.

'And how about you?' Paul asked her. 'How are you feeling?'

Debbie's gaze dropped. After that inexplicable but

joyous phone call from Kate in the village, her phone had gone silent again. Until they'd arrived in Banjul that is, whereupon it had exploded into bleeping life, signalling a plethora of messages in her inbox. All of them from Adam. Begging messages, promising her the world. She'd read the first two, then deleted the rest of them unread and switched her phone off.

'I'm all right,' she said, feeling embarrassed and ashamed. 'Looking forward to a new start when I get home.'

But Paul wasn't really listening. Once again, he was looking towards the doorway. 'It's your mum,' he said, getting to his feet. 'She looks a bit … Janet, are you all right?'

Debbie turned to see Janet walking towards them, still dressed in the African outfit she'd worn to travel in. She looked strange; as if she'd had a shock or something. 'Mum?' she said, getting to her feet. 'Are you all right?'

It wasn't until Janet sniffed that Debbie realised she had tears in her eyes. 'Mum?' she said again, going over to her. 'What's wrong?'

'Nothing,' Janet said, shaking her head and blowing her nose. 'I was just thinking, that's all. Remember when you were a little girl, and I … I used to show you the moss growing on walls when we were walking along? We'd always stop to stroke it because it was so soft.' She laughed shakily. 'Took us an age to get anywhere.'

'Yes, I remember,' said Debbie, smiling slightly at the memory, mystified as to why Janet was bringing this up now. 'I still it do it all the time. But, Mum, why are you so upset?'

'I don't know,' Janet said, making an attempt at a smile and reaching up to wipe her eyes. 'Because when you think about it, there's absolutely no reason to be upset is there? You're here. You came out here for me. And I'll never have to see Scott again if I don't want to. Never have to consider his opinion. Or accommodate him. Or try to keep the peace. It's ... it's wonderful really, isn't it?' And she burst into noisy tears.

Thirty-Eight

Time seemed to have stopped. Corrinne had no idea how long it was since Nessa had left. She was beginning to lose hope that she would ever move on from limbo.

Why had she ever bothered to try to help people anyway? Maybe she ought to have been a cleaner instead of a therapist. Yes, if she'd known about having to go through this crap when you died, that's what she would have been. Unless there was another purgatory somewhere for all the cleaners who'd cut corners during their working lives. If there were such a place, then a few of the cleaners Corrinne had employed herself would be in there for sure. Especially Elsie, who had never hoovered around the skirting boards.

But then, what did clean carpet edges matter in the scheme of things? A lifetime of trying to look good, to outdo the neighbours, or to get on the best-seller lists. It was all a useless waste of time, and Corrinne wished there was some way of communicating that truth to the people who were still alive. The people who still had the chance to live their lives differently.

The door opened, and she looked up, suddenly filled with hope. 'Nessa?'

But it wasn't Nessa, it was a man, who looked to be in his late twenties, with sandy-coloured hair and a moustache. A man who looked exactly like her father had looked at that age.

Corrinne put a hand up to her mouth, feeling as if someone had punched her in the stomach. 'You look exactly like my dad,' she said weakly.

The man smiled. 'I do hope he was considered to be handsome.'

Tears were streaming down Corrinne's face. 'Oh, yes,' she sniffed. 'Very.'

The man looked concerned. 'I'm sorry. Does my being here upset you?'

She quickly wiped her eyes on the edge of the duvet, pulling herself together. 'Oh, no. Please don't go. You can't imagine how nice it is to see another person. I've been going crazy in here, waiting.'

He sat down on the edge of her bed. 'Your representative is out there gathering evidence, is she?'

'Yes, that's right. I suppose you're waiting too? What was the focus of your work?'

He thought about it for a moment. 'Peace and love, I suppose. But somehow, wherever I went in the world, wars seemed to break out.'

Had he been some sort of news reporter? She didn't like to ask. 'Oh, my goodness. How awful.'

'Sometimes our life's purpose can feel like a bit of a lost cause, can't it?'

She nodded, gazing into his grey eyes. Eyes that somehow told her how much he'd suffered. It was selfishly reassuring to know she wasn't the only one. 'Yes,' she said. 'It can feel like that.'

There was a pause. Corrinne continued to look at him, hungry to absorb his similarity to the man she'd adored; the man who'd left her life so young. He was smiling gently back at her, not seeming at all bothered by her scrutiny, and it was comforting to bask in the remembered feelings of being securely and unconditionally loved.

'Your work was about responding to events, I believe?' he said, his smile deepening when she looked surprised. 'My apologies. I overheard your representative talking about you. Nessa, isn't it? I only listened in because it sounded interesting.'

'It's nice of you to say so.' Corrinne sighed. 'I felt passionate about my work once, I suppose. Before my life fell apart. Then I forgot about everything I believed in and went crazy.'

He nodded, as if he understood. 'Would you do things differently then, if you had your time over again?'

Would she? 'Oh, yes,' she said with feeling. 'Definitely.'

'How?'

Corrinne plucked at the duvet, suddenly vulnerable.

'I'm sure you don't really want to hear about my stuff.'

He shrugged, and she imagined him on earth suddenly; in a country pub with a pint of bitter, a trace of beer foam lingering on his moustache. 'I don't mind at all, if you'd like to tell me about it. I understand you had a phone call? An anonymous woman telling you that your husband had a secret life? A second family?'

It still hurt now, almost as much as then. 'Yes. Yes, that's right. I went … well, I went ballistic. Completely off the rails. Which probably nobody could blame me for.'

'Except that you'd made your living from encouraging women to believe that everything that happens – each event – is neutral, and that we can choose how we react?'

He seemed to know so much. He must have been hidden away somewhere for ages while he listened in on Nessa's conversation.

'Yes.'

He nodded, as if he understood. 'And, if you did have the chance to replay it all and to make different choices? What would you do?'

'Oh, well, then …' Corrinne closed her eyes, trying to imagine it. She saw herself put the phone down on the coffee table when the anonymous call ended. Sit down on the sofa – the sofa her husband had insisted they buy, and which she had never found comfortable, being, as she was, prone to a bad back.

She saw the vulgar over-sized television and a pair

of his smelly trainers over in one corner. Listened to the birds through the open window, which was only open because her husband – who viewed fresh air as something to be avoided at all costs – was out.

'I'd take my time, before I reacted,' she said. 'I'd take a series of deep, calming breaths. Then I'd imagine what my highest response to the situation could be. And after I'd done that, I'd go into the kitchen, to the fridge. I'd take out the magnum of champagne my husband had put in there ready to celebrate a big business deal he expected to go through at the end of the week, and I'd pop it open. Pour myself a glass. Giggle as the bubbles went up my nose.'

Corrinne smiled to herself, almost able to feel the sensation of the bubbles, taste the deliciously-expensive liquid in her mouth.

'Then … I'd go out to a pet shop, and buy myself the puppy I always wanted. A golden retriever with big brown eyes. And all the stuff for him – a bed, a lead, some toys and little coats. Then we'd go home and play together for ages.' She laughed, feeling the softness and warmth of the puppy's squirming little body in her hands. His needle-sharp teeth, and the wetness of his tongue as he licked her ear.

'And then?'

'And then, when the puppy fell asleep, I'd fire up my laptop and I'd book a long stay in a cosy cottage on the Cornish coast. We'd drive down there, the puppy and me, and I'd light fires in the evening and sleep with the window open so I could hear the sea. I ... I'd start living again.'

When she opened her eyes, he was smiling at her, and something about the combination of his smile and her visions filled her with a profound contentment. It was true, she hadn't always lived by the words she had written in *Staying in Neutral - Responses to Change Your Life*, but they were helpful words nevertheless. Her life hadn't been a waste of time. Whatever conclusion God came to.

'It sounds idyllic.'

She sighed. 'Doesn't it?'

'Describe it to me some more. All the little details.'

So she did, but somehow she must have fallen asleep while she was talking, because when she next opened her eyes, the light in the room had changed, and the man was gone.

Had she dreamt the whole thing?

'Hello, Corrinne,' a woman's voice said, and Corrinne sat up to see Nessa seated in a wicker chair, facing her.

'Nessa! You're back.'

Nessa smiled. 'Yes, as you see.' Corrinne thought Nessa looked healthier somehow, which was probably impossible, since she was dead.

'How did it go? Was your mission successful? Did you manage to convince them all?'

'Two out of the three women – Janet and Debbie – really benefited from your book.'

Corrinne's face fell. 'Only two?'

Nessa nodded. 'Yes, but the third woman, Kate, came round to your way of thinking by herself, almost entirely without your help.'

'Oh,' said Corrinne. 'D'you think that counts?'

Nessa got up and came to take Corrinne's hand, her smile glowing as much as the evening sunshine, which was drifting into the room from the high window. Far from recoiling as she might have done a few weeks ago, Corrinne found she relished the touch of another human being … or whatever Nessa was now that she was dead.

'I'm reasonably confident I can persuade God that it does, yes. Especially after your chat with him this afternoon.'

'My chat …?' Corrinne's hands flew to her mouth. 'You don't mean …? You aren't telling me that man was …?'

'God, yes.'

'But he looked exactly like …' Corrinne broke off as everything snapped together inside her head.

'Your father, when you were young. A man you worshipped.'

'Yes, I did worship him,' Corrinne said, her mind busy replaying what she had said about champagne, puppies and cottages in Cornwall.

Nessa squeezed her hand. 'Sweetie, the important thing is that the theories in your book work. They really do, you know. I've seen it with my own eyes. And, well, I only wish I'd read your book before I died.'

Corrinne looked at her. 'Do you?'

Nessa nodded. 'Yes. You see, I drowned. I used to love swimming in the sea, but that day the current took me, and it was just too strong for me to get back to the shore. There I was, struggling to stay afloat, with nobody around, and nothing to hold onto, and I knew I could only tread water for a short amount of time. That I had two minutes at the best before I died. And Corrinne, if I'd been able to view my approaching death as a neutral event, it would have helped me so very much. I wouldn't have panicked and cried. I wouldn't have regretted that I'd never had children or that I stole money from my brother's piggy bank when I was four years old, or all the other horrible things that flashed before my eyes in those last few moments. I would have known that all those events were neutral, and that I could choose to be accepting of what was about to come. To be grateful for all the times the sun had shone on my back or I'd seen a beautiful flower. For my wonderfully loving Gambian family.'

Corrinne's eyes were filled with tears. 'Really?'

Nessa squeezed her hand again. 'Yes,' she said, 'really.' She looked sad again. 'As it was, they never even knew I'd died, my Gambian friends. It has been so lovely to see them again, and I'm confident now that I've introduced Janet to them that they'll be all right. I'm very grateful to have had the chance to reassure myself. Yes, everything's turned out very well.' She stood up.

'Where are you going?'

Nessa smiled. 'It's time for my audience with God. You'll know his decision very soon, Corrinne dear.' And, with one final glowing smile, Nessa vanished.

Corrinne was flying. She could feel her face pushing through the breeze, her nightdress shaping her body with the forward force, her hair streaming behind her. She smiled, spreading her arms out to fully embrace the wonderful feeling, but when she looked again, curious to see where she was, she could see neither her arms nor her hands. In fact, she could see nothing of her body at all.

Was she gone then? Just spirit? Moving on from limbo? If so, then surely this must be a good thing? It felt like it. Except she had no idea where she was going, and it didn't feel as if she were controlling her direction of travel herself.

In the distance, a silver streak of the sea was visible on the horizon, and a huddled little red-brick town. Quickly, it grew closer. Was she speeding up? Yes, definitely. But oddly, as she swooped down and along an unfamiliar car-filled street, Corrinne didn't feel scared. Not even when she headed straight towards the window of a shop, *Janet's Dreams.* Suddenly, she was inside, hovering somewhere just below the ceiling, observing two women below – one older than the other, but with enough similarity for Corrinne to guess that they were mother and daughter. Everywhere, around them, the shop interior was filled with batiks, brightly-coloured fabrics and African carvings and pictures. The two women were bent over a piece of paper, their heads close together. Corrinne moved in closer and saw that it was a letter. One of the women – the older of the two – was reading out loud from it.

'Thank you so much for my bicycle. I love it. It only takes me forty-five minutes to get to school now, and in the afternoons, when I get back, I can help Mama as usual. I am learning so many new things. There is a book at school all about oceans. When I grow up, I think I want to be a marine biologist...'

Corrinne watched the older woman pause from her reading to smile at the younger one.

The younger woman returned the smile. 'I must phone Paul to tell him the bike's arrived,' she said. 'He'll be so happy.'

'He will,' the older one agreed. 'Oh, look, there's a letter from David too.' She bent her head, perusing the letter's contents. 'He's asking if we could sell hand-woven baskets in here. Look, he's sent a photo. I think we could, don't you? They're lovely.'

The younger woman took the photograph and looked at it. 'Oh, yes, definitely. They'd make excellent linen baskets. He's got a good eye.'

The older woman laughed. 'Even better now it's turned strictly towards business.'

'Come on, Mum,' said the younger woman. 'You

can't tell me you were never tempted.'

The older woman smiled. 'Ah, well...' she said, but Corrinne didn't hear the rest of her sentence because some force was pulling her back out of the building, out into the street again, then up, up, across the roof tops to a small, prettily-designed park.

A couple were coming down the hill to the park entrance; a rather well-built couple with a young baby in a buggy. Corrinne watched them negotiate the buggy through the park gate, and wheel it towards the pond, where a group of ducks immediately woke from their slumbers on the bank to approach them.

The man reached into the buggy to undo the clips and scooped the baby out, positioning him in his arms so that he would be able to see the ducks. 'Can you see the quack quacks, Bradley?' he said in a soppy voice. 'I think they're hungry.'

'They wouldn't be hungry, if Daddy hadn't forgotten to bring the bread, would they, Bradley?' the woman said, pulling the baby's blue hat further down over his ears.

'Bread isn't good for them anyway.'

The woman began to laugh, then suddenly stopped. 'Blimey, Geoff,' she said. 'Look who's just coming into the park.'

Corrinne glanced over towards the park entrance and saw another couple with a buggy entering through the park gates.

'Want to scarper quick?' asked the man called

Geoff. 'Pretend we haven't seen them?' And he put the baby back into the buggy and quickly tucked a fleecy blanket around him.

The woman sighed and shook her head. 'No, let's get it over with. We're bound to keep meeting them, living here, going to kids' places. If we speak to them now, we never have to do it again if we don't want to, do we?'

'All right. If you're sure.'

Another sigh. 'As sure as I'll ever be.'

The couple made their way slowly over. Corrinne followed. The newcomers, who had stopped to do something for their baby, hadn't seen them yet. When the woman spoke, they both looked up, startled.

'Hello, Ian.'

'Kate!'

There was a pause, as they all observed each other. Then Kate said, 'I'm glad she pulled through.' And Corrinne saw her nod towards their buggy, then deliberately turn her head towards the other woman. 'You too.'

The woman's face flushed bright red. 'Oh, thank you. And many congratulations on your birth too!' she gushed. 'He's beautiful. Did you have a hard time, or was everything straight forward for you?'

'Thanks,' Kate said briefly. 'It was fine. We must be off now. Just wanted to … you know. Anyway, bye.' She nodded to her husband, and they walked on towards the park exit.

'Well,' said the woman with the red face, standing looking after them. 'I never thought …' But Corrinne didn't get to hear what the woman had never thought, because she was being sucked upwards again, away from the park, and found herself travelling – at great speed this time – over land and trees, roads and towns.

A minute later, she recognised some of the landmarks of London – the Olympic stadium, the Gherkin and the Shard – but before she could properly register it all, she was descending again, entering a large building through the automatic doors and swooping on, along a corridor to a meeting room, where dozens of women were gathered. Here, for the first time, as she descended, Corrinne felt the floor beneath her feet. There was an empty chair next to her, and she sat down on it and turned towards the front. And saw that the speaker was her daughter, Verity. Not only that, but behind her, on a huge banner, was Corrinne's own picture, next to an image of her book, with the words, *Staying in Neutral - Responses to Change Your Life.* Over five million copies sold.

Goodness. What was this?

Verity was speaking. 'Welcome to today's seminar. It's my absolute honour and privilege to be here with you, sharing the work of my late mother. Many thousands of women have had their lives transformed by her wisdom, and my only regret was that she didn't live long enough to see what a huge difference she made to people.'

Oh. Oh ... Oh! Corrinne screwed her eyes tight shut in an effort to contain the mass of pure joy her daughter's words had brought her; to stop herself from running screaming to the front to wrap her arms around her and to sob and blub her very heart out. She had never thought her children were in the least bit impressed by her work, but here was undeniable proof that this wasn't the case.

Try as Corrinne might, the intense joy refused to stay stuffed inside of her. Too big to be contained, it erupted from her to fill the entire room with a golden, shimmering light. And Corrine laughed until she was light and the light was joy. Forever.

Author's Note

My heartfelt thanks go to Heather Donaldson, Bev Sayles and Sarah Van Haght, who were all so very generous with their time and information, helping to bring The Gambia and its people vividly to life for me. Any mistakes or uses of poetic licence are entirely my responsibility.

Thanks also go to Jenny Eaton and the EOS Programme, without which, Corrinne Walker and her teachings would not exist. Caroline Mayers and Victoria and Chris Penrose all helped to jog my memory about antenatal classes – thank you so much.

And as always, I have to thank my trusted beta readers and others who have given me such useful feedback, support and encouragement about earlier drafts of this book – Ann Warner, Juli Townsend, Wendy Janes, Laura J Novak and the members of the Women's Fiction Critique Group.

Finally, much love and thanks go to all my family and friends who put up with me shutting myself away to write and who listen to me when I go on about my writing.

Also by Margaret K Johnson

The Goddess Workshop

Four very different women have one thing in common – and they're determined to put it right!

When Janet, Kate, Estelle and Reenie sign up for a workshop at the village hall promising women a 'garden of earthly delights,' not all of them know exactly what they've signed up for. And when they discover that a giant reproduction from the Kama Sutra has replaced the usual portrait of the Queen, more than one of them contemplates doing a runner before it's too late.

Jade Gate, their mysterious and charismatic workshop leader, wants to sweep them into the adventure of their lives. But can they trust her? And can they overcome their personal struggles for long enough to become the happy, sensual beings they deserve to be?

The Goddess Workshop comes before this book, *Perfect Responses*, but both books are standalone reads.

Margaret K JOHNSON

THE GODDESS WORKSHOP

ARE YOU READY
FOR AN ADULT
EDUCATION?

The Dare Club

Aleysha, Nick, Colette and Emma are on a mission to scare themselves into for-getting their problems. But will it work?

When four very different people meet at a Lift Up course for the newly divorced or separated, there are initial tensions. Aleysha hasn't accepted the fact that her seven-month marriage is over. Nick is struggling with being a single parent. Colette is still dealing with the health problems that caused her husband to walk out on her, and Emma is a dumper, while the others are dumpees.

As the group get to know each other, Colette suggests they start a dare club. If they're cavorting several metres off the ground, or on stage, standing in a spotlight, it's bound to help them to forget about their troubles, isn't it? At the very least, they'll have some fun, and who knows? It might just change their lives forever.

But is saying how you feel actually the scariest thing of all?

Margaret K JOHNSON

THE DARE CLUB

HOW FAR
WOULD YOU
GO?

For Hannah, With Love

Jen's partner Michael has never been in a relationship for more than four years, so with their fourth anniversary coming up, she's getting understandably nervous. Especially as she's just discovered she's going to have a baby.

She means to tell him straight away, but then he turns up on the motorbike, full of dreams of the two of them riding through the Pyrenees on a care-free trip of a life time. Somehow, Jen ends up keeping her news about the baby to herself. Is Michael having an early mid-life crisis?

Determined to save her relationship, Jen takes drastic action. Aided and abetted by her two very different best friends, she sets on a journey to discover why all Michael's other relationships failed. If she knows this, then maybe she can stop the same thing from happening to her.

But, as her pregnancy clock ticks, and Jen's investigations take her to Cuba, she has no idea what she's about to discover. **What's the big secret he's been hiding from her? And will her quest to provide a happy family for her unborn child be a success?**

Margaret JOHNSON

FOR HANNAH, WITH LOVE

WHAT WOULD YOU
DO TO SAVE YOUR
RELATIONSHIP?

A Nightingale in Winter

It is 1916, and The Great War is raging throughout Europe. Eleanor Martin is traveling to France to serve as a volunteer nurse. She only wants to bury herself in her work on the Front and forget her traumatic past. But when her ship is torpedoed, Eleanor has to act quickly to save an American journalist's life. As she cradles Dirk Loreson's broken body in her arms, speaking to him to keep him conscious, the possibility of a whole different future begins to open up for her.

Leo Cartwright, an ambitious artist, is also en route to the Front. A ruthless man who will stop at nothing to find inspiration for his paintings, Leo's path is destined to cross with Eleanor's. As she comes under his spell, will she find the strength to resist his demands? Will she trust her growing love for Dirk?

A Nightingale in Winter is about courage and searing ambition at a time when the very foundations of the world have been shaken.

MARGARET K. JOHNSON

A *Nightingale* IN WINTER